TENANTS & TYRANTS

Book 5 of
THE WARDEN

FELICIA JEDLICKA

Felicia Jedlicka (FelJed)
Find me on Facebook: www.facebook.com/feljedauthor
Visit my website feljedauthor.wordpress.com

For those who expect more of themselves than others do.

SISTER WITCHES
THE DEVIL'S SHADOW
THE DEVIL'S SOUL

DESTINY REJECTED
DESTINY RECLAIMED
DESTINY RAZED
DESTINY RESTORED

DÉJÀ VU

SAVE THE HUMANS

THE NECROMANCER'S CHILD

THE NEBRASKA APOCALYPSE NOVELS
CORN COWS AND THE APOCALYPSE
COW TIPPING AFTER THE APOCALYPSE
CORN HUSKING AFTER THE APOCALYPSE

THE WARDEN SERIES
SUCCESSORS
RIVALS
LOVERS AND LIARS
BAD BLOOD
TENANTS AND TYRANTS
THE RING BEARER
GODS AND MONSTERS
BEASTS AND BURDENS
MAGIC AND MAYHEM
FORK IN THE ROAD
DETAILS AND DEADLINES
*CURSES AND SACRIFICES**
*WITCHES AND WOLVES**
*SAINTS AND SERPENTS**
*ENEMIES AND ALLIES**

MARRIED TO DEATH*

Tenants & Tyrants

Felicia Jedlicka

1

DANIEL McGRATH SPRINTED UP the second-to-last flight of stairs. His throat burned from the effort of sucking in excess air while ascending the five flights of hospital stairs. He was convinced if he made it to the top without puking it would not be viewed as a triumph by his stomach.

On the last landing before the roof Heaton popped out of the sixth-floor door looking alert and un-winded. Daniel conversely thought his heart might explode if it thumped any faster. He pointed a finger at Heaton, threatening to say something as soon as his breathing was not overpowering his vocal cords.

Heaton looked up at the next flight, and back at him. He had finally abandoned his long dreads and floppy mops and settled on cornrows to manage his thick black hair. Daniel had objected fervently to this new hairstyle. Not because he wasn't pulling it off, but because it, along with his new black leather sport coat-style jacket, made him look like a mobster thug. However, since this look had increased the attention he got from women at the pubs, he had no intention of making any changes. He had even threatened to grow a goatee like Daniel's.

"Where the feck have you been? I thought you were right behind me," Daniel spat out between breaths.

"I was. I took the elevator," Heaton answered, motioning to the door he'd just arrived from.

"What? I thought you said we had to chase it up the stairwell."

"Yeah," Heaton said, implying the *no duh*, "not both of us."

"Are you off your nut? I just ran up five flights of stairs."

"Yeah, you did good. Jordan said he popped out onto the roof. Let's go get him."

"You wanker! You made me climb these stairs?" When Heaton didn't respond, he clarified his outrage. "You run marathons, you plonker!"

"Yeah," he offered the *no duh* implication again, "on roads, not stairs. Who wants to run up stairs?"

Daniel opened his mouth to let loose a deluge of Irish curses, but his cell phone interrupted him. The ring was a high twittering noise. It was annoying as hell, and he had chosen it with the very specific intention of pissing himself off every time he heard it. So far, it was working.

He tugged it from his pocket and clicked to answer it. "What?" he griped into the phone.

"Are you two coming?" Nevia asked on the other end. They had only been working together for three months, but she was already ruling the roost. She made the plans while they did all the dirty work.

"Yes, we're fecking coming, you narky woman!" He clicked the phone off and shoved it back in his pocket. "Whose damn idea was it to keep her on?"

"Yours," Heaton answered, jogging ahead of him on the stairs.

Daniel felt hot in his long jacket, but as soon as he got onto the roof, the night's early autumn breeze cooled him down. Most people hated to see summer go, but he was much happier in a cold climate. If he hadn't hated the idea of being nearly celibate, he might have considered opting for Ethan's job. He was basically an indentured servant, anyway.

"Where is the blood-sucking bastard?" he asked, scanning the roof. There was a helicopter landing pad just to the north of them and a secondary entrance for the emergency staff to enter the hospital. However, those doors required I.D. badges, so the bugger couldn't get away from them through there.

"He has to be up here. He's not a flier." Heaton surveyed the roof, taking in the scene with the precision of a soldier. Daniel only knew a little about Heaton's military background, but it was enough to know not to ask about it. Heaton wasn't exactly proud of the roles he had played. The glory of heroism was always contingent on perspective.

"Then he's hiding. Search or lure?" Daniel asked, not sure which answer he would have preferred. He was tired enough to hope for lure, but no one really wants to be vampire bait.

"I'm up for search, if you take the cut."

"Damn it, I always take the cut," Daniel grumbled.

"You heal faster."

"Barely!" Daniel didn't really heal faster, but something about his system allowed for quick clotting. It was a pretty useless talent, but it had saved his life on one occasion. The occasion was New Year's Eve. The life-threatening offender was a broken bottle that he impaled himself with when he passed out. Even with the quick clotting, it wasn't a happy new year.

"Fine, I'll do it," Heaton said, pulling out his knife. "Can't feel anything on this arm, anyway." Heaton rolled up his sleeve to reveal his melted flesh. Ever since he had confronted Daniel about it at the prison, he had been passive-aggressively taking shots at him about it. However, Daniel no longer held any sympathy for his affliction. Rule one: stay the fuck out of a *disperser's* way!

Daniel had never known what to call himself. He had rejected the phrase *exorcist*, for obvious reasons of blasphemy and inaccuracy. He hadn't really thought of himself as worthy of an official title, but Nevia had started referring to him as a disperser and it just sort of stuck.

Heaton cut through his scarred flesh before Daniel could voice an objection. It was just another in a long list of things that he would complain about later. It was getting tiresome, but Daniel wasn't in a position to take the high or low road, so instead, he would just sit in the middle and ignore it all.

"Walk it around. I want to get to the pub before closing."

Instead of walking around, Heaton milked the wound, letting the gash pour blood onto the graveled roof. Daniel looked away as he did. He wasn't particularly sickened by the sight of blood, but he was sickened by Heaton's severity. He was generally a calm mediator, but recently his sudden outbursts of bravery, violence, and on occasion sexism were starting to push the envelope. He had even had Nevia sniff-check him for parasites. No luck. Heaton was just becoming an ass.

"Maybe if I gash my throat, I could get you there before the good tarts are taken."

Daniel turned back to him. His face was smiling like he was joking, but his voice had said otherwise. "Really." Daniel nodded, lowering his voice to a level that allowed him to keep his temper in check. Outside of being mad drunk, he didn't have a problem keeping his anger management issues in check. He always wondered why it was so important for him to keep himself under control when no one else did. "Was that supposed to be funny?"

"I don't know. Are you laughing?"

"No, as a matter of fact, I'm quite the opposite of laughing."

"I don't see any tears." Heaton weaved his head to see.

"Crying is not the opposite of laughing," Daniel objected.

"What? Yes, it is. Have you ever seen drama masks: happy, sad?"

"Laughing is not happy."

"Of course it is." Heaton raised his voice to help make his point. "You're happy when you laugh."

"Not always. I've laughed when I'm sad. You laugh when something is funny. You laugh through tears. Laughing is just an extension of an emotion. Just like you can cry when you're sad, or you cry when you're happy."

"Only women cry when they're happy."

"Only women cry when they're sad," Daniel pitched. "Men drink when they're sad and laugh when they're drunk. They might be sad and laughing, and still not crying. So, no, crying is not the opposite of laughing."

"So, what is the opposite of laughing?"

"Yelling!" Daniel technically raised his volume for that statement, but only for effect.

"In what world is yelling the opposite of laughing?" Heaton asked, going so far as to get in his face.

"Laughing—" Daniel heard his cell phone tweet from his rear pocket, but he ignored it so he could finish explaining. "Happy and sad are the polar opposites of one spectrum. That's why you can laugh when you are happy or sad. Angry and jealous are opposite ends of a completely separate spectrum of emotions, and those emotions cause yelling. Therefore, yelling is the opposite of laughing."

"Son of a bitch!" Heaton yelled.

"Hey, don't—"

"Behind you!" Heaton pointed with his wide eyes.

Daniel whipped around, hoping that Heaton would have a good laugh at his well-played joke, but the stark white elongated face behind him was no joke. The open mouth mere inches from him held sticky yellow fangs. The creature hissed and dove for his neck, even as he stumbled back into Heaton.

Daniel heard a pop and the creature's head bobbed to the right, followed by its body. Daniel fell back as the creature fell to the side. Heaton caught him and steadied him. A small pool of blood gathered around the head of the vampire. There was no need to check for a pulse—not because the vampire was undead like the story books said, but because he had a bullet through his brain, and that just wasn't survivable.

Daniel cleared his throat and straightened his jacket as he righted himself. He turned back to Heaton and looked him over. "You, okay?"

Heaton looked at him with the same concern. "Yeah, you?"

"Good, good, never better." He pushed his fingers through his hair reflexively to check for flyaway strands. "That was a good shot."

"Yeah." Heaton nodded.

"Nice to have her around," Daniel said, surveying the damaged body.

"Yeah." Heaton did the same. "I'm glad I decided to keep her on."

2

I T WAS ALWAYS AMAZING to Daniel how often they could walk out of buildings with dead vampires and have no one notice. This time they used a hospital wheelchair, a gown, a "borrowed" baseball cap, and sunglasses to disguise their vampire corpse. The outfit made him look like a frail old man slumped over into sleep.

In terms of discretion, this was pretty high in their repertoire. Heaton had once walked out of a police station with an unconscious Japanese fire demon slung over his shoulder. The creature was only a baby, and looked like a bald fox with red skin, but it wasn't Halloween and the thing smelled like charred flesh. Not one policeman questioned him on the way out.

That was one of Heaton's many great moments of stupid bravery. Sure, it was dangerous and against so many regulations, but like he said, if he didn't look suspicious, no one would question the sizzling pile on his shoulder. Considering it worked, there wasn't much arguing with him after that.

Heaton opened the back doors to the van, and Daniel helped him toss the vampire into the back. "How can you separate the spectrums? Jealousy can make you angry and sad." He continued to argue with Daniel's dizzying logic—if it could be dignified with the title of logic.

"No, jealousy is its own emotion. You can feel multiple emotions, but jealousy only spawns yelling. Imagine you walk in on your girl screwing another guy. What do you feel?" Daniel shoved the wheelchair into a bush at the edge of the parking lot.

"Pissed."

"No, first you feel jealousy. Then you add to it either anger, or sadness, or both, and sometimes neither; sometimes you just stand there gawking like a dumbass, not sure what to do."

"That makes no sense," Heaton said, pulling a cigarette from his jacket pocket. He rarely, if ever, smoked, but he occasionally lit one up just to remind himself why he didn't want to be a smoker. Lately, he had been reminding himself a lot.

"Okay, take the chick factor out of it." Daniel scrunched his nose at the first puff Heaton let out after the initial light. It was Heaton's favorite part. It was Daniel's least favorite part because he usually blew it right in his face. Yet another passive-aggressive move. "Let's say you want a car. A nice sporty number, but you can't afford it. You see some twenty-something twat driving one just like it that his daddy bought him. What do you do?"

Heaton nodded. "I yell profanities at him to make me feel better."

"Ah-haaa, you see?"

"You might be onto something, but I still think you're talking out of your ass."

Daniel shrugged, not necessarily disagreeing with him. He heard footsteps behind them and turned to see Nevia slowly making her way over to the van. She was a self-confessed un-athlete. She hated running and only did it in emergencies. He couldn't blame her; the stairwell had been enough exercise to last him a week.

The barrel of her sniper rifle rested gently on her shoulder. Her on-the-job fashion put her in another pair of khaki slacks, an off-the-shoulder white cotton top, and a black ammo vest that, when buttoned all the way up, emphasized her breasts. Sadly, the vest was unbuttoned; no doubt she needed to un-corset her ladies to get the best control on her aim.

"That is so fecking hot." He couldn't help but say it out loud regarding the casual gun-toting vision coming his way.

"Yeah, she is quite a package," Heaton agreed. "You know, I was thinking of shagging her."

"What?" Daniel turned his attention back to Heaton. "You and her?" Daniel figured he was just kidding, but the straight face that was eyeing Nevia's approach as fondly as he had just been told him otherwise.

"Yeah, what do you think? Think it'll screw up the mojo?"

"No." Daniel had meant to say "no" to the first question, but the interpretation was already established. He couldn't backpedal without making himself sound... jealous.

"Good, unless you had eyes on her."

Eyes, hands, mouth, and then some. "Nah, I just don't know if she would go for you."

"What is that supposed to mean?"

"Nothing, man. She's just a pretty straight shooter, you know? Plus, she's pretty young. You're in your thirties."

"Dude, you shag women her age all the time, and you're older than me."

Heaton had a point. Daniel was no one to give advice on relationships, and he certainly wasn't one to judge him about the age difference between him and Nevia. Especially when he was skirting his forties and had already slept with her twice.

"Yeah, I guess I have no room to judge," Daniel conceded, trying not to let himself get territorial over a woman. He rarely remembered the women he slept with, let alone took issue with sharing them with Heaton. In fact, Heaton had pointed out quite a few women for Daniel to follow him on.

"So, I take it you guys didn't want to take that vampire alive?" Nevia asked as she arrived. Her hair at her forehead was pushed up, giving her the slight spike that changed her professional FBI agent façade into a rebellious woman who defied the standard for long hair. He wanted her to wear it like that all the time, but the spike was usually incidental.

"We were distracted," Heaton said.

"You were arguing." Nevia threw the rifle into the back of the van without concern for where it bounced. She was usually careful with her weapons, for safety reasons, but also because she loved them—oh so much. She must be mad. "Again," she stated as she looked Heaton over.

"Sorry." He shrugged. The sarcasm in the apology was far from hidden. Nevia eyed his cigarette like she wanted to say something about the filthy habit, but she didn't. She turned and faced Daniel with as much authority as a five-foot woman could muster against a six-foot man. Her clout increased significantly, however, when she pulled a Glock from behind her back.

"What is going on with you two?" She popped the clip and stuffed it in her back pocket. She released the loaded shell, kissed it, and stuffed it in her bra. He wasn't sure why she had placed it there, but he was more than happy to watch her do it. "I keep hearing stories of your single-minded triumphs, but all I see are two bickering children."

Daniel wanted to have the answer to that question as well, but he knew asking in the middle of a parking lot wouldn't get the answers he wanted. He knew that whatever was bugging Heaton had started when they had gone to free Cori for Ethan three months ago, and had slowly escalated to this passive-aggressive, sarcastic, asinine behavior.

"Is it me?" Nevia looked back at Heaton, but he just puffed on his cigarette all the more. Leaning against the van billowing smoke, he was more the thug than before. "Am I coming between you? Am I screwing up the dynamic duo?"

She looked back at Daniel for the answer, but he had none. She had to know that he didn't have the answer. She couldn't be blind to Heaton's behavior, not to mention she must have been able to smell whatever was bugging him.

Daniel looked at the wafting haze with new eyes. Heaton wasn't just taking back an old habit. He was protecting himself from Nevia's nose. She had mentioned once that being in a crowded smoky room was like wearing blinders. It was why she enjoyed hanging out at the pub with them so much. Whatever Heaton was feeling, he didn't want her to know about it. Even though she was looking at Daniel for the answer, he knew the question was really directed at Heaton.

"Are we going to dump this body, or what?" Heaton interjected, completely ignoring her query. "Daniel wants to get to the pub." He crushed out his cigarette on the van and slammed the doors shut.

"Hear, hear," Daniel responded half-heartedly and shrugged at Nevia before heading to the passenger seat.

Nevia got in the back, and Heaton climbed in to drive them to their first stop.

3

THERE WASN'T MUCH TO do with vampire bodies. They didn't really try to kill them, but they were such a pain in the ass sometimes that they couldn't avoid it. They prided themselves on taking live prisoners, but vampires came in many varieties.

The standard photophobes, those that drank blood, were more like an infestation of humanoid ticks. They bred like rabbits and drank blood from anything or anyone. Livestock was generally their preferred fodder, but they did occasionally venture into the cities. Hospitals were prime targets because they could drink from blood bags, coma patients, and the recently dead.

It was general policy to take them alive and relocate them. If they were one of the brave that dared to go after live, conscious human blood, they were sent to Danato. The policy, however, left leeway in dealing with an overpopulation of the buggers. When relocation was not an option, due to stressed food supplies, hunters were advised to... hunt.

Sunlight caused the creatures' tissues to decompose rapidly, making body disposal easy. A day in the sun and a vampire corpse looked more like a roadkill animal than anything supernatural.

The first stop, therefore, was essentially just a busy road that they could dump the body on the side of. Ditches were always a good bet. If the sun didn't make them disappear fast enough, the bugs would. Vampire corpses were like candy to ants and earthworms. They were also good fertilizer, a product idea that had yet to find an entrepreneur.

The second stop, and last stop, was their usual pub. It wasn't a cool dance club, and it barely fit more than forty people, but it was within walking distance to all three of their flats, so they could pretty much drink themselves stupid and not risk lives on the roadways. The sidewalks had a tendency to slam into them on the way home, but that was usually just caused by a lack of determination.

Daniel stepped into the bar and paused to greet it with open arms. "Home at last." Heaton bumped past his arms, not the least bit amused by his display.

"Let's get a table," he said on passing.

Daniel lowered his arms and stared after him. He really wanted to deck him for that. Bad mood or not, the bar should have been off limits to outside stresses. He could feel Nevia looking at him, and he looked at her.

The thin smile that she usually offered him was gone. She wanted to know what was going on with Heaton, and the fact that she couldn't smell him through his skanky habit was probably driving her nuts. He wanted to talk to her about it, but there were two things working against him. One, no matter what, Heaton was his friend, and he didn't want to gossip about him behind his back. And two, he was trying to keep his distance from her.

After two hot incidents at the prison, Nevia had put the damper on any further requests for sex, and there had been many. It took him a while to realize that him begging her for sex was not just pushing her away, but turning her off. The more he wanted her, the less she wanted him. In the end, he just had to avoid being alone with her, because, try as he might, he couldn't stop making advances.

"Table for three." He shrugged and prompted her to lead. He wasn't usually a gentleman, so it was no surprise that she narrowed her eyes at him before moving through to follow Heaton.

Heaton had chosen a table in the midst of everyone. The remaining empty glasses on the table would sit there for hours before the barmaid would come get them, and even then, it would only be because they were running low on clean ones. As he sat down, he saw Nevia reach for the glasses. She would pick them up and take them to the bar and fetch them all fresh pints. He grabbed her wrists and shook his head. "Don't do that, Nevia."

"Jordan!" Heaton hollered over the din and bad selection on the juke box before Nevia could say it. He rolled his eyes and threw his head back. "She's only told you three billion times."

"You know, I'm really in the mood for a dark beer, if you wouldn't mind, Jordan." He gave her a certain look that he hoped implied, "please take your time." For good measure, he wiggled his finger along the underside of her arm, where he was still holding her wrist. She glanced at Heaton before pulling her hands from the glasses and heading up to the bar. "What's up, man?" Daniel dared to let honesty take a turn at chiseling away at Heaton's bitterness.

"Nothing," he said, avoiding Daniel's eyes.

Daniel leaned on the table and regretted not letting Nevia take the glasses. He didn't like her cleaning up after people. She was better than that. She was better than a beer-fetcher too, but it was her way of hazing herself into their little group. After the last three months, she was more a part of the group than she realized. Heaton was dangerously close to losing his position, though. Pretty soon they would be colleagues instead of friends, if he kept his crap up.

"Did I do something to piss you off?" Daniel asked. Heaton looked at him like he should have already known the answer to that, so he wouldn't tell him. "Ever since the transmorph incident when we saved Cori, you've been... a dick." Daniel didn't want to add insult, but the description was apt.

"You mean when you and Jordan saved Cori?"

"Whatever." Daniel leaned back again. "Is this not working? Nevia, you, me; do you want to go back to the dynamic duo?"

Heaton scoffed. "You know I don't have to stay in this job."

"What?"

Heaton leaned forward to voice his thought more clearly without hollering. "I can transfer out any time I want. This isn't a prison sentence for me like it is for you."

"Is that what you want?"

"I've been thinking about it."

Daniel couldn't help but feel the knife in his back. It was surprising how painful it was. Heaton was right, he was under no obligation to stay with him. He had essentially been assigned to him as a parole officer, but he could be replaced. Daniel just hadn't thought that he would want to. Four years with someone in a life-threatening job made for an intense bond. The fact that Heaton was saying this to him so casually was more than a slap in the face. It was a wound to his heart.

"Lot of history to consider."

Heaton shrugged. "It's just a job."

Daniel could feel the heat of anger rising inside of him. It was not the kind of anger that came from being insulted. It was the kind of anger that came from being injured by betrayal. It was not a good anger for him to have.

He looked over at the bar to Nevia. She was sitting patiently with three beers, waiting for some kind of signal to return. The look he gave her must have indicated urgency, because she was off her stool and through the crowd in three seconds flat.

She set the two pale ales and the dark ale on the table and slid them to their destinations. "Heaton, you want to dance?" Nevia asked, but he just shook his head and drank his beer. He saw right through her attempts to get close enough to read him. At this point, Daniel was willing to strip him to bare balls and hold him down so she could find out what was driving his rogue behavior.

"Yeah, he does," Daniel said, intending to goad him into it. "Heaton would love to dance with you, Jordan." Heaton glanced between them. "He was just telling me how he wanted to shag you." Daniel did an internal cringe when he saw Heaton stiffen with shock.

"What the fuck, dude?" Heaton set his beer down.

"It's alright, Heaton," Nevia said, sitting down. "It's not like I haven't considered it."

Heaton and Daniel both looked at her, slack-jawed. She shrugged. "What? If it's crossed your mind, don't you think it's crossed mine?"

"You would do him?" Daniel pointed at Heaton.

"Again, dude, what the fuck?" Heaton glared at him.

"Sure. I don't think we *should*, but I *would*."

Heaton's attention returned to her, as if he was trying to calculate what he needed to say to get past the "I don't think we should" part of her statement. "I'm flattered."

"Don't be, you're hot. Asking myself if I would consider sleeping with you is like asking myself if I'd like to have another beer. Of *course* I would, but when that beer is offered and how drunk it's going to make me must be taken into consideration."

Heaton must have understood that, or at least pretended to, because he gave her a head bow of appreciation. "Truthfully, the only reason I told him that was to watch him panic." Heaton motioned to him, and for a split-second Daniel wanted to defend himself, but forced his face not to react. "He didn't much care, though. He pretty much told me to go for it."

"I didn't say that." His eyes flashed to Nevia to see if she was mad. Her damned blank stare of observation told him nothing. "I said I have no room to judge. I never implied that he should or shouldn't. If anything, I suggested against it." Daniel looked back at Heaton and saw the smug smile of a man pleased with his turn of the tables. He gave him a glare and turned back to Nevia, but she was already scanning the room.

He sat back and drank his beer, annoyed that he had just embarrassed himself on cue. He was usually suaver than that. Heaton was putting him on edge with his aggression. Nevia was putting him on edge with her frigid temperament, which, for whatever reason, was so damn alluring to him. He couldn't be himself, at least not with them. With a stranger, however...

4

I T DIDN'T TAKE LONG for Daniel to find someone to cruise. He had developed a reputation as the pub man-whore. All he had to do was wait for a woman drinking off a bad day to wink at him, or smile coyly, and he was up from his chair offering to buy her a drink.

Tonight's fancy was a tall, big-haired blonde. Her bosom was big, her butt was round, and she had plush lips and clean teeth. It was a pub-crawler's paradise sitting across from him. He breathed in her clean, powder-fresh scent.

Best of all, she wasn't about pretenses. She had all but told him she needed to get laid. Normally, he would have skipped the next round of drinks and suggested they go back to his place so he could accommodate her, but there was one problem.

Heaton had long since left the bar. He always had a few women on speed dial, and didn't like messing around with foreign waters at the pub. He liked consistency to Daniel's variety. Nevia, on the other hand, had not headed home. She had caught the eye of a twenty-something, and he was fishing for his own invitation from her.

Daniel couldn't help but be disgusted by the way the lanky blond turned his chair around to straddle it in front of her. She was still relaxed at the table with her feet up. He couldn't see her face, but the twenty-something kept smiling at her and laughing whenever she said something he thought was funny.

Nevia was fun when she drank, but she was also a little candid. She might have simply been speaking honestly and he might have decided that it was a joke and laughed at it. If that was the case, her thin smile would soon vanish and she would make an excuse to use the restroom and not come out for a long while.

He had seen her do it with several men over the last few months. She would come out holding her stomach, looking uncomfortable. When they saw her again, their overly happy smiles would fade, and they would inevitably ask what was wrong. He wasn't sure what excuse she gave: stomach flu, diarrhea, or menstrual cramps, but he could see their faces turn green.

It was an ingenious way to get rid of the men. First off, any man willing to screw a girl with bathroom sickness of any kind was total slime. Second, if they weren't slime, they didn't get offended when she wanted to leave without them. Third, and most important, after such a turnoff, the guys would never try to hit on her again.

There were only a few times she went home with the guy, or at least left the pub with them. He had been making a habit of sticking around until last call just to see if she was going to or not.

"Hello," his would-be one-night stand waved her hand in front of his face. "Are you still with me?"

He turned back to her and smiled sheepishly. "I'm sorry, I was just checking on my... cousin. I don't want her to get taken advantage of."

The big-haired blonde shifted to get a good look at the back of Nevia's head. She turned back to him with a wry smile. "Look, I'm game for whatever you want to do tonight, but if you'd rather be sportin' slim over there, then let me know. I can always catch a ride somewhere else." She winked, implying the type of ride she would be finding.

Daniel looked her over, admiring her features. He was a fool not to take her home with him right then. He took her hand and kissed it. "I'm going to regret this in the morning, but could I get a rain check?"

She looked disappointed, but she nodded politely. She leaned over and kissed him on the lips, giving him a taste of what he was missing. As she slipped off the bar stool to find another suitor, she murmured in his ear, "I hope she's worth it."

He smiled on the outside, but he cringed on the inside. He was an idiot. Nevia had made it perfectly clear she didn't want him, and yet he was pining for her like a damned schoolboy. He had not been loyal to one woman his whole life—aside from his mother, but that never counted.

What made him so damned irritated was she wasn't even his type. He liked bountiful bouncy busts and butts, not boney little girls. He tried to remind himself of that, but every time he tried to disillusion himself about her beauty, he just wound up thinking about how good she felt on top of him while he kissed her petite, pert breasts. The whole exercise always left him more entrenched in his obsession with her.

Daniel heard Nevia laugh. She rarely laughed. He stared at the twenty-something with venomous thoughts. He wondered if she could smell his irritation. He wanted her to.

Disgusted with his waste of a perfectly good lay, he slipped off the bar stool and went back to the table. It was time for him to give up on this game. He was losing miserably, but what was worse, she wasn't even playing.

He half set, half dropped his glass on the table. The sound made Nevia jump and a little part of him was glad. She pulled her feet off his chair and pushed it out so he could sit. He glanced down at the chair as if it were another temptation to an addict. He looked at the twenty-something. He was young and stupid, but he looked harmless enough. Nevia could smell if he intended to do her harm. She didn't need his protection.

"I'm going home. You need anything?" he asked, hoping that maybe the answer to that question might be, "yes," followed quickly by, "I need *you*."

She didn't say that. She just shook her head, as if it was strange of him to ask. He locked eyes with her for a moment, hoping that some part of her sensed how painful it was to leave her there with that guy. She waited for him to speak, since he had opened his mouth to do so. "Good night," was all he said, but it might as well have been, *goodbye forever*, as final as it sounded.

He couldn't say goodbye to her forever, since they were partners, but he could say good riddance. He could finally give up and walk away with whatever dignity she had left him. He could bury this emotion in a pile with all the rest that he didn't want, didn't need, and hadn't even felt until she came along. She probably gave him a nod or a wave, but he had turned away and walked out before he saw it.

Outside of the pub, he paused, feeling the brisk air wake him up. He hated walking home from the bar. It was better than running over pedestrians with his car, but he hated losing the buzz.

He headed around the block and made his way toward home.

5

I T TOOK HIM A few blocks before he stopped clenching his jaw in anger. He was still mad, and the little boy inside of him wanted to cry, but he felt better. He was done with her at last. It was going to be a hard recovery, but admitting you have an addiction is the first step.

A block from his house, he heard feet pounding on the pavement. He rarely worried about muggers, since he could shed their skin with a strong-enough look. Since they got back from the prison, Nevia had been sniffing out transmorphs left and right. He had gotten so much practice with his skill in the last months that he was confident he could shave a cat without so much as a burn.

Granted, he was still dangerous, but at least he could keep from killing and maiming people. The only skill he hadn't improved on was his reversal power. He still couldn't heal the damage he had done. At least not to the extent that it could be considered healing.

It took him a few seconds to realize that the light-footed trampling was right behind him. He turned, prepared to flay whoever it was, or at least disintegrate their clothes, but it was Nevia. She skidded to a stop at his threatened stance and held up her hands. "It's me!" She knew very well what he was capable of. She was fascinated by it, and perhaps a little turned on by it, although she didn't act on it... anymore.

"What are you doing coming up behind me like that?" he scolded.

"Sorry," she panted, and he realized she must have run all the way from the bar to catch him before he got home. Not only did she hate running, but she also hated losing her buzz too, and running was a surefire buzz-kill.

"What's wrong? Why are you running?"

She shook her head. "To catch you, duh."

"Yes, but why? Aren't you supposed to be walking Mr. Smiles home?"

"That didn't work out." She swallowed hard. She was probably trying to make the dry burning feeling in her throat go away. He resisted the urge to offer her a drink at his place.

He also resisted the urge to ask her about the twenty-something. He just shook his head and continued on without her. This seemed typical of a woman. He had just said "be gone with you," and now she was here. He didn't know what she wanted, but the fact that *now* she wanted anything from him pissed him off.

She stepped in line with him, just a half step behind him, but still within his peripheral. "I wanted to talk about Heaton."

"No, just get over it."

"Why are you being so pissy?"

"Scratch-and-sniff, not working tonight?"

"I can smell that you're mad, but I can't read your thoughts. I can only make educated guesses based on what I know of you. Most of what I get from people is from my profiler training."

"Fine, I'm pissed because you ran all the way up here to talk about Heaton, and I have no intention of discussing him with you." He picked up his pace, just to make her work a little harder to keep up.

"What did he say at the table to make your eyes go pinpoint?"

He swung back around so fast she ran right into him. She backed away to recreate the distance she needed not to have to crane her neck looking at him. "What about my eyes?"

"What did he say?"

"Tell me about my fecking eyes."

"Tell me what he said first. I couldn't smell you in there. What were you feeling?" He looked her over carefully. He'd thought she was running after him to keep his interest in her. He'd hoped she wanted to have a nightcap with him. He hadn't expected that she was doing another one of her science experiments with him.

"Go back to your twenty-something scanger. I'm not your lab rat." He was about to turn around, but she grabbed his coat collar.

"There! You just did it again." Before he could respond, she ripped open the few buttons that were actually buttoned on his black shirt and started smelling his chest. He didn't know what to do. Should he push her away in disgust? Should he be turned on? Before he could decide, her face popped up from her investigation of his scent. She stepped away and examined him. "You're hurt."

He looked down at his chest to check for blood. The skin was unharmed. He looked back at her. She looked confused, and a little guilty. "Let's go to your place," she said quietly.

His heart beat a little faster. He didn't acknowledge the request, but he knew what his face looked like; like he was afraid and hopeful. He hoped that maybe tonight she would finally give in and sleep with him. He was afraid she really was playing the game, and that he was still losing.

"Come on." She grabbed the cuff of his coat sleeve and dragged him along. She didn't have the strength of muscle to actually force him to go with her, but she did have his balls firmly gripped, and that was likely to get leverage for any short- or long-distance traveling.

When they reached his apartment, he unlocked the outside door, and thought about jumping through it and slamming it in her face. It was cowardly and childish, but he thought about it. The only thing that stopped him was Nevia's hand gently pressing on his back, ushering him through.

He wondered what else she had smelled on him. Could she smell how much he wanted her? She already knew. He had made it obvious, but did she believe him? Did she realize just how much he wanted her?

He released the deadbolt, and they entered his one-bedroom apartment. Even though it was a one-bedroom, he treated it like a studio. The large living room they entered was where he kept his bed, and no other furniture. A constant bachelor never offers his overnight guests the option of assuming the night can end anywhere differently than where it began—in the bedroom.

He used the bedroom for storage and always kept it locked. He didn't have many personal items, but what little he had he kept in there. The kitchen was just off the living room, separated only by a pass-through with Indian-style carved wood shutters. From the bed, he could see just a glimpse of his stove and kitchen table. The bathroom was immediately right of his bed. He liked the quick access in case the walk home from the bar hadn't sobered his guests up enough not to puke all over his bed.

Nevia came straight in like she owned the place. She had only been there a few times for "nightcaps" but she had never been bashful past the second time. She went straight to the kitchen and chugged some water. The run must have made her thirsty.

She came back into his bedroom/living room and stood sipping her glass of water. She watched him remove his coat and hang it up in his coat closet. He also removed his shoes. He didn't remove anything else, even though his shirt was basically off, anyway.

He glanced at her before lying down on his bed. He normally lay on it sideways on his stomach, so his companions would feel comfortable lying beside him, without thinking that they had to immediately start making out. He always found that to be the key to getting women into bed. Put them in a situation that would normally put them on the defense, and then wait. Once they realized you wouldn't pounce, you could take the next step. Each step had to be casual, though. If it was too calculated, it made them feel cheap.

With Nevia, however, there was no point. He lay down as if he planned to fall asleep in her presence, only above the covers. He closed his eyes and leaned his head back on the pillows. "Where do you want to do this?" she asked, setting her glass on the side table, leaning against the bed, and kicking off her shoes. He opened his eyes and watched her unbuttoning her pants. Normally this would have sent any man into internal cheers of hurray, but he knew she wasn't removing her pants for sex.

It was true Nevia had come up a few times for nightcaps, but that wasn't all. She had been goading him into practicing his healing power more. Since he didn't have any volunteers stupid enough to take up the role, she'd designated herself.

Three times he had tried to heal her.

He watched her remove the slacks, to reveal the bubbled, shiny tissue on her upper thigh that made Heaton's forearm look like a stove burn.

Three times he had flayed her.

He cringed at the scar tissue. He cringed because he knew how badly he had hurt her. He cringed because if Heaton knew about this, he would send him back to Danato in a heartbeat. He cringed because Nevia's beautiful, youthful skin was in ruins because of him.

"Come on." She crawled over him to get onto the bed. When he didn't open his eyes, she kneeled in front of him and touched his cheek. He felt that little boy inside start to cry, and a few tears wet his eyelashes. "Daniel, it's okay."

"It's not okay." He opened his eyes, intending to yell at her, but with her face so close he couldn't muster anger. "How could you let me do that to you?"

"I asked you to. Don't pretend this abuse was on your part. I'm the one aiming the hammer; you're just swinging it."

"I don't want to hurt you. Please, Nevia, don't ask me to do this."

"I know you don't want to hurt me, but you need to practice. Unless you want to hang out at a morgue at night, you aren't going to get any." He shook his head. He was about to get indignant, but she kissed him. It was the first time she had done anything remotely sexual with him since the prison. He wanted to devour her lips and pull her on top of him, but it wasn't that kind of kiss. It was a "do this for me" kiss.

It should have been sweet, but it was sour. He knew she was still just using him as a lab rat. She really was playing the game. He just didn't know which one. A little kiss was enough to harden his resolve and make him consider what he was doing just practice.

"Just focus on that feeling, Daniel," she said as she leaned back on the bed, her head opposite his. She looked like she was giving herself to him, which she was, but just her body, and not for pleasure.

He decided just to get it over with. The sooner he started, the sooner he could tell her he tried, and she could leave, limping. He rolled over to straddle her, with his head facing her feet. He pressed his weight on her hips to pin her down and focused his attention on her right thigh.

He hadn't been concentrating for more than a few seconds when he felt his heart slow down. The wave of heat that hit her made her squirm. He knew he was hurting her, but he couldn't help it. The process started here. Even if he wanted reverse, he still had to start by damaging the tissue first. He didn't know why.

She clutched at his back, wringing her hands in his shirt. "I want you to think about what Heaton said at the table. I want you to think about how much what he said stung your heart. Think about how much what he said hurt you." She was panting and grunting through the words, so he wasn't sure if she was serious, or just wanted to talk to distract herself from the pain.

He thought about Heaton like she said. He remembered how he acted like it would be no big deal to leave him behind. Heaton was his best friend in the world, and he was willing to transfer like this job was nothing to him. Like *he* was nothing to him.

Daniel felt the coolness that accompanied his actions dissipate into a warm glow around him. His heart started beating normally and then faster. For a moment, he thought he had stopped using his power, but as he concentrated on the tissue, it frosted over.

He knew the heat was excruciating in this process, but he couldn't remember a time when he'd made his subject/victim feel cold. From his perspective, though, it was hot. He felt like he was running up the stairs again, only in a heat wave. He started panting to compensate for his increased heart rate. He didn't like it at all, but he pressed on, willing his eyes to look beyond the layer of frost on Nevia's leg.

He could feel her scratching at his back, but it was less insistent than it had been before. Whatever he was doing was hurting, but not as badly. Her hands gripped and released completely. He thought he might have been mistaken about the pain. She might have passed out from it.

His brain felt too hot. He got an instant headache, and the sweat beading down his forehead was making his eyes sting. He felt faint and eventually he lost track of everything. He wasn't unconscious, but his vision was patchy, and his hearing was one long muted dial tone.

6

H E HAD A VAGUE sense of coolness. Someone was yelling at him. He opened his eyes and saw Nevia standing over him. She was blurry and her mouth was yelling his name, but the sounds were barely audible. She slapped his face.

He didn't feel it, but he smiled, or at least he tried to smile. He looked down at his body and found his shirt was gone. His pants were still on but they were wet, sopping wet. He looked up and saw the torrent of water that was keeping him wet. He was in the shower.

He got the sense that the water was cold, but he couldn't feel it. Nevia was still talking to him. He was sure she was cursing and yelling at him to snap out of whatever trance he was in, but he just watched her face. It was etched with worry for him.

"Daniel." Her voice pushed through as if he'd just needed his ears to pop. "Say something. Do you still feel hot?"

"I feel wet," he said, finding his voice.

"Open your mouth," she ordered, and shoved a thermometer in when he did. He didn't remember having a thermometer, but it had been a while since he cleaned his bathroom. After a minute or so the device beeped and she took it out. "104," she said as she slumped back onto the toilet. "Fahrenheit," she clarified. She sounded relieved.

"Isn't that kind of high?" he asked.

She crossed her leg and tossed the thermometer on the counter next to the sink. Her pants were still off. She hadn't taken the time to dress before dragging him into the bathroom. "Yeah, but it was 115. You were burning up. I didn't know what else to do."

"What happened?" His head still hurt, but the water was clearing the fogginess.

She looked him over. "You did it." She must have expected a certain response from him, but he didn't really get what she meant. "You..." She started to say it again, but she stood up instead and gestured to her right thigh.

He looked over the unmarred leg. Convinced he wasn't getting it still, she presented the left leg. They both looked perfect. If anything, the right leg had more supple and glowing skin. He looked up at her, and she was smiling. It was a real smile. She was excited, or proud, or just thrilled to have her own personal plastic surgeon.

He almost told her to get out right then and there. He couldn't understand her. Why was she doing this? What did she gain from him expanding his abilities?

He was certain that the water would impede her sense of smell, but her smile faded none the less. She shut the water off and helped pull him out of the tub. She had to brace herself on the toilet to get the leverage to assist him. He wondered how she had even got him in there in the first place.

"Stand up," she commanded. He did so, and she undid his wet pants and slipped them off his feet when he stood. He tried not to fantasize about her kneeling before him for another purpose, but his resolve was shattered when she removed his boxers, as well. If it weren't for stepping out of a very cold shower, he may have embarrassed himself further.

She grabbed a robe off the back of the door and slipped it on him, tying it in the front. He wondered if all this pampering was necessary, or if she was just being helpful. When she instructed him to walk, he realized it was necessary.

His right knee buckled, and he fell sideways against her, pinning her doggy style to the counter. He stammered out an apology, and between the two of them, managed to get him upright again. He wanted to make a joke about wanting to try that again when his legs worked, but he wasn't in the mood for comedy, even his own.

She helped him back to his bed, and he begged her not to put any covers on him. He was still too hot and thirsty. "My throat is dry," he said.

"I'll get some water." She jogged into the kitchen, her bare feet slapping on the linoleum. She poured a glass of water from the sink, and as an afterthought, poured another glass and added ice to it from the freezer. She sped back without spilling more than half the contents of the glasses and gave him the iceless water to guzzle first and then handed him the ice water to sip on so he could continue to cool down.

She sat down on the edge of the bed and watched him. She wasn't really so much looking at him as examining him. Something was rattling through her mind. Her logical brain was busy at work, while his had long since shut down. "I felt cold this time. The reversal must really reverse everything. Which is strange, because—"

"Stop!" He hadn't meant to yell it, but he did. "I don't want to talk. I don't have the energy to fuck. So just shut up or get out." He shook his head, wanting to take back all of it.

"Do you have a preference?" she asked. "Because I really think I should stay a while, just to make sure you're okay."

He knew she was only speaking as a person concerned with another person's safety, but if his gruff attitude and indifference wouldn't scare her away, he was going to start pushing the envelope again. "Will you let me hold you?"

It must have been the last thing she'd expected him to say. It was as outlandish as him randomly asking her to blow him, but it was innocently romantic. "I... uh..." She paused a moment as if she were trying to sense his smell. She must have sensed him by now. He may have been attracted to her, but his body was a wasteland of dead muscle. Cold shower aside, he still wasn't making any moves tonight. "Let me just refill your water and shut down some lights. I'll stay until you're asleep."

She did as she said she would. She brought back the water, shut down the remainder of the lights in the apartment, and checked the door locks. She put her pants back on and crawled into bed with him. She tossed around a bit, trying to decide how to position herself.

When she finally settled in on her side, he slipped his arm around her waist and under her pillow. He rested his head next to hers and pressed his body as close to hers as possible. "You're still really warm."

"I run pretty hot, anyway. Don't worry about it. Just sleep."

"I'm not sleeping, you are," she scolded, or at least tried to sound scolding. He could feel her heart thumping hard. She was nervous about being this close to him.

"Hmm-mmm." He kissed her gently on the neck. "I want you to stay. Will you stay with me tonight?"

He heard her take a deep breath and her heart started pounding harder, but she didn't answer. He didn't press for a promise, but he did thread his fingers with hers before he passed out from pure exhaustion.

7

THE NEXT MORNING, HE woke up alone in bed. He cringed, thinking how pathetic it was to beg her to stay. If she had stayed, he could have at least held onto the thought that she was still attracted to him, and he might be on the right track by forcing the issue a little more subtly. Since she had left, it was just another one of his attempts to beg for something she wasn't offering.

He heard sizzling from the kitchen, and he wrenched his head to see what was going on. Nevia was still there. She was in the kitchen making him breakfast, or at least, she was making breakfast. He may or may not have been officially invited.

He suddenly realized how hungry he was and found the strength to push through sore muscles to get closer to the food. He was glad that the after-effects of his reversal work didn't leave him partially paralyzed, but then again, it was just tissue on a leg. He might have only scratched the surface of his potential recovery time.

"Hey, I thought you never cooked," he said, resting against the entryway. She turned around with two eggs in her hand like she had been debating whether to crack them against each other or just throw them into the skillet and pick up the shells later.

"I rarely cook." She cracked the egg on the side of the pan with the sizzling bacon. Some of the egg dripped in the pan, and some out, before she could drop the egg with broken yolk in with the bacon. "With good reason."

He knew he should take over for her, since cooking breakfast happened to be his specialty. He was a big egg man: omelets, Benedict, poached. He also had a minor love affair with bacon. The fact that she was even attempting to cook for him was ranking high on his hotness scale. More than that, though, he was just happy to have her in his apartment. Sex or no, he just wanted to be near her. He wondered if that would be enough for him. Not likely, but denial is a pretty happy place.

"I hope you like your eggs with bacon stuck to it?"

"That's my favorite kind." He smiled when she looked back at him. He detected a note of amusement, but she hid whatever smile she had from him. "Actually, my favorite kind is…" He was about to say something regarding being prepared by a hot woman, but he bit back his overbearing flirtation. "Eggs Benedict," he said simply. "I love the tangy, salty, creamy mix."

"Have you ever had it with asparagus?" she asked, not turning around.

"Yeah, asparagus was made for hollandaise," he said.

She turned around. "This is probably going to suck."

"I'm really hungry. I would eat a shoe right now."

"Then this will taste like a really good shoe."

He chuckled. As his smile faded, he didn't take his eyes off her. It was a bad move for someone trying to be subtle.

"Listen, Daniel... we need to talk about last night."

He turned away from her. He couldn't handle another rejection.

"Just forget it. I can't do this anymore. I tried to be done with you last night, and you're over here in an instant. I tried to be subtle, and not a horny ass, but the bottom line is I want you so bad, I can't even think straight. I know how ironic it is that I'm having issues with this and you're not, but whatever. Serves me right, I guess."

She looked embarrassed, but he didn't realize that her embarrassment was on his behalf. "Actually, I meant Heaton."

"Oh," he said, feeling another crown of pathetic-ness being placed on his head. He was the reigning king of wretched, unrequited lust. "What about him?"

"What did he say to you at the table? You looked mad and... hurt."

"He said he's thinking about getting a transfer." Daniel clenched his fists, wanting to punch something.

"Just like that? Why?"

"I didn't get into specifics after that. I asked him why he was being such an ass since we saved Cori. He said you and I saved Cori."

"So, this is about me? He's mad about having me here and instead of talking about it, he's having a baby tantrum."

"Maybe, I don't know. I don't want to talk about this."

"Daniel, he's my partner now, too. You can't just play the boys' club card and shut me out."

"Yeah, actually I can," he said, firmly pinning her with his eyes. "He's my best friend, and he's known me for the four hardest years of my life. When you can claim the same, we'll gossip, but until then, you don't get to criticize him."

He saw her shift under his gaze. He hadn't managed to fluster her since they first met, but he was intrigued that he could still do it. She was a strong, determined young woman, but she was still young; young enough to feel the discomfort of being scolded.

He stood up and pulled her to one side to move the pan off the burner behind her. The eggs were irrevocably hard, but he would eat them, anyway. He pulled her chin up to face him and traced her jawline. "Why did you stay last night?" he whispered.

Her eyes flickered over his. She was panicking. She didn't have an answer prepared. She didn't have any excuse to leave suddenly. She opened her mouth to speak, but nothing came out. He wanted to kiss her, but he knew she would find the strength to object to that. He may have been losing this game, but he was starting to get the hang of the rules.

"Thanks for the eggs, Nevia." He leaned down and kissed her neck instead of her cheek to remind her of last night. He found a fork and dug into the eggs and bacon straight from the pan. As he did, his cell phone rang. He followed the sound to the living room/bedroom and found it on the nightstand. He saw the caller I.D. and pressed to answer it. "Heaton, what's up, man? Another vamp?"

"Annette is here. She needs more blood," Heaton said on the other line with a smile that Daniel could almost hear in his voice.

"Oh, happy freaking day," Daniel chimed. "I'll be there as fast as I can." He hung up and ran into the kitchen, tossing his half-eaten pan in the sink. "Go home, pack your bags, and for the love of all things fuzzy, bring a coat that an animal died for and not a pillow."

"Why?" Nevia asked, watching him frantically searching for a duffel bag in his over-stuffed coat closet.

"We're going back to the prison," he said. "You'll get to meet Danato this time," he added as an afterthought.

"Why are we going back?"

"Because Annette needs blood." He bit his lip, trying to contain what might have been a girlish squeal if he didn't have testicles to prevent such things.

"Blood?"

"Dragon's blood!"

8

Cori maneuvered out of Penelope's way as her jaw snapped the air where she had been standing. It was the sixth time that week Belus had pitted Cori against the dragon. Neither of them was happy about the overexertion.

The newly named Penelope was in a particularly foul mood that day. Her name was not official, and according to Danato, never would be. He was adamant that, like the prison, she should have no name. Names were written evidence and invitations to curiosity. For good reason, Danato did not want curiosity. Nevertheless, Cori was tired of referring to the beast as an article rather than a being.

Regarding the incessant training, Belus insisted that the last three months of torment were standard protocol for anyone taking his job, but she didn't believe him. First off, no one had ever had his job before, so whatever he decided was standard was just his own expectations. Second, there was no way he wasn't taking revenge on her for shooting him.

Justifiable or not, shooting one's friend and mentor had to come with consequences. Belus might deny his feelings about it, but she knew how dearly he had held onto his umbrage for her after she'd betrayed him during the elemental escape. He had to be harboring animosity toward her, especially since she had never technically apologized for it.

It would have been easy to beg for forgiveness from him, but he wouldn't respect that any more than he would *not* receiving an apology. She was stuck—if she apologized, she was admitting that she had done something wrong, which she for once was certain she hadn't; if she didn't apologize, she was left with inconsolable feelings of guilt. Without an apology, how would she know if he'd really forgiven her or not?

Penelope's temper hit a summit, and she wailed in Cori's direction, twitching her tail. Cori braced herself for an attack, but the cumbersome dragon wheeled around and went back to her airplane hangar cave. Cori ducked the tail as it whipped over her head. Penelope let out one final moan, which Cori could only interpret as a cry, before she settled down to sleep.

Cori looked back at Belus and his two recruited man-slaves. Duke, the Texan guard that always treated her as if she were a priceless porcelain doll that might shatter if he took the lord's name in vain in front of her, and his best buddy, "Guardsman" Chuck, as she had for some reason labeled him—though she was certain he had no military experience. He was generally posted on the time bubble level, and helped her out of the den at her designated time increments. A minor duty, but still vitally important and worthy of the added designation.

Duke and Chuck had been brought around several times in the last few weeks to help her with her hand-to-hand combat training. She had mistakenly mentioned that she was disappointed that Efrat had so easily kicked her ass the first time they'd encountered each other. Belus took that as an invitation to get her hand-to-hand combat skills up to par.

Cori pointed her sword at Penelope, who had curled up into a ball like a cat and was staring out at them with pouting eyes. "Look at that, you broke her!" she scolded Belus. "She's going to be mad at me for weeks now. Poor Penelope."

"Don't call her that," Belus said, moving to the lever to close the hangar door. "She'll be fine in a couple of days, but I would advise against trying to cuddle with her. She might snap your neck instead."

"Way to go, sensei," she scolded again, just to make sure he understood this was his fault and not hers. "Are we done then?" She balanced the hilt of her sword on the palm of her hand. She knew they weren't, but there was always hope.

"No, Chuck and Duke haven't had their go yet," Belus said, pointing to the men. They both stiffened up as if they'd forgotten they were still on the clock.

"Which one first?" Cori said playfully, directing them over with her index fingers.

"Both," Belus said sternly.

"What? I've only just started to put up a decent fight with one..."

"No mats either."

"Are you kidding me?" Cori looked at the hard surface of the glossy white floor. It was hard concrete. Without cushioning she was going to bruise every muscle in her back and probably get a concussion. "Belus, that's not..."

He looked back at her with piqued interest. He was just begging for an excuse to make it worse for her. "Yes?" he asked, further twisting the knife of temptation.

"I can't beat them, you know that. Together they outweigh me by... hopefully a person and a half. They just have more leverage. It's just not going to happen." She had hoped that was the right way to approach this. Honest and humble about her abilities. It wasn't.

The look that crossed Belus's face was no less threatening than the look Penelope gave her right before she attacked. He stepped forward, meeting her halfway. "Then fight me."

He was definitely serious, but she laughed anyway. She looked at Duke and Chuck behind him, but they weren't laughing, and Chuck was vigorously shaking his head. She let her laughter die and cleared her throat as if it was just a tickle that had caused her insolent outburst. When her eyes returned to Belus, she regretted laughing.

"Put your sword down, or keep it. Attack me," he said flatly. "I am smaller than you. I do not outweigh you. If your skills are such that weight and height will save you, then we will finish for the day, and you can go home early." He gave her the tiniest of smiles, but it wasn't a friendly one.

He knew how much of her time he had been commandeering. Between her standard duties, her gardening project, and his training, the only time she had at the end of the night was to eat and sleep. Some of which happened simultaneously. She was fortunate to live in a house with two abnormally strong men who could take turns carrying her up to bed when she fell asleep at the dinner table.

The permission to end the day early was almost worth whatever it would take to beat Belus. She knew it was underhanded to wonder if his shoulder wound was still raw enough for her to use it to her advantage, but she really wanted a break. "Okay, but I'll keep the sword."

He nodded and waved her to come at him. She paused a moment to think about her attack. She knew he had to have something up his sleeve, but she hoped that, like with all of her other endeavors, she could hold out to the end and get the upper hand at the last second.

She came right at him with a slashing motion. She expected him to jump back out of her range, but he jumped forward, caught her wrist in the movement, and she was airborne and landing before she even understood that the fight was over. When her comprehension surfaced with the searing pain in her shoulder, she screamed.

In between pants and yelps, she noted his foot braced on her elbow. Her arm was stretched out behind her with the sword still in her grasp, because she didn't have the function in her hand to release it. Her eyes were tearing from the pain, and she could hear herself whimpering for mercy.

Belus pressed a little harder with his foot and she screamed. When he eased the pressure, he spoke. "Am I weak?"

"No!" she yelled.

"Do you pity my size?"

"No!"

"Do you think I should pity you for yours?"

"No!"

"Do you promise to never use your size or your sex as an excuse again?"

"Yes, sir," she ground out, trying to sound in control of her emotions, even though all she wanted to do was cry.

He released her, and she pulled her arm back into a more comfortable position. She took a moment to bawl quietly, hoping that he would not begrudge her a moment to recover. She felt hands on her, and she looked back. Duke and Chuck had rushed over to help her up. The sympathy on their faces was more than from just witnessing the scene. They almost seemed to understand what she had been through. Belus must have trained them as well.

"Leave her!" Belus barked when they tried to get her to her feet. "Go back to your posts." They didn't object, but Duke hesitated. She imagined that asking Duke to leave a damsel in distress was like asking him to shoot himself in the foot. Sure, he would do it, if ordered, but it might take a little mental preparation, and he'd regret it.

When they were gone, she used her legs to stand up. A little more difficult, but it got her up. Her arm was still searing with pain, but she was pretty sure it wasn't dislocated. She did her best to not cry, but the tears just fell from her eyes, whether she sanctioned them or not.

Belus watched her sit down on the bench, careful not to disturb her arm. "Lift your arm."

She couldn't help but cry then. He was just being cruel. She lifted it, but the pain was too much and she let it down. He moved to her. "You probably have a pinched nerve." He stopped in front of her and reached for her shoulder.

She grabbed his shirt with her shaking left hand. "Please, don't." She was sobbing so ridiculously hard, she remembered what it was like to be a little girl flooded with emotions she didn't know how to deal with. Though at that age it was usually in regard to a broken toy, now it was in regard to a broken ego. "Please." She let her hand slip away.

It was pointless. He was already reaching for her arm. He raised the arm, which was painful enough, but after it was up, he palpitated the shoulder joint and pressed firmly into it. She screamed as the pain peaked and released. She took in a few gasping breaths as he let the arm drop. "Now raise it."

"I hate you." She mumbled so quietly she wasn't sure he would hear it. She didn't hate him. He knew she didn't hate him, but the statement was the only spectrum of their love-hate relationship he was comfortable hearing from her.

"Raise your arm," he prompted again. She did, and it didn't hurt. It was sore and would be for a few days, she imagined, but whatever had been pinched was un-pinched. "Better?" She nodded. "Do you still hate me?" She looked up at him to see the smirk he had only recently allowed to surface in her presence. She smiled and nodded. "Good girl." He squeezed her shoulder and let his hand drop away. "Come on, I'll buy you a cup of coffee. I know a good coffee shop."

9

T HE COFFEE SHOP WAS just the cafeteria, and there was no payment since money was a non-issue, but Belus did bring her coffee to the table for her. Not before flirting with the hair-netted attendant behind the counter. She was not very tall, and not very slim, but even with the hairnet, Cori could tell she was cute as a button, especially when she blushed at whatever Belus said to her.

Cori eyed Belus as he strutted back to the table with their coffees and a tiny tin pitcher of cold cream that he'd finagled for her instead of the powder packets she usually settled for. He set it before her and sat down, giving the attendant a wink before turning his attention to Cori. The smile he gave her was just a leftover of what he had been directing at the attendant, but it made her smile reflexively.

"Here, I thought you had your eye on that cute brunette nurse upstairs," she said.

"No one said I didn't," he said, changing his smile into a smirk. "And it was more than my eyes."

Cori laughed at that. She had already been shocked once today by Belus's fighting ability. He had told her once that she was stronger than he was, but she had doubted it.

Whether it was true or not, it didn't matter, since he could apparently kick her ass with deathmatch skills. Now she was being confronted with the image of him as the prison playboy.

Her laughter faded as she thought about how much she would have missed him if he had not survived her gunshot. How many things would she not have known about him? Her eyes watered just thinking about it, but she concentrated on paling her coffee to a palatable bitterness.

She wasn't much of a coffee drinker, but she could hardly stand the childish image of her drinking a soda pop while her mentor drank a coffee. There were apparently many things she would drink just for the privilege of socializing with Belus. That thought made her want to cry as well.

When she looked up with the intention of asking about their agenda, she found him staring at her. It was confusion and sympathy, and just a teaspoon of disgust. She looked away and drank her coffee, which was too hot, but she pretended it wasn't. "What's next, sensei?"

"Don't call me that."

"Why not?"

"Because you're saying it as a joke. I'll take respect or I'll take sass, but not some half-ass version of both."

"Yes, sir," she mumbled, before torturing her mouth with another drink.

"What were you just thinking about when you lost your sense of humor?"

"You," she answered honestly. "My bullet. My gun. My hand." She shook her head and growled, willing away the grief and guilt that were pressuring her to cry. Why did she always have to cry?

"That still bugging you? I thought you would have gotten over that by now. You gave it a shot, but you missed. Better luck next time, kid."

He intended it as a joke and she knew he did, but it didn't stop her from glaring at him for it. "I could have killed you. Doesn't that scare you, or at least bother you? How can you joke about it?"

Belus rolled his eyes. "Kid, you are too emotional. You criticize me for being a stick in the mud, but you are as tightly wound as a politician on voting night." He stood up, taking his coffee in hand. "Come on." He nodded for her to come with.

"Can't I at least finish my coffee?"

"No, bring it with," he said as he headed to the door.

He led her to the elevator instead of the gym, and they went up one floor to the animal level, which housed the infirmary down its center.

As they entered, the four nurses at their hub station beyond the four-chair "waiting room" looked up at her. They abruptly started arguing and debating who would get whose shift. "I'm not injured," Cori rebuked them with a high whine in her voice.

They paused and looked at Belus. The arguing started again. "I'm fine too, ladies," he said. Their shoulders slumped, and they continued to read magazines or paint their nails. The heavy workload of a prison nurse was the time between animal and human injury. Without television or the internet, it was an exercise of the mind just to find something to occupy the time.

One nurse, the cute brunette that had been eyeing Belus the last time he was in, leaned over the counter, showing off her cleavage, which was ample. She was not overly tall or slender either, but perhaps that was Belus's type. Cori could easily draw assumptions about whether Belus was a butt man or a breast man, but she la-la-la-ed the thoughts away before she delved into territory that even she wasn't comfortable with.

"What can I do for you?" the nurse asked.

"A number of things," Belus said with a smirk that made the nurse giggle.

LA-LA-LA-LA!

"But for now, why don't you get me my file," he said seriously. The nurse scooted off to get the file, and Cori followed Belus into the lab that had a long table in it. He got comfortable just as the nurse came in with his file.

The manila folder was nearly an inch thick and looked more like a businessman's taxes than a medical file. Belus winked at her, and she left them alone, shutting the door behind her. Belus waved Cori to sit, and she sat cattycorner to him, since he, of course, took the head of the table.

"Do they know about each other?" Cori whispered, thinking that it might not be gossip if she didn't say it loud enough.

Belus narrowed his eyes at her. "Monogamy isn't as ideal in this environment as in the real world. Done respectfully, without machismo, it can be a beneficial arrangement and a pleasurable distraction."

Cori cleared her throat. Her words were sticking before she had even thought of them. "I wasn't judging. I just wasn't sure if I should be careful what I said around either of them."

"Don't worry about it, Cori. I doubt you want to get to know me *that* well." He raised his brow, and she smiled, satisfied that she hadn't completely insulted his character. "This is my medical file. Take a gander."

Cori pulled the file over to her and flipped through it. She wasn't sure what she expected to see. She thought perhaps it would contain a long list of injuries followed by doctor's notes of prescriptions and diagnoses, which it did, but a short distance through she started seeing paper drawings that mapped his wounds like one might map the dents on a rental car before borrowing it. She gasped at one photo that very clearly showed an alien creature lodged in his mouth. Cori instinctively covered her mouth when she saw that.

She flipped through further and started reading the highlighted portions of the documents, the specified low survival rates, compromised immune system, and lowered brain functions. As she flipped through, Belus pointed at one picture of him she was certain he could have been a corpse in.

"This one was fun. Danato had to kill me with a voodoo pin to keep me in stasis while he figured out how to remove a Balan demon that had attached to me." Cori's eyes widened and he misinterpreted the meaning behind it. "Don't worry; we have all sorts of things to protect us from that... now."

"You were dead, for real."

"Yeah, for like three days. Your little bullet is not the only time I've been close to death, Cori. It certainly isn't going to be the last."

She leaned back in her chair. This wasn't making her feel better. Belus was so much braver than her. He had practically told her to let him die for her. "I should have chosen to let myself die."

His brow furrowed.

"If I had let myself die, then..."

"Then you would be dead. How is that better than me getting shot?"

"I didn't know if you would survive!" she yelled, slamming the file shut. "I only knew that Efrat would try to save you. I didn't see the end result. I just took the gamble. I risked your life, Belus! You should be pissed!"

"And yet I'm not the one yelling," he said sarcastically.

"I hate myself!" She gritted her teeth. "I hate Efrat! I hate him so much for making me have to make that decision. I should have just shot *him*!"

"That may have been the easy choice, but not the right one," he scolded with more volume than he'd probably wanted to be using, but when she was yelling, it was hard to compete with mere statements.

"Don't defend me! I was stupid and arrogant!"

"You explained it all to me, Cori. I don't disagree with your decision. Why are you beating yourself up about this?"

"Because I love you, you jerk!" She pulled her feet up on the chair as if they would protect her from his look of annoyance. He didn't give it to her. "I just..." She needed to backpedal and find the path to that statement, so he didn't assume she was being uselessly sentimental. She brought her feet back to the floor and sat closer to the table to explain herself with some hint of maturity. "I know I made the right choice, but it still hurts. Before all this, I respected you. I considered you part of our twisted little family. I knew I cared about you, but not how much. I hate you so much sometimes, but I love you too. I know you don't like hearing it, but..."

"I never said that," he interjected.

"Well, I know it makes you uncomfortable..."

"I never said that either," he added.

She scrunched her brow, not sure what to say to describe the offish way he handled her affections. "Fine, whatever it is, then; I just don't want anyone to hurt you. Least of all me."

Belus took that in for a moment before leaning forward to take her hand. "Listen Cori, I understand what you're saying. I know, more than ever right now, you need to express that to me, but I need you to stop doing it, okay?" She ripped her hand away and tucked it under her arm. She couldn't believe how cold he was being.

He stood up and loomed over her. "Cori, look at me." She kept her eyes down. There was no point in continuing this discussion. He was going to step on her heart, whether she looked at him or not. He sighed and sank down to one knee, resting his hand on her leg. She was so taken aback, she almost pushed him away to avoid the strangeness of the situation. "Cori, I love you too, but I can't keep assuring you of that and you can't keep reminding me of your love."

"I said it like three times," she wailed. "One of which was right before I shot you, so it kind of negated it." She could feel the shaking in her voice as her anger took a greater hold over her throat than her pain.

Belus squeezed her leg and shushed her. "I know, but listen, you need to understand something. Danato was very unwilling to put me in charge of you. One of the reasons is because he doesn't want to share you." Cori shook her head. She didn't like that she was being referred to like property. "He cares for you a great deal. The deeper reason behind that isn't permissible for me to discuss." She opened her mouth to ask about that, but he just shook his head. "You know how Ethan jokes about me being the crazy uncle of your little family." She nodded. "Well, I need to stay *Uncle* Belus.

"If Danato thinks that I've replaced him in your eyes in any way, he would be mortified. I can't claim he would do any harm to me, but my friendship with Danato has never fully recovered from a woman coming between us." Cori wanted to ask about that too, but she didn't bother trying since she suspected it was on Belus's zipped-lip list as well. "So, when we are around Danato, just make sure all your affection is directed at him, so he doesn't think that I've usurped his pater status. Can you do that for me?"

"Yes." She tried not to sound bitter, though she still felt a little rejected, but it wouldn't be a day with Belus without feeling a little dejected in the end.

"Do you want to go home?" he asked.

She checked her watch. She usually didn't wear one, but since she had been in and out of the time bubble so much, Danato had given her one. It was apparently a big deal to get it, too, because he'd threatened that she couldn't lose it. The device was a simple digital watch, but it kept time with the real world while she was in the time bubble, so she knew within a minute of her departure time.

"Shit!" She threw her head back. "I can't. The next batch of crops are going to be done in an hour. I'm going to miss dinner again."

"Oh." He seemed disappointed that the generosity of his offer had just been wasted. "How long will you be in?" He stood up and took his file.

"A day and a half, at the most. The fields are so big now, I'll be picking and handing food through for about two hours."

Belus checked her watch. "You will miss supper. Danato won't be happy about that. How have the wizards been treating you?"

"I haven't encountered one since I started this project."

"Really?" he asked incredulously. "Is it the spot, you think?"

She shrugged. "I thought maybe they didn't like the water, but the fields aren't even that close to it anymore."

"Well, you should probably take your pistol in anyway. Two hours is a while to be without some protection in there."

"Danato hasn't given me permission to use it yet," she said, standing up.

"That's my call now, kid," he said.

"Oh, right. I'll get used to that sooner or later," she said. "Who do I ask about requisitioning a puppy?" she asked as they headed out.

"I'll leave that one to Danato," he answered.

10

ETHAN COULDN'T HELP BUT be giddy as he ran to the loading docks. He had only just gotten word of Daniel and Heaton's arrival, but he was already thinking about a beer and poker night. He already had one scheduled, but with Cori stuck in the time bubble, he needed another player. Three more would be even better.

"Daniel, Heaton," Ethan yelled as he entered the cavernous room. He hugged Daniel and Heaton and found his way to Nevia. "Jordan," he said with the same enthusiasm. She presented her hand to shake, but he took her up in his arms and gave her a squeeze before putting her down. "Good to see you. These guys haven't scared you away yet?"

She pinched her fingers together with a paper thin space. "Any day now," she said with a smile.

"Where's Cori?" Daniel asked. "I thought saving her life meant I had earned the right to arrival hugs and kisses."

Ethan shook his finger at him. "Cheek kisses, maybe, and only if she offers." Ethan took Nevia's duffel from her without asking and slung it over his shoulder. "No, she'll join us later. She's picking vegetables. She's single-handedly put a thousand dollars a month back into Danato's budget," Ethan gushed as he led them to the door. "She might even be able to produce enough to supplement the bulk feed for the animal level, which will be another few thousand saved."

"Ethan, wait up," Heaton said, stopping him at the door. "Annette is still coming."

"Who's Annette?" Ethan asked even as a spiky-haired blonde emerged from the back of the truck with an army duffel bag hanging from her shoulder. The spiked hair and firm protruding biceps had already convinced him that she was gritty, but the bubblegum she was chomping, behind a shimmering pink smile, screamed *playful*.

She sauntered over, letting her hips sway in her ripped stone-wash jeans. Ethan could see just the tiniest bit of her belly under her gray cutoff t-shirt that read "Naughty or Nice," except the "or" had been crossed out, to write "and" next to it. Ethan smiled, wondering if Cori would get as much of a kick out of this woman as he did.

She jumped gingerly off the platform as if she didn't quite know how to do it gracefully. When she landed, she leaned back to inspect Ethan up and down. "Well hello, Mr. Pierce." She shook her head. "I had no idea you were so young." Ethan pinched his brow and smiled politely. She couldn't have been more than thirty. "I have been so excited to meet you. The circuit says you and your Miss Reiger... or is it Mrs. Pierce?"

"Um, either—Cori is fine, though, and Ethan for me," he suggested.

"Rumor has it you two are shaking this place up."

Ethan lost his smile. "I'm sorry, but who are you?"

"Annette." She put her hand out to Ethan and stepped forward. She was a bit taller than him. Her handshake was firm, almost unfriendly, or perhaps just not as feminine as he'd predicted.

"Annette what?" Ethan asked.

"What Annette, actually. Annette is my last name. Mabel is my first name, but since I'm not eighty-two yet, I refuse to use it."

"I understand. Annette it is. So, Annette, why are you here?"

"I've come to see a man about a dragon. I take it Danato hasn't given you the rundown on me yet."

"No, as a matter of fact, he hasn't. Why don't you give me the short version?"

"Well, the short version is: I give you money, you give me dragon blood." She smiled widely and spread her arms. "How's that for concise?"

"Why do you want dragon blood?" Ethan asked. He heard a distinct snicker behind him and he caught Daniel hiding behind Heaton. Heaton himself was holding back a smile.

"I'm a witch, Ethan." Annette put a hand on his shoulder, drawing his attention back to her. "I use your dragon's blood for all sorts of things, but I am also a businesswoman. I have a broad range of clientele who like to use the blood medicinally and recreationally."

The snickering continued in duplicate, with Heaton joining in, but Ethan didn't look back. "You sell it to people as a drug? What does it do?"

"It's different for everyone. Most people enjoy a drunk or high feeling. Others feel a clarity that allows for meditation. Some just don't feel anything, but that doesn't mean that they never will. It just means the dragon isn't compatible with that person."

"And Danato lets you take blood?"

"Danato lets me *buy* blood." She rubbed her fingers together. "I pay very well. As I said, I have a varying clientele."

"Dude," Heaton said behind him. Ethan looked back to see him containing himself enough to speak. "She's cool. We bring her around about every other year to collect. Danato knows her well."

"I do." Danato entered the docks with a smile Ethan hadn't seen outside of Cori's presence. "Hello, Annette."

"Danato!" The blonde stalked across the room and gave Danato a big hug and a warm but innocent kiss on the lips. "How wonderful to see you again! You look well."

He scoffed. "You look radiant, as usual. This is a new look for you."

"Oh, I think I went back too far. Eighty just hit me so hard. I don't know what I was thinking."

"I do." He winked at her.

"Oh, shush." She playfully slapped his chest. "I absolutely have no idea what you mean."

"I see you've met Ethan." He pointed to Ethan.

Annette turned around and looked at him with the same appreciative scan she had before, but now Ethan thought it might not have been as motivated by attraction as he had thought. "Yes, he is just the bee's knees, isn't he? I can't believe how strapping he is. Your praise was not exaggerated."

"Yes, he's come a long way. His greatest attribute is his constancy, but I sure as hell didn't teach him that."

Annette laughed and slapped his shoulder this time.

Ethan took in the appraisal scene with bafflement. He felt like he was a child, being doted on by two adults who forgot he had ears. "Excuse me," he said, interrupting the dialogue. "I don't mean to break this up, but should I be getting a little more information about this?"

Annette smiled at him warmly, while Danato's attention wandered to Heaton and Daniel. "Heaton, good to see you again," Danato said, ignoring Ethan's question.

"Sir." Heaton shook his hand.

"And Daniel." Danato shook his hand, but held it for an extra moment. "I hope you're staying out of trouble."

"Not even a little, sir, but nothing illegal anyway." Danato gave a grumble before releasing his hand.

"Sir, this is..." Heaton waved Nevia forward from her hiding place along the back wall. "Nevia Jordan, Jordan, as she prefers."

Danato smiled and met her halfway for a handshake. Her hand disappeared into his as they shook. "Jordan, Ethan has raved about your talents."

"I had only just begun when I was here last. I was unfortunately not as much help as I would have liked to have been," she stammered humbly in the face of the big man.

"Not according to Ethan," he said. She glanced at Ethan, and he gave her a smile. No matter how much she tried to downplay her role in saving Cori, she had been the key to it. Whether it be narrowing the playing field, or simply forcing him to relax enough to come up with the last puzzle piece.

"Ethan is a generous and brave man. It's been my honor taking over his position," she said.

Danato looked back at Daniel and Heaton. "Are you sure *honor* is the word for dealing with those two?" She laughed, but said nothing more on the subject. "Annette, why don't I show you to your quarters for the evening?" Danato raised an arm for her, and she wrapped her hands around it like she would have been just as comfortable with an evening gown on as her jeans. "Ethan, I assume you can handle your guests," he said on the way out.

"Yeah, and hey, don't forget we have poker tonight," he yelled after him, but he could hear Annette laughing, so he wasn't sure he had heard him.

11

CORI COULD FEEL THE ache in her muscles from two days of picking cabbage, peas, green beans, corn, and tomatoes. She had left the cleaning, de-podding, and husking to the cafeteria staff, but the bundles of food that she sent out of the bubble would be enough vegetables to feed the entire prison staff for a month or two. The staff would be busy for the next week, just with preparation and preservation.

She knew her face was probably covered in all sorts of dirt. Despite wearing gloves, her hands were raw. Her forearms looked like she had been scratched up by a feral cat, not to mention two days in nature without a shower left something to be desired beyond what deodorant could provide.

She hadn't really given much thought to going home to clean up versus cleaning up in the lake in the time bubble. All she knew was she wanted to get home. When she stepped through the front door, she realized she should have cleaned up before coming home.

There was nothing worse than coming home to a party that had started long before you arrived. She looked over the faces at her husband's weekly poker night. The house had accommodated them with a table to seat eight instead of six, and it was full.

Daniel sat at the far end—she hadn't expected that. Belus had his back to her at the other end. She was surprised to see Danato, to his left, had given up his usual chair. Duke and Chuck, whom she *had* expected, were to Danato's side, while Ethan, who sat on the opposite side with his back to the kitchen, was flanked by Heaton to his right and the woman she assumed was Nevia Jordan to his left.

At first, no one heard her come in. The boisterous conversation and smack talk left the room feeling crowded and smoky, even though no one was actually smoking. She hung up her coat, silently wishing there was a back door to the house, so she could have slipped upstairs to freshen up before facing guests.

"Hi sweetheart," Danato said first, giving her a sympathetic smile. He must have noticed the wreck her hair and face were.

"Cori!" several voices chimed in, along with one "Ma'am" from Duke and an uninterested glance from Belus, who gave her an additional short cursory check from the feet up, as if he was checking for injuries.

"Hi, everybody," she said in what she hoped was a friendly tone.

Danato held out his hand to her to come to him, and she moved away from the coat rack, happy to let him embrace her so she didn't feel like she was intruding. He caught sight of the pistol on her hip and his warmth faded. "Why do you have that?"

Cori paused in her step to look at the gun. For half a second she panicked, trying to remember why she did have it. "I told her to take it with her," Belus said as he put a few chips in the pot. "For protection," he added, in case he needed to rationalize his orders.

"I see," Danato said, looking a little put out by the first impact of his dethronement.

Cori moved forward and touched his shoulder, hoping to snap him out of his irritation, and to remind him, as Belus had suggested, that he was still important to her. He smiled up at her again and hugged her body to him. He always squeezed a little too hard, but he wasn't the best at expressing himself, so if it was uncomfortable, it just meant he cared that much more.

When he released her, she kissed his cheek. "How did it go?" he asked.

"Fine, most everything survived. We should have another month's worth. Although I think everyone is going to get tired of sauerkraut. I think I'll have to see if I can put together a rotation for spinach. I think that will go over well." Cori scanned the table, which was full of empty chip bags and remnant plates with yellow, dried cheese. "Speaking of vegetables..." She looked between Ethan and Danato. Ethan wasn't paying much attention to her, but the smirk he was wearing was probably at her expense.

He was probably resisting the urge to comment on her appearance. "Did you guys actually eat supper, or did you just nuke up nacho dip?"

"Nachos!" Daniel and Heaton bellowed in sync and tapped their beers together. She imagined she could have said burritos or chili and gotten the same response.

"It's alright, sweetheart. The boys are filling up on beer." Cori perked an eyebrow at him. "I'm fine," he defended. She knew very well snack foods would do little to please Danato's palate, let alone fill up his cavernous belly. Not to mention salty chips and fatty cheese were not on his diet plan as far as she was concerned.

"Mmm-hmm," she said and moved away from him.

Ethan practically spat his beer out to catch her before she left the table. "Cori, I want you to meet Nevia Jordan. We call her Jordan."

Ethan put his hand on Nevia's back as if the only other woman in the room would be hard to identify. Cori tried not to find fault in that. She also tried not to be jealous that the cute, petite brunette that he had regaled her about was sitting next to him. It shouldn't have made any difference since she was going to be in reach or eye shot, no matter where she sat.

"Nice to meet you." Cori leaned across the table in front of Belus to shake her hand. Belus leaned back to cover his cards, in case this move was a plot to look at his hand. She should have known he would take his card-playing seriously. "And I guess thank you."

"I'm sorry we didn't get a chance to meet last time. Duty called."

"I understand." Cori released her hand and looked down at Daniel. He wasn't particularly paying attention to anything but his cards, but his eyes fluttered up to her as if he felt her looking. She gave him a smile and a nod. She wasn't sure what else to do, but she felt a man that had saved her life deserved a little more acknowledgement.

He must have felt the same tenuous obligation, because he gave her the same nod with an added wink for flirtation. She'd expected no less. She found it amusing that because of conversations with Ethan, they each probably knew more about each other than they realized, but until they spent more time together, they would still feel like strangers.

She headed into the kitchen to wash her hands and put together a proper supper for Danato and the others. She should have resented having to do the duty even after just getting back from two days of manual labor, but she was happy to have an excuse not to stand around like an intruder. She could have just gone straight upstairs, but she didn't want to seem unsocial. Plus, she was starving and wanted her own supper.

"Hey, where's my kiss?" Ethan whined, looking back at her.

She smiled as she pulled lunch meat and tomatoes from the fridge. "You want a kiss? You can come get it."

Heaton and Daniel groaned at the biting remark. "What?" Ethan whined, though he was smiling still. "Danato got a kiss first thing, brought right to him. I'm your damned husband, woman. Bring me my kiss." Ethan slammed his fist into the table theatrically.

Cori tried to keep her smile under control. "When you have a bum leg and walk with a cane, I'll bring you kisses, but until then you can come around this island and *try* to get a kiss from me." She emphasized the *try* more for entertainment, which worked, since Heaton and Daniel were roiling with laughter. Even Chuck and Duke were not immune, despite their loyalty to Ethan.

"Oh, sweetness." Ethan shook his head at her. He licked his lips. "I bet I could..." He paused, not wanting to finish whatever vulgar line of thought he had in front of everyone.

"Does the kiss offer apply to everyone, or just Ethan?" Daniel asked.

Ethan whipped his attention back to Daniel. "That's where the try part comes into play." Ethan waggled his finger at him.

"Danato, what did you do to get your bum leg, anyway?" Heaton asked.

Danato looked over at him. Cori continued to spread mayo on her bread slices, but she glanced up to see his reaction to the question. She had never asked him about his leg; she had just assumed it was a sore subject, like the rest of his past. He glanced around before answering, as if he wasn't sure if he wanted to share his story with this crowd. "I disrespected my wife one too many times." He gave Ethan a stern look, and everyone laughed.

Daniel dealt the cards, and Nevia stood up. "Deal me out this time."

"What?" Daniel objected. "No way, I only have half your money. There's room for at least three more rounds of humiliation for you." Heaton and Ethan started laughing, tucking their faces into their hands. At this angle, Cori could see a slightly prideful smirk on Nevia's face. "What? What's so funny, you plonkers?"

"Dude," Heaton drawled, "when are you going to get this?" Ethan started laughing again as Daniel's face fell befuddled. "She's a bloodhound on steroids. She knows when we are bluffing."

"Bollocks, I've beaten her like four times." Daniel looked at Nevia, who was smiling a little broader.

"She let you win," Ethan explained.

"What?" Nevia turned away from him and joined Cori in the kitchen. "That's fecked up, woman!" Daniel called after her.

"Can I help you with this?" Nevia asked, starting to place meat on the dressed bread before Cori gave her an answer. She was glad she did, since she would have instinctively said no, even though she wanted to be done with the task.

"Thank you." Cori felt a little uneasy about speaking to a woman who had probably spent a good amount of time with Ethan in this house without her. She knew it was irrational, but the fact that Nevia and Ethan were closer in age made her feel like she was an outsider to them. Like when best friends from high school take on a college friend. They are all friends, but you still can't compete with history. "My husband has said a lot of good things about you." Cori regretted saying "my husband." She may as well have pissed on the furniture while she was at it.

"He's said better things about you." Nevia touched her hand, just for a moment, to make her catch her meaning.

Cori chuckled as she started to understand how intuitive this woman could be. "I'm sorry. I must seem like such a bitch."

"You seem like a hard-working woman who has just come home to a bunch of rowdy men and one strange woman in her house." Nevia placed one finished sandwich on a napkin and presented it to Cori. "Why don't you get started on this one, and I'll hand the rest of them out as I finish them."

"Oh... I..." Cori started to object, but she wasn't exactly sure why she wanted to. She was hungry enough to eat three sandwiches. Postponing out of some hostess code didn't sound appealing.

"You'd be doing me a favor." Nevia leaned in a little to whisper. "I hate poker."

Cori laughed. "Alright." She took the sandwich and slipped around to sit next to Ethan. He looked over, probably expecting to see Nevia. He did a double take and glanced to the kitchen to see what Nevia was up to. He smiled, approving of the changing of the cooks.

Ethan leaned over for a kiss and she took that opportunity to take a big bite of her sandwich. His eyes gleamed with silent reproach, and his smile stopped being about amusement. He turned and wrapped his feet around her chair legs and scooted her chair closer to him.

"Ethan? You in?" Heaton elbowed him from the side.

"I'm out." Ethan set his cards down without even looking at them.

"Well, Ethan's off the radar. Belus?" Heaton said, keeping the game moving.

Cori took another bite of her sandwich, even though she hadn't technically swallowed the first. Ethan reached to pinch her leg in just the right spot to make her squirm. She held back the girlish squeal she wanted to give out of respect for the disgust of their neighboring card players.

Ethan leaned into her ear and whispered. "I will make you beg for my lips," he threatened. She chuckled and pulled away from him, not wanting to put anything else on display for the poker night. "Don't forget whose ring that is," he grumbled with a smile that was still more guile than delight. As a general rule, a woman being treated like a man's property was intolerant to her, but somehow Ethan managed to find that playful line where submitting to his dominance implied unending ecstasy for her.

"Where did you get those rings, Ethan?" Danato asked. Cori froze in mid-chew. Apparently, tonight was the night for bringing up awkward questions.

"I got them at a jeweler," Ethan said, perhaps a little too quickly. "Where else?"

Danato wasn't stupid. He caught the subtle undertone of fear between the two of them. Cori continued to chew, hoping that she didn't have to answer for stealing property from wizards. The gold medallions Ethan had used to melt into her rings were once the property of an unconscious wizard. If Danato knew about that little detail, he might have objected to them, which is why they never brought it up.

"Why? Did you want one?" Ethan asked, trying to be casually funny. Danato didn't fall for it, but he returned his attention to his cards.

Cori felt Belus's eyes on her, and she looked at him. She furrowed her brow at him, but he just looked over her rings inquisitively like he was putting together puzzle pieces. Unlike Danato, he seemed to be on the verge of understanding when Nevia stuck a sandwich right in his face. "Sandwich, Mr. Belus." She presented him with the platter of sandwiches in her left hand like a woman familiar with waitressing.

The sudden appearance of the food startled and baffled Belus. "No, thank you, Miss Jordan."

"Just Jordan, please."

"Just Belus, please."

"Sure thing." She turned to Danato. "Mr.—"

"Danato," he corrected before she could finish.

"Sandwich?" she asked.

"Yes, two, if Belus's isn't spoken for."

"You betcha." Nevia smiled and gave him both.

Cori glanced at Ethan, giving him a questioning look. She wondered if Nevia had prompted her sandwich distribution just in time to diffuse any arguments about her rings. Ethan smiled and gave her the slightest nod. She could see now why Ethan had given Nevia such high marks. She was a handy friend to have.

With food as the distraction, Cori slipped upstairs to better acquaint herself with a bar of soap.

12

E THAN WATCHED CORI HEAD upstairs rather mournfully. He knew she wanted to get cleaned up, and he knew it might be better to get her out of there so no more questions were brought up about his ill-gotten gold, but he really wanted to get that kiss from her.

He had not had more than a half dozen nights with Cori since Belus had taken over as her superior, and he resented him for it. He knew Belus wasn't trying to wreck his sex life, but he also knew he wouldn't have any sympathy for it.

"Did Cori seem a little upset to you?" Danato asked.

Ethan looked up from his freshly dealt cards. "What's that?"

Danato shrugged. "She seemed a little off to me," Danato commented, scratching his scruff as he put his attention back on his cards. "I wonder if she had a lot of troublesome nightmares while she was in the time bubble overnight?"

Ethan was about to object that Cori was tough and could handle her nightmares, but he changed tactics. "I don't think she'll ever be able to completely shut out her dreams there." He glanced back at his cards.

"Maybe someone should check on her," Danato suggested, as if the thought had just occurred to him. "Although I'm not sure I want to leave this hand behind." Danato looked through his stack of chips like he was preparing for a big win.

"This isn't much. I'll check on her." Ethan folded his hand and gave Danato a small smile as he left the table. There was a little grumbling from Daniel, but for the most part his escape seemed spontaneously necessary.

He ran up to his apartment and slipped into the bathroom. They still didn't have a tub, but their stand-up shower was roomy enough for two. He slipped out of his clothes with his natural stealth and slipped through the curtain.

Cori, in her gloriously naked state, was letting the water pound on her head to rinse out her conditioner. It was probably long since out, but she was letting the water cascade over her head, neck, and back.

He reached around her and slipped his hands between her legs. She bucked back with a gasp, and he caught her neck before she could head-butt him. He could feel her pulse speed up, and her breathing hastened. "Ethan?" she questioned, not able to open her eyes through the torrent of water on her face.

She knew it was him. The house would not allow anyone in this room apart from them, unless by invitation.

He pushed his body, which was as rigid as a board, closer to hers. He massaged his finger over her, sending her heart rate up even further. "Ethan?" she asked again, quieter.

It was probably wrong to let her fear be their foreplay, but he knew the difference between her fear and her *irrational* fear. He would never taunt her when she was actually afraid. He knew she knew it was him, because she was not fighting against him. She could at any point turn her head to check for sure if it was him, but she didn't. She was letting the fear skirt the edge of arousal until one or the other demanded to be answered for.

He whispered in her ear from behind, "Do you want my kiss now?"

Her body instantly relaxed against him, and he was reminded of why he liked to press the fear button. He loved feeling her body relax for him. He liked to think of it as she was his, and her body would only yield to him.

Cori nodded, but didn't speak. He resisted the urge to give her that kiss right away, and guided her to brace against the wall, while he continued tending to her needs. When she begged for more than his dexterity, he turned her around and lifted her up to him. He gave her a deep kiss that matched the intensity of their desires. She latched onto him and found as much relief with him as he found with her.

After they released each other, Cori stepped out, and he finished showering, since he was already there, anyway. Outside the shower, she dried off. "I'm surprised you managed to escape your poker game. Didn't Daniel have a hissy fit?"

"Not really," Ethan said, scrubbing out his shampoo. "Danato kind of asked me to check on you. If I didn't know any better, I'd say he was trying to support our sex life."

"He might be," she said, muffled, like her towel was over her head. "I think he wants us to have a baby."

Ethan froze, waiting for a scoff or sarcastic statement to follow that. "Really?" He shut the water off. "Why do you say that?" He pulled the curtain aside and saw her robed with a towel twisted around her head. She was applying a moisturizer to her face.

"I didn't feel good the other morning. He asked if it was morning sickness, but he asked it like he was asking if I had bought him a Christmas present. You know?"

Ethan slipped a towel around his waist and watched her for a moment. He wasn't sure about kids, but a pregnant belly and a cute little baby were appealing to him. At first, he thought it might just be a desire to see Cori plump and glowing with hormones, but he liked the idea of them creating a life. He liked the idea of Papa Danato, the ogre, cooing over an itty-bitty baby. As long as the baby was safe and Cori was safe, he was all for it.

Cori must have seen the admiring expression he was giving her in the mirror. She turned around and raised an eyebrow at him. "What?"

"How do you feel about that?"

"What? Danato's interest in our sex life?"

"No." He stepped closer and crossed his arms. All he was missing was his uniform, and he could have been speaking to one of his men. "A baby, Cori. How do you feel about babies?"

Her eyes glazed, and she was lost in thought. This was apparently the first time she had actually examined the question. "I..." She turned around. "I don't know. Things are just so busy right now. I don't even want to know what precautions I would have to take as a pregnant woman. I'll probably have special restrictions to keep demons and sprites away. I'll have to have protection for the baby, because more than likely some creature out there will do something to hurt it."

She sounded nervous, like he had just asked her to perform a one-man play a week from today. He stepped in close behind her and gripped her shoulders a little tighter than he needed to. "Cori, I didn't ask you to figure out the implications. I'm just asking you if you like babies." He moved his hands under her arms and pulled her robe open. He caressed her stomach and whispered in her ear. "Would you like me to give you a child?"

She looked down at her stomach as if she were picturing the same big round bulbous, almost freakish belly. She smiled and looked back at his reflection. "I'll see what Belus thinks."

Ethan coughed and sputtered as he pulled away from her. "What did you just say?"

Her face shrank like she just realized what she'd said as well. "No, I didn't mean it like that."

"Good, because it sounded like you were going to ask Belus's permission for us to have a child."

"Well, I just need to understand the implications before…"

"I think you need to understand that we are the only two contributing to this creation. Belus needs to stay the fuck out of it."

Her guilt for her statement vanished, and she tied her robe. "It's my body. I just need to get a little advice from someone who can warn me about the dangers."

"Great, why don't you talk to Belus? We've got my vote and Danato's, so if you and Belus stalemate us, then we'll let Cleos be the tiebreaker!" Ethan couldn't believe he'd said it, but he also couldn't believe she had played the "my body" card. Like he wasn't as equally concerned for her body as she was.

He expected a raging fit over the statement, but it must have cut her pretty deep. "I'd like to stop talking about this for now. I need some sleep." He moved forward slightly in an attempt to embrace her and apologize. "Please go back down and join your friends," she said quietly and waited for him to leave, which he did.

13

D ANIEL HADN'T EXPECTED TO see Ethan back for the game. He dropped into his chair like it was a recliner and waved to be dealt in. He looked annoyed and the fact that his eyes never met anyone's was a sure sign that he wasn't sharing why.

"Everything go alright?" Danato asked in a low tone to make it sound like a private question, even though everyone was listening for the answer.

"Yeah, she's just tired," Ethan said, handing back two cards to Duke to exchange.

Daniel wasn't always the best observer, but he could see Ethan's hair was wet. He had been gone long enough to give his wife that welcome back kiss, but what happened after that was the question.

He glanced over to Nevia, who had moved to the couch to read a magazine she had had the forethought to pack. Her eyes were fixed on Ethan. She turned her attention to him, and she gave him a taut frown before disappearing into her magazine again.

The game played on until the house turned cold. Nevia started a fire without being asked, but the warmth and gentle cracking only made everyone yawn. Duke and Chuck were the first to bail. Belus seemed determined to play until his chips were out, but after Danato announced his desire to head to bed, he seemed to snap out of his obsession and make the same claim. Heaton made the excuse of heading out for a cigarette, which Ethan glared at him for, but didn't actually reprimand him for.

When it was finally just the two of them, plus one innocuous bloodhound on the couch, Daniel threw a chip into Ethan's face. He looked up at him with the same level of annoyance he had been holding for whatever happened between him and Cori. "Talk," he demanded.

"None of your business."

"You're my business."

"My marriage isn't." Daniel leaned back to swig his beer. He waited for his friend to do the same. Ethan rested back and guzzled down the remainder of his beer. He glanced over at Nevia as if debating if she should be included in this conversation. He spoke low, but he had to know she would hear him. "What do you think about kids?"

"Me?" Daniel poked his chest. "Love 'em," he answered honestly, without thinking of what Ethan's stance might have been on it. "I love the cuteness, and the loud screaming for no reason. I think I'd go insane if I had one, but oh yeah, love the little buggers. I used to be one, you know," he added, which made Ethan smile.

"Yeah, I'd heard that."

"So, what are your thoughts on the little ones?" Daniel asked, wondering if Ethan was being pressured into fatherhood earlier than he'd planned.

"I think I'd like to have a family," he said as if the idea was sound, but hadn't yet solidified as a full-on statement.

"Sounds good to me. I would love to corrupt your little snappers," he said. When Ethan didn't smile, he added, "How does Cori feel about that?"

"She feels she needs to consult with Belus." Daniel nodded, not sure what to say about that. "I'm thinking that was just her way of saying no. We never discussed children before we got together. I guess I had never thought of it one way or another until... recently."

Daniel was curious about what had made him suddenly think about children, but he wasn't good at multitasking, so he let it go. "So, when did you bring babies up to Cori?"

"Tonight."

Daniel laughed. He let the full extent of his laughter balloon too far, but he knew exactly what had happened upstairs. "Oh, my stupid young friend." He wiped away a tear. "I do recall telling you that I am the last person to give you relationship advice, but please allow my years of experience to guide you on your path to potential conception." Daniel raised a finger while he took a drink of his beer, which turned out to be his last.

"Damn." Ethan rolled his eyes and headed to the fridge for a fresh one, which he even popped the top off of. "Bless you, lad."

"Seriously? *Lad*? Are you in father mode?"

"Hell yes, I'm old enough to be your father. Granted, I would have had to have started very early, but..." He took another drink. "Before my father passed, he was considered a priest-slash-doctor-slash-therapist." Although Daniel recalled telling Ethan how his father *passed*, he didn't want to relive it. "As you well know, we are none of those things, but it's not like anyone really understands what I am now, so I can imagine what people thought of him then.

"My father was often invited to home births. The midwives did their thing, but my father was there as kind of a good luck charm. People believed if he was present, there was less of a chance that a child would be born with a demon on its back. There was some folklore for this back in the day, and where I grew up, people still believed in the superstitious mumbo-jumbo. Granted, my mother believes in it whole-heartedly and would slap my face for calling it mumbo-jumbo, but that's just my mother.

"Once I hit the age where dear old dad thought I should learn about the birds and bees, instead of sitting me down for a talk, he took me with him to a birth—first of many to come." Daniel made the sign of the cross, even though he wasn't necessarily a churchgoer anymore. "I would love to tell you that it's beautiful and miraculous, but frankly, at the age of fourteen, it was the scariest fecking thing I had ever seen. The image of what that poor woman went through to release that child kept me a virgin until I was twenty." Daniel took a swig of his beer.

"Was there some advice in there?" Ethan asked.

Daniel grimaced. "You damn plonker! You get a girl up a pole and she has no choice. You ask her to choose to have her body ripped apart in childbirth. You got to let her stew it over." Daniel watched Ethan slowly come to terms with his words, but he didn't like the wait. "Ethan, you just brought up the idea of babies tonight. Let her think about it. If she needs to talk to Belus, let her talk to Belus. If she needs to consult with a Ouija board, a Magic 8-ball, and a fortune cookie, let her do that. It's the biggest decision of both your lives, and she's the one to make all the physical sacrifices, so let her think. Let her decide and thank your lucky stars if she lets you do it to her, cause the only reason she'll thank you for putting her through so much pain is because she'll fall madly in love with that baby the instant she sees it."

Ethan leaned forward, as if the words had doubled him over. He looked up at Daniel and suddenly took off to his room for the night. Daniel smiled, glad to have provided him with a little sage advice.

"That was sweet," Nevia said from the couch.

He jumped, surprised by her. He had forgotten she was there. She was peering over the couch, watching him.

His smile faded unintentionally. "I'm always willing to tell my friends they're being thick as a brick."

"No, I mean your sympathy toward women. I didn't think you had any chivalry."

He paused, seeing the opening for him to make himself look good in her eyes. "I don't." He wouldn't take it, but he saw it. "I think women are a bunch of scrubbers who deserve what they get."

Nevia's eyes narrowed in anger. He was almost pleased to see it. He wasn't sure if this was a new game or cheating at the old one, but he just needed to do something to change the dynamic between them. At this point, being back where they first were together, he was just as likely to slap her as kiss her.

"You're lying to me," she growled, crawling over the back of the couch, which she somehow did gracefully. "Why would you say that to me?" she asked, closing the distance between them. He shook his head and looked away. He didn't have a good reason. "Do you seriously prefer hating me to wanting me?"

Her interpretation of him was dead-on, as usual. He shook his head. "I'm sorry. I just don't know what to do with you."

"You don't have to do anything with me. We've..." She glanced at the door, debating if it was solid enough to mask their conversation from Heaton. He understood the house to be soundproof, but he didn't mention it. "We've had our fun. It's pointless to keep trying to repeat the experience. Just let it go and move on. I'm sure you want to get back to your normal routine."

He didn't bother to lower his voice as she did. "I just love how intuitive you are, but yet you keep bypassing what I'm actually saying to you. I already told you I'm not ready to move on." He leaned forward slightly just to see if she would retreat. She did. "I still want you. I want to bend you over this table. I want to plow you on that couch. I want to find out what that goddamn twenty-something touched on you, and lick it clean."

Even though he didn't actually get up, the threat of the statements made her turn tail to the couch. She leaned on it and crossed her arms like it might protect her from his lascivious attention. "I get that, Daniel, but why? I thought you were the love 'em and leave 'em type. I thought that this would be easy to walk away from. What do you want?"

"You!" he stated again.

"Yes, yes," she ground out, trying to maintain volume control, "the table, the couch, but then what? What do I do when you've had your fill and want to go back to just being partners?" She raised her hands in surrender before he spoke. "Look I get it. I feel how much you want me, and I'd be lying if I said I wasn't tempted, but Daniel, I'm not a one-night stand kind of gal. I haven't slept with anyone since you, and frankly, until I am on the path to marriage, I probably won't."

"No one since me?" he asked, trying to remember how many men had left the bar with her. Had they just walked her home and left her at the door like gentlemen? Was he seriously the only person who knew her body biblically?

Nevia rolled her eyes. "Is that all you heard?"

"No, I just thought otherwise. I don't know what I want from you beyond sex. I'm in uncharted territory here, too. You may have only been with me, but I've never been with a woman I didn't want to be rid of the next day. Wanting you goes against my natural compulsion." He pushed his hands through his hair. His gel had long since worn off and his hair was flipping up like one unending cowlick. "I probably would have a better time getting over my little obsession if you would stop coming over and offering yourself as a sacrifice in your damned experiments."

"I'm not trying to tease you, Daniel. I legitimately want to help you with your powers. I think you have so much potential."

He could see the sincerity in that statement. She didn't have an ulterior motive. She found him fascinating, and forcing him to hurt her was her way of encouraging him to try harder. She didn't want him to be satisfied with just dispersing people. She wanted him to be able to heal them as well. "Thank you. I suppose someone has to be my cheerleader, especially if I won't do it myself."

Heaton chose that moment to return from his cigarette break. He came in smelling of smoke and warming his hands. He looked over the scene and perked an eyebrow. "Am I interrupting something?"

Daniel was about to say no, but Nevia jumped on the opportunity. "Heaton, do you really think you can hide from me forever? If you have a problem with me being your partner, just say so. Don't hide behind your disgusting habit."

Heaton's face blanked, and he opened his mouth a moment before speaking. "I actually like you quite a bit, Jordan. I think you're an excellent marksman and you are welcome on our team."

Daniel could see her accusation had stunned him. Although he said it rather perfunctorily, he got the sense that Heaton was being honest.

"Really," Nevia said. "Then why did you tell Daniel you wanted to transfer?"

Daniel cringed as Heaton's face changed from shock to disappointment. "Because that was a private conversation between us, and I often say things to Daniel that only pertain to the moment. That's why he and I are such good friends. We don't talk about each other behind the others' backs."

Daniel wanted to explain, but there was nothing to explain.

"But you've been—" Nevia started.

"Jordan!" Daniel didn't mean to yell it, but he wanted to make sure she understood. "Four years." The expression on her face was a mix of understanding and shame.

"I'm sorry, Heaton. I made him tell me. I thought…" She looked at him as if the apology was as much for him as Heaton. She shrugged. "I thought I could help. I'm just not used to the dynamic of this partnership yet."

"You'll get it," Heaton said as he walked through to the stairs. "Hell, after four years, Daniel's still figuring it out," he called behind him.

Daniel closed his eyes and prayed that this incident would not ignite a new level of passive-aggressive behavior. When he felt Nevia put her hand on his, he fluttered his eyes open and stood. "Good night, Jordan." He stormed off, not willing to turn around and listen to an apology. This was the reason he didn't want a female partner. One minute he was trying to convince her to sleep with him, the next he was trying to stop her from ruining his relationship with his friend.

C ORI WASN'T SURE WHAT time Ethan had finally crawled into bed. She expected he would stay on his side of the bed to punish her for her offense. She understood why he was angry, but not the degree to which he was. They had never spoken of children before, and frankly, the idea was still a little startling to her.

She hadn't meant to upset him by suggesting she should speak with Belus, but he was objective and taciturn. He would not be reluctant to give her the truth about the risks of raising a child in this place. She hadn't meant to take the decision from their hands, but simply to prepare them for the burden.

As soon as he was in the covers, his arms wrapped under and around her, pulling her to him. If she had not already been awake, the sudden shift may have scared her.

His face tucked in next to her ear and he kissed her cheek before whispering, "I'm sorry." She knew he was, as was she, but it still didn't take away his reaction. She nodded, but didn't voice her apology. She didn't want to just smooth this over, only to have it come up again later as a bigger, sorer issue.

"I shouldn't have brought up something that big and not let you have time to absorb it," he continued.

She nodded again. She liked the sound of that better; at least he was thinking about her perspective. "You should talk to Belus." She turned back to look at him.

"I thought—"

"I was wrong," he jumped in. "If this is something that you want, then you should find out what the risks are. We both know this place is a circus of dangers. You can't ask Danato about it if he's baby crazy. You need someone who can honestly tell you what we're getting into." She smiled at him. She wasn't sure what had happened between now and before, but she was glad he was seeing her side of things. "That is... if you want to have my baby."

His eyes set on hers with a desperate need for satisfaction. She still thought it was unfair for him to spring this on her when he had clearly been thinking about it for a while, but she knew if he wanted something that badly, she could hardly deny him just because she was busy.

She twisted a little further and kissed him. "I'll talk to Belus about it tomorrow... discreetly." It wasn't exactly consent, but it put a smile on his face and he settled himself in to his pillow. His hands were still firmly wrapped around her with no hope of release, but she didn't seem to have trouble falling asleep now that she knew he wasn't angry at her anymore.

15

DANATO DIDN'T KNOW HOW the day had gotten away from him so quickly. The morning breakfast seemed more like the cafeteria in the prison. With three extra mouths to feed, he was tossing French toast on the griddle for nearly a half hour, just to get enough for the four men. Cori had taken sausage duty and Nevia jumped in to start another round of coffee and get water going for Heaton's tea. In the end, he wasn't sure he liked having guests as much as he thought he might.

He called everyone into the office shortly after he arrived at the prison, because he got a call from his communications officer, aka "the taps man." They were getting an unexpected visit from the Council of the Moon. Along with the group that he had planned on arriving today, and the impromptu visit from Annette, he was about to go cross-eyed keeping track of visitors.

Belus arrived shortly before everyone else and he filled him in. He took his spot on the file cabinet just as the others arrived. Cori and Ethan came in, holding hands. They looked over the two seats and decided to share one. He sat down first and gave her a quick pinch on the butt that he probably thought no one noticed before guiding her down to his leg.

Heaton came in and found a spot to lean against the wall. Danato had not seen him in a good number of years, but he had changed quite a bit since the last time he was there. Heaton had always struggled to find an exterior identity. He liked to keep up with style and trends, which in and of itself was not a bad thing, but always changing his look made him seem discontent with himself.

Daniel strutted in, taking the open seat and letting his long legs splay beyond the reasonable space that a body should take up when sitting. Danato had never liked him. He wasn't sure if it was just the memories that coincided with his arrival at the prison, or if he just detested any man who openly flaunted his shortcomings.

He was about to advise Nevia against bringing her gun into the room, but she stopped promptly at the entrance and removed her firearm from under her blue blazer. She released the cartridge and placed it in her back pants pocket. She popped out the loaded bullet, kissed it, and tucked it into her bra, before placing the Glock in the bin. She did it so fast Danato almost didn't catch the kiss. She must have done it that way a thousand times, and probably didn't even know she was doing it.

She came in and shut the door behind her. Heaton watched her settle into the wall beside him before kicking his partner's chair. "Dude." Heaton put enough emphasis on that one word that Daniel looked at him with concern.

"Think you might want to offer the chair?" Heaton glared. Nevia, for her part, stayed quiet and blank-faced. If she cared whether she had a chair, she didn't show it.

Daniel looked her over and turned back to settle into his chair a little deeper. "Nah, I only give my chair to women I hope to sleep with some day." He leaned forward and turned toward the other chair. "Cori, love, would you like my chair?" Either the absurdity of the statement or what she knew would follow gave Cori warrant to laugh at him.

"Flirt as much as you want," Ethan said with as much amusement as threat on his face and in his voice, "but try anything and I'll cut your balls off with fingernail clippers."

Heaton groaned and shook his head. Daniel hissed, presumably with feigned pain, but his smile returned as fast as it left. "Oh, my friend, you don't realize what you've done." Daniel reached over and picked up Cori's hand with his index finger and thumb. His slow movement must have kept her from ripping her hand away. "You just gave me permission to flirt with your wife." Daniel smiled and put Cori's hand to his lips. She smiled, and let him kiss it once, before she drew her hand back to tuck it into Ethan's.

Ethan perked an eyebrow at his friend. "I'm not really worried."

"If I had known you would be a perk of the job," Daniel said with a smarmy tone, "I would have applied for Ethan's position in a heartbeat." Cori rolled her eyes at that. Danato glanced at Belus. He wondered if Daniel knew how vehemently Belus had fought to get him considered for the position. In the end, the board would not approve of someone with such a violent criminal record and Danato had put the brakes on long before that edict, anyway.

Daniel looked like he was going to say more, but Danato had had enough of the boys' club for one morning. "Gentlemen, can we get on with what I called you here for?" Ethan and Cori snapped to and shut up.

"Yes, sir, let's have it." Daniel smacked his hands together and rubbed them.

"We've got a full house today. As you know, Annette is back." Heaton and Daniel exchanged smiles. Cori abruptly raised her hand.

"I'll explain later, Cori," Belus said, and she put her hand down.

Danato tried not to let that bother him. He had always enjoyed being the one Cori came to with questions, but he needed to make an effort not to interfere with Belus's command. It wouldn't do anyone any good if she wasn't sure who she could turn to for answers. If she was even remotely concerned about offending either of them, she might opt to keep to herself, and history had proven that Cori, guided by her own deductions, was risky. "Thank you, Belus," he said, as if *he* was the one who had suggested he explain things to her later.

So much for that effort.

"I have two groups arriving today. First, the Council of the Moon has decided to drop by."

"Council of the Moon?" Ethan leaned forward with interest and nearly pushed Cori off his lap. "What are they here for?"

"Ah..." Danato searched through the paperwork on his desk and found the file he needed. "The werewolf, Callin, has requested an audience with them. He wants his sentence revoked, and he wants custody of his child." Danato skimmed the document again to make sure that was right. "That ought to be a short visit." Nevia shifted on the wall like she wanted to say something, but decided not to.

"Why is that?" Ethan asked.

"Well, for one, he formed a pack, and that means an automatic six-month sentence. He's already served nearly three. We aren't going to release him early unless the council can prove that we were in the wrong to secure him, but since Leona hired us, it was pretty open and shut."

"What about custody?" Ethan gripped onto Cori as he leaned forward again.

Danato shrugged. "It's preposterous. It's a hundred-year-old doctrine; he's not going to convince them in one trial to change their policies."

"Why not? Someone has to start the change," Ethan rumbled, apparently offended that Danato was not supporting this man's rights.

"I don't control the council, Ethan, but I was going to suggest that you help get them situated when they come in. I think Leona might be joining them, since the custody in question is involving her child. I figured Cori wouldn't mind missing that meet-and-greet again."

Cori scoffed. "No doubt."

"Cori," Danato continued, "you can help Annette with the dragon. You'll need to—"

"Ahh..." Cori interrupted and looked back at Belus, "*can* I help with that?"

Belus looked at her squarely. From anyone else's perspective, they would have thought he was glaring at her, but he was just trying to figure out what she was talking about. "No." His face abruptly lit with understanding and he shook his head at Danato. "Pen..." He set aside a glare for Cori for that misspoken start. "The dragon is irritated with Cori. I think Ethan will have better luck with her."

"I don't want Cori to deal with Leona," Danato objected.

"Who's coming in on the second truck?" Cori asked. "I could help with them."

"No." Danato flashed eyes to Belus, looking for backup in this, just as she had gone to him for it.

"No, Cori, they're nonessential guests," Belus joined in with his usual diplomacy that bordered on indifference. "Daniel and the others can get them situated. Right?" Belus hollered to the back of Daniel's head. "Right, Daniel?"

Daniel looked back behind him and saw the sternness in Belus's face. "Right!" He sat up straight and leaned forward on his elbows. "Yes, sir, whatever you need," he said to Danato. "We are far from guests. In fact, Heaton and I could help with the dragon."

Heaton nodded, but both Danato and Belus chimed in with a resolute, "No!" Daniel slumped back in his chair like a rain cloud had just settled on the remainder of his visit.

"Are you sure Cori can't help with the dragon?" Danato asked Belus.

Belus shrugged. "If I bring her back without an arm, you won't be any happier with me."

"*I* won't be happier with that," Cori added, since no one was bothering to ask her opinion about dealing with a grumpy dragon.

"If Leona's anywhere in this building, I don't want Cori near her," Ethan interjected. "Daniel can handle werewolves. Why can't Cori take the non-essentials?"

Belus and Danato both chimed again, "No!" They weren't always on the same page with things, but he was happy that they could still put up a uniform front.

"I'm not sure I prefer Cori to be armed again outside of the time bubble," Danato stated carefully, "but this might be the time." He looked at Belus, although he didn't think he should have to. "Belus, thoughts."

Belus's face blanked. It was admirable and slightly amusing that Belus actually thought about his answers when they really counted. Before Belus could answer, Nevia, who was barely present in the room as a body, made everyone's head turn with a simple statement. "I can go with Cori."

A small exchange took place between Belus and Danato, Heaton and Daniel, and Heaton and Danato. "She's better with a gun than anyone in this room, I guarantee it," Heaton assured Danato.

"Not to mention," Ethan added, "she'll sense any aggression before it can even be acted on."

Danato looked at Nevia. She seemed like a regimented young woman, but he still couldn't get over someone so young and so small, being Cori's bodyguard. Then again, he had learned from Belus never to judge a man by his size, so he could hardly deny the idiom to a woman. "You okay with that?" he asked Cori unceremoniously.

Cori glanced at Nevia and smiled. She could hardly turn down the woman's protection, even if she wasn't okay with it. "Yeah, sure, bring on the Council of the Moon." She said it with a smile, but Danato sensed that something about the situation bothered her.

16

I T MORTIFIED CORI THAT she had to be assigned a bodyguard just to do her job. She understood everyone's reluctance to give her gun back, and she understood that female werewolves were beyond dangerous, but when it came right down to it, she wanted to remind Danato that at one point she had been considered a potential candidate for Warden. When did everyone forget that?

"It's hard to shake an image you didn't mean to cultivate," Nevia said, interrupting her mental conversation. They were on the docks waiting for the first truck to arrive. Given the nature of the cargo, Danato didn't want them to just wait for a call.

Nevia was standing against the wall behind her while Cori sat on a stack of pallets. She wondered if she had something against sitting in general, or if she was concerned the pallets might put slivers in her nice trouser pants.

"What?" Cori said, unconsciously touching a pocket on her black cargo pants.

"Danato and Ethan seem very concerned for your safety. I'm sure they don't realize how frustrating it is for you to excel through coddling."

Cori looked her over. Could she really smell all that from her? "They can't help it. They've spent a lot of time cleaning up after me. I've made a lot of mistakes."

"We all make mistakes. It doesn't mean we have to pay for them forever."

"Three months ago, I helped one of our most dangerous inmates avoid capture so that he could help me save Belus after I shot him in the chest."

Nevia raised her brow, taking in the statement. "Oh, so their concerns aren't without foundation." Nevia's eye sparkled and despite the seriousness of the statement, she started laughing. Cori joined her, allowing the ridiculousness of her life to tickle her funny bone. "I guess I don't have any advice for that after all."

Cori wiped away her tears of laughter. "They mean well. I just don't know why I work so hard if I'm not going to get any respect."

"Oh, they respect you," Nevia corrected. "I think they put you higher than you realize."

"You can tell all that from smell?"

"Not exactly." She looked down as if she was embarrassed. "I was training to be a profiler for the FBI when I got... sidetracked. I had a knack for it. Part of it was my ability, but another part is just being able to read people. I'm a good observer."

"I can see that, but you can tell if people are lying though. I mean, if you were around for the lie."

"Yes, but only if they are willfully lying."

"What's the difference?"

"Someone might say 'I'll be there in a minute.' That isn't true because it never really means a minute, but they aren't lying because they aren't actually trying to deceive you. For me to detect a lie, the person has to be consciously saying something that goes against what they believe is true."

"So," Cori shifted herself so she could face her, "if I took you to a prisoner, and they said they were wrongfully imprisoned..." Cori let her finish.

"If they believe they are wrongfully imprisoned, I won't detect a lie." Cori's disappointment was obvious. "However," Nevia added, "if we asked that prisoner if they had done whatever it was they were incarcerated for, their answer could be determined true or false."

Cori nodded. "Interesting."

"Did you have anyone in mind?"

Cori shook her head. "No, not really."

"And that would be a lie." Nevia smiled.

Cori laughed. She hadn't intended for Nevia to use her detection on her. "I do, but it has nothing to do with my current duties, and frankly, just saying that prisoner's name would get me into trouble."

"Is it the one who helped you save Belus?"

Cori could feel prickling heat travel down her spine. She felt like she had opened Pandora's box, and she didn't know how to close it. "Um…"

"Don't worry, Cori. It's none of my business. I just can't help trying to solve the puzzles in front of me."

"I guess that's all I'm trying to do. I just don't have the skill to solve them like you do." Cori could hear the truck backing into the loading bay outside. Workers started moving around, prepared for whatever cargo was accompanying this shipment of visitors.

Cori jumped off the pallets, with full intentions of not being scared or seduced by Leona. She glanced back at Nevia. She was right behind her. The woman was small, but like Belus, had a rock-steady presence. She wasn't sure what her opinion was of her personally yet, but professionally, she already respected her.

Cori stepped onto the dock rather than let them wander for even a few feet to get to her. "Let them off before you start wheeling boxes about," Cori scolded the eager dock workers.

When the dock door opened to reveal the back of the truck, she took in a deep breath, and reminded herself that she was second only to the warden. She was pretty damn important to this place and, female werewolf or not, Leona was going to treat her as such.

The truck door slid up, and Cori heard the sound of babies crying. Leona emerged from the truck with an infant car seat hanging on one arm, and a colicky baby and a diaper bag in the other. Her hair, that had looked stylishly messy the last time Cori saw her, was just plain messy this time.

A sixties-style box dress in a boring shade of mocha replaced her usual tailor-fit inappropriate gray business suits. With the right accessories and makeup, Cori could see the dress being flattering for the slender French woman, but with beige flats and none of the accouterments, it just made her look dowdy.

"Leona," Cori said as the disheveled woman came at her full speed.

"Cori," Leona looked around. "Do you... there, that will do." Leona gave her a quick cheek-to-cheek kiss before lumbering down to the stack of pallets Cori had just been sitting on. Leona pulled an armada of baby stuff out of the diaper bag and proceeded to change diapers at the warp speed of *mom*.

Cori wasn't sure what to do with any of that. Her arch-enemy was too preoccupied to even make her uncomfortable with a semi-lesbian lip kiss. She was a little disappointed. Not so much at missing the discomfort of the aforementioned kiss, but because this time she had been prepared for their meeting, and it didn't matter.

"You must be Cori."

Cori looked back to see a flock of fem-wolves coming out of the back of the truck in perfect formation, with the tallest straight-haired blonde right in front. The others varied in details, but in the end they were just as they were meant to be—an amalgam of all-female types, uniformly dressed in the same mocha box dresses. Unlike Leona, though, they were all pulling it off. And not with jewels or makeup.

They were all pulling it off with pristine natural beauty: their hair long, shimmering, lying gently on their shoulders, as if each strand had been polished and placed; their nails manicured into firm lengthy almond shapes with a high gloss peachy pink nail polish that didn't distract from anything else. If they were wearing makeup, it was only foundation and powder. A little shimmer on their lips was the only thing Cori could see.

The woman at the front stood out because of her 6'2" height and silver moon necklace. To say she was beautiful would have been like saying you preferred red M&Ms over blue ones. All the women were beautiful. To see them all at once was the only thing that took away from the experience. That much beauty is likely to nauseate anyone.

Cori threw out her hand to the woman. "You must be the Council of the Moon?"

"I am Frederique. I am the head councilwoman." Her French accent was even thicker than Leona's. The musk that came off of her when she shook Cori's hand almost made her cough. "I am also Leona's sister," she said with a smile.

Cori glanced back at Leona. There was no doubt in her mind that Leona had probably relayed all of their association to her sister, as any sister would. "I think very highly of your sister," Cori said, in case the translation of the story had missed the finer details of their encounter.

"Yes, she speaks very highly of you as well." It took Cori a moment to realize that Frederique still had a hold of her hand, but when she gently tried to tug it away, she started massaging her hand with her thumb.

"I understand that she is fighting for custody of her children."

"Nothing to worry about." Frederique stepped closer and Cori found herself freezing in place like she often had with Leona. She tried to pull herself out of the ridiculous trance, but the desire to stay right there was so strong. "I think Leona will get everything she wants, and more." Cori heard the distinct sound of a pistol chamber being loaded. The frozen feeling she had struggled with left, and she looked back at Nevia.

Nevia's eyes were narrowed into fine slits and her target, although not actually being aimed at with the gun yet, was Frederique. Likewise, Frederique had the same narrowed eyes on her. Cori wanted to step between them to stop whatever was about to occur, but she wasn't exactly sure standing between a fem-wolf and a Glock was a good idea.

"What do we have here?" Frederique drawled, not taking her eyes off Nevia as she sniffed the air. "What are you? You don't smell like fear. That must be stupidity I smell."

"I would advise you to release her before I confirm or deny that assumption."

Frederique dropped her hand and side-stepped so she was in front of Nevia. They each looked cool and calm as they glared at each other. The only one who was in the least bit of discomfort was Cori.

"You smell like a mutt."

"I've got a little bloodhound in me," Nevia said. "And I can smell just what you're up to. So, I'll need you to continue to keep your distance for the duration of your visit."

"Do you have any idea who you're talking to?"

"Yes, ma'am, the head of the Council of the Moon. I could make more impressive observations, but we both know it doesn't take my abilities to smell what you are. That musk you emit is as repugnant as skunk, but it doesn't cover up your intentions, so keep your distance or I'll shoot you dead."

Frederique laughed, and her entourage had a little chuckle themselves. Cori cringed at the insult. She knew as well as they did that bullets wouldn't even penetrate their thick muscle fibers. Even completely relaxed, the bundled tissue was constantly in preparation for the next time they would change into full werewolf form, expanding their muscles into abnormal and painful proportions.

"Oh, you stupid mongrel, do you not know that I can't be affected by bullets? My muscles would ricochet it." Cori wondered if that was an exaggeration or knowledge from personal experience.

"Actually, I did know that," Nevia said, tapping her gun against her leg. "That's why I would shoot you in the eye. The ricochet inside your skull would do nicely to lobotomize you, even if it didn't outright kill you."

Frederique paled at that statement. Cori pinched her lips back so she wouldn't smile at Nevia's ballsy retort.

"Evidence has found that a long knife, or shiv of sorts, can be thrust into the nasal cavity," Nevia continued. "It doesn't kill right away, but werewolves have extensive blood vessels in their nasal cavity to accommodate for a heightened sense of smell. You have a major one right above your left nostril. Since you can't apply pressure to the area, you'll likely bleed out in about ten minutes.

"Also, if my aim is good enough, which, by the way, it is, I could shoot you in the hollow spot where your throat meets your chest. The soft spot will allow just enough penetration to either cut off air flow or blood flow. If it's removed outside of surgery, you would drown in your own blood. The intercostal muscles between the ribs are pretty flexible and if all else fails, there are always a few orifices that allow bullet penetration.

"But to get back on point, yes, I know you are bullet-*resistant*. So, let's just leave the pissing contests to the males of the species and get you ladies to your destinations."

Frederique took a moment to decide whether it was better to concede for now, or challenge Nevia's aim. She decided against it and turned back to Cori. "If you wouldn't mind, Cori, my ladies are parched from the trip. Could we make a detour for some water?"

Cori nodded. "Of course. I'll show you to the cafeteria. You can have whatever you like." Cori glanced back at Leona. "Should I have the staff prepare some baby food?"

"That would be most generous of you," Frederique said with a sweetness that she never would have suspected for insincere without Nevia's reaction.

17

E THAN EASED THE DRAGON that had recently been dubbed Penelope out of her airplane hangar. He understood why Belus was reluctant to let Cori near her. The great beast was agitated and difficult to coax out without the invitation of a battle.

Penelope's cacophonic roar had become a lugubrious moan. He rarely sympathized with her since she had all too often broken his ribs, but his heart clenched at the sight of her big eyes tearing. She did not want to come out, and was pouting to get her way.

Despite Ethan's strength, there was no fighting with a dragon. Well, there was, but there was certainly no dragging a dragon. Once the beast was down, the only thing you could do was wait her out, or lure her out. He threw down the big chain that was laughably called a leash. Laughably because of the aforementioned conundrum.

He approached the big head and touched her snout. She let out a curt puff of air. Despite her lack of fire-breathing ability, it smelled like charcoal. He leaned forward and rubbed the spot between her eyes, above the nose. It wasn't his favorite technique to calm her, because it usually left his pants covered in snot.

Penelope groaned appreciatively. Despite her character being more recognizable as a cat, her leg twitched, as if she wanted to help him with his efforts. Her mouth opened, and she licked him up the side of the leg. As if snot wasn't bad enough.

Behind him, he heard Annette laughing. Her throaty laugh didn't quite match her physique. Nothing about her matched. She was feminine, but well-muscled. Her hair and makeup were mature and reserved, but her ripped jeans and t-shirt were almost pubescent. She was attractive, but something about her was extremely asexual to him, like kissing her would be like kissing a sister.

He looked back and saw Annette wearing a long, black-hooded robe. Although he didn't question her when she'd said she was a witch, he kind of took it more literally than symbolically. Given his experience at the prison, he expected she would simply raise her hands and call down the power of an ancient god with a chant and dance.

What he hadn't expected was an hour's worth of murmured prayers, frankincense, crushed flower petals, and bowing. That was just to clear the room of any unwelcome spirits, demons, and all-around bad vibes. After that, she began lighting candles, chanting, and meditating.

"You do that very well," Annette said, looking on from her makeshift folding-table altar.

"I've known a few dogs in my time. Granted, they were never quite this slobbery."

"You should feel privileged. The saliva of a dragon has many medicinal properties. In a pinch, you should come to her if you're hurt."

"Like dogs when they lick their wounds?"

"Yes, only not just coagulants, add antibodies, anti-inflammatory. To be perfectly frank and gross, if one were willing to drink the saliva of a dragon, it would be as effective as a whole-body cleanse. It would repopulate the flora in your gut. It would balance your pH, reduce inflammation to your joints, and purge toxins with one glass."

"Sounds like a miraculous cure-all," Ethan said. In the mere distraction, Penelope huffed again, and he was promptly reminded to rub again. "Why don't you bottle that along with the blood? I could put a bucket down right now and get you a gallon in a few minutes."

"I've tried it many times. The curative properties start degrading the instant they leave the dragon's mouth. You can maintain most of it by keeping it at body temperature, which is why when I speak of drinking the saliva, I really do mean straight from the lips to the lips."

Ethan gagged. There was no way he was going to drink warm dragon spit, especially when he saw it dripping into his glass directly from the source. He still had trouble drinking the dragon semen. The only reason it was remotely tolerable was because wheat grass was the dominating taste.

Wheat grass was also disgusting, but it was honest in its unpalatable flavor. Had the dragon semen been mixed with berries, it wouldn't have worked. First off, no one should ever do such a thing to a berry. Second, having something repulsive blended with something appetizing would not result in him liking dragon sperm, it would just make him hate berries.

"After a few hours outside of a bodily environment, the liquid becomes useless," Annette finished.

"So..." Ethan was interrupted by Penelope giving him another grateful kiss. He took the opportunity to walk away, which prompted her to follow, like any animal would when they thought there was more petting to come. "You said you have many uses for the blood. I take it you don't just use it to get high."

She smiled at him proudly. He wasn't sure how a woman he had just met could be proud of him, but he imagined she took a vested interest in Danato's understudy. "Dragons are magical creatures. Everything in this prison is magical, or supernatural, or at the very least, an aberration to what humans consider normal. But unlike all the other creatures here, dragons are immortal."

"What?" Ethan must have said it as dead-panned as he meant it. The word wasn't registering. She smiled and let the word sink in deeper. "That's not possible." She smiled and bit her lip. She waited for him to formulate an argument. "Are you saying their spirit lives on, or are you saying they literally don't die?"

"They don't die." She said it simply, but the number of questions that were stacking up behind him like a pile-up on a freeway were making his head shake without any verbal objection to back it up. "There are currently eight dragons on Earth today. I imagine there were more at one time, but I detest the dinosaur-dragon debate. Frankly, it's the chicken and the egg all over again."

"Eight? Where are they?"

"As you well know, your upper management keeps one male for your... supplements. The other three males that I have never had the privilege of seeing are god knows where. And the other three females are housed at my facility in China. I'm not aware of anyone who has seen all eight. In fact, seeing the four females at regular intervals probably puts me pretty high on the totem pole."

"Why only eight? Don't they breed? Why have sperm if you aren't going to breed? If they never die, would they overpopulate?" Ethan threw out just a few of the questions he had rolling around in his mind.

"Only eight, because that's what is left after many years with humans as hunters. They will breed, but..." Annette came around the table and placed her hands on his shoulders. She turned him around to look at Penelope, who was sitting up properly, twitching her tail like a cat.

Annette wrapped her arms around him like she was about to point stars out to him in the night sky. The warmth of her, and the sweet floral perfume, made the embrace seem maternal. He wasn't sure if he should feel uncomfortable at the sudden closeness to a stranger, but he didn't. He relaxed against her and let her hold him.

"Those dragons will live forever, unless they breed. It's kind of like the phoenix. The female, in order to be fertilized, must receive... shall we say, a lot of attention from the male. I won't get into details, but when people brag about going all night long, dragons could brag about going all week long." Annette chuckled, and he smiled to let her know he was amused, but still listening.

"The male eventually dies to impregnate her. Her pregnancy can last years. It depends on a number of factors that none of us really know, but in the end, the female will give birth to one male and one female."

"Twins?" Ethan asked.

"Oddly, no," Annette said, distracted, like that topic was one that had baffled her time and again. "The female is almost an exact replicate of the male, with the only variation in DNA being the sex, and vice versa with the male."

"So they just flip-flop, but come out predesigned to be potential mates again."

"Precisely," Annette pitched with pride for his quick mind.

"I take it the female dies in childbirth?" Ethan asked, following the thought process of the phoenix idea.

Her hands slipped from the embrace and she moved behind him, now leaning on him more than holding him. She sighed. "Well, sort of. I would love to romanticize it, but... the offspring eat her as nourishment for the first weeks of their life. And when I said that the male dies to impregnate her, I meant that after she conceives, she becomes so ravenous that she eats him in order to gain the energy to grow her babies."

Ethan turned around to look at her. He felt like his pleasant bedtime story had just turned into a horror movie. Annette looked sad at having to tell him the truth. "Wow, so not so much like the phoenix, but more like a praying mantis?"

Annette nodded. "I'm sorry, they are such beautiful, miraculous animals, but... they are animals."

"So even if you let them mate, you would never be able to get more dragons, just different versions of the same dragons."

"Correct," she said, rubbing the back of her neck under the hood. "So, we just don't breed them."

"They live forever?" Ethan verified.

"Yes, forever. Or at least well over five hundred years. We know enough to tell their age and our oldest dragons are 650 years old. There is some speculation that breeding will become necessary at some point, but so far we haven't had a reason to. The dragons are healthy, and for the most part, they prefer their solitary lifestyle."

Ethan wondered if she was an advocate for or against breeding. "If they can't reproduce multiple times, how did they ever come to be eight, and not just two?"

"Oh," Annette shook her head and headed back to her altar, "now you're just getting into the chicken and the egg. All we have are theories: random quadruplets, orgy mating, and a whole slew of things I don't waste my time arguing with, because no one is ever going to try it, anyway."

Ethan chuckled at the frustration she got even from the mere mention of the theories, let alone what she might have felt sitting between two bickering biologists or animal behaviorists. "Okay, so getting back to my original question. What do you use the blood for?"

"If the saliva is a cure-all, then the blood is a magical primer. Everything I do is enhanced by the blood. Without the blood, I'm just a religious hack. With the blood, I can tap into natural and magical forces. I draw on that power and do... essentially whatever I will it to do."

"But... you're a good witch, right?" Ethan smiled tersely.

She came around the table again and planted a sincere, motherly kiss on his forehead, which he readily leaned in for. "I am an Earth goddess witch." The way she said it, he expected the candles in the room to flicker against an unseen breeze, but they didn't. "I tap into the energy that the Mother Earth uses to grow and nourish the plants and animals. However, I can also tap into the volatile energies that create storms, earthquakes, and volcanoes. This energy doesn't have to be used for evil, but it is power, and I can't honestly say that I've never held a grudge before."

"How powerful are you?" Ethan couldn't help asking.

"I have no power whatsoever. But the Earth is the largest source of coalescent energy outside of the universe and you'd have to be a god to tap into that. I'm just a witch, a witch with very good connections. And as you know, the most dangerous trait of anyone is who you know."

"So, I should keep you on my good side."

Annette smiled broadly and pinched his cheeks. "Oh, honey, I'm already your biggest fan. As long as you keep Danato happy, you'll keep me happy."

Ethan grimaced at that stipulation. "How happy?"

18

AFTER CORI AND NEVIA got the werewolves situated in the guest quarters on the north side of the prison, they headed back inside via the back entrance. Cori waited until they were inside the prison, free from chattering teeth and deafening wind gusts, before speaking.

"Do you mind telling me what that was all about?" she asked as they headed through the lines of useful and useless storage closets. Nevia rubbed her gloved hands together and shivered relentlessly. Cori hadn't really thought about it, but somewhere along the line, she had become immune to the cold. It still sucked, but she wasn't as traumatized by it.

"I'm sorry, Cori, I was wrong to imply your coworkers were being overly protective of you. They were right to want you away from those women." They continued, turning past the prop room.

"I know they're dangerous. I'm not stupid. I don't think Leona would actually hurt me."

"Cori." Nevia shook her head as they headed by the gym. Cori caught a glimpse of the famous Annette.

Ethan was watching her sprinkle rose petals all around the dragon. Penelope, for the most part seemed to be content, albeit fascinated by the little red spots that were appearing around her. "I know what you think those women think of you, but you're wrong. I can see you respect their feminine ideals and strength. You probably assume they see a kindred spirit in you."

"Yeah, sort of." Cori thought that sounded about right.

"They don't." Nevia stopped in the front foyer to give her a stern but sympathetic gaze. "I don't mean to insult you, or disappoint you, but I feel obligated to protect you and prepare your emotions. They think of you as a chew toy."

Cori quirked a smile and crossed her arms, already prepared to dismiss the statement, but she quickly remembered how intuitive Nevia was. She had never viewed Leona as anything but her arch-enemy, but somehow hearing this was hurtful. She thought they at least respected each other as enemies. "I don't really know what you mean by that. Do they want to kill me?"

"No, they want to torment you. They want to manipulate you. I don't know what happened between you and Leona, but whatever it was, your interpretation and hers are completely different. Those women do not view you as a friend or an enemy. You are entertainment for them, and that is all."

Cori felt so stupid. She'd thought she could be considered a rival to fem-wolves. It was like she just found out that the only reason the cool kids were hanging out with her was so they could pour pig's blood on her at a school dance. Unfortunately, she didn't have any cool powers to take revenge on them.

"I'm sorry, Cori," Nevia apologized again.

"I don't know why I'm so bothered by it," she said, trying to find something else to do with her hands.

"Fem-wolves are notorious bitches," Nevia said flatly, like any good girlfriend would. Cori was now pretty sure that she liked Nevia professionally *and* socially. "You are one of the unfortunate few that can't block out their hypnotic abilities."

"Ethan said they have no particular seduction skills."

"It's not magical; it's just a soothing voice, strong smell, and the right combination of look and touch. It is rare to be affected as much as you are, but it's nothing against you."

Cori could hear the defense in her voice. "They consider me weak. They think I'm a weak-minded human that they can manipulate." She could hear herself saying it, and it just sounded like she was saying, "the sky is blue." *No shit, Sherlock!* Of *course*, these women thought she was weak. Of *course*, they had no respect for her. Of *course*, they thought she was pathetic.

"Fortunately, you live in a prison with many talented psychics," Nevia interrupted her internal dejection. "That one that helped Ethan. Mezula. She could put a simple hypnotic suggestion in to block their influence. Like I said, theirs isn't magical, so it's easily overridden."

"That's a good idea, but Mezula and I don't really socialize."

"Almost any reader could do it, if you can trust them not to mess with anything else."

"I think I can find one," Cori said with confidence. "How do you know all this, anyway?"

"I've been doing a lot of research since... I got hired. I don't like surprises."

"Nothing surprises me anymore," Cori said flatly.

19

DANIEL SAT WITH HEATON on the pallets, waiting for the truck to arrive. The dock manager had been giving them both a nasty glare, but Daniel lowered his tinted glasses to show him who had the better chance at winning a staring contest. He wasn't in the habit of flaunting his eyes for the upper hand, but he didn't appreciate Heaton being lumped in with that glower.

Heaton had at least eased off the cigarettes when it was just the two of them. Unfortunately, that proved he was only smoking to hide his emotions from Nevia. Considering they usually didn't need a third party to interpret for them, it was disappointing he felt he needed to hide anything from anyone.

"Were you serious the other night... about transferring?" Daniel asked, hoping he was being casual enough not to set off a temper tantrum.

"I don't know," Heaton said without actually looking at him. "I was just talking. I think about stuff. I don't always think it through before I act on it."

Daniel looked around to see if anyone was going to observe if the conversation went a little sappy. "What's up with you, Heaton? *Is* it Nevia? Cause say the word and she's gone."

Heaton scoffed. "She's the bloodhound, dude. You guys have put more transmorphs in this prison in the last three months than we have in four years. Not to mention you're totally besotted with her."

"So, what... no, I'm not... Look, say the word and the bird is out."

Heaton shook his head. "She's good, Daniel. She's really good. And yes, you are."

Daniel examined his friend. "Do you have a thing for her?" Heaton didn't react. He kept looking at his shoes with interest. "Do you?"

Heaton looked up at him and shook his head. He looked frustrated, but too tired to get mad. "It's nothing to do with her, Daniel. It's barely got anything to do with you. I just don't know if I can be your partner anymore."

"That's got every fecking thing to do with me." Daniel resisted the urge to use volume. "You're like a brother to me, Heaton."

Heaton shook his head. "I'm not trying to fuck up your life. I'm just trying to get me back in control of mine."

"I don't accept that as an answer."

"Well, you're going to have to," Heaton said with a little more volume. "Let's just forget this, please. We've got more important things to deal with."

"Not to me," Daniel grumbled and slipped off the pallets to stretch his legs. "When you remember that I'm your best friend, be sure to catch me up on whatever screw is loose up there to think you couldn't just be honest with me."

Heaton rolled his eyes, but the sound of the truck pulling in distracted them both from the semi-heartfelt conversation. Daniel headed up the platform to help unload the passengers within.

Danato had warned them both that what was inside was top secret, so no one, not even Ethan and Cori, were to know about it. When Daniel asked why they could see it, he said it wasn't a secret for them.

The garage door opened just as Heaton came up to stand beside him. "Shouldn't there be a drum roll for this?" he said, crossing his arms. Daniel chuckled, thankful that Heaton could always joke with him, even if their friendship and partnership was struggling.

The dock manager opened the back of the truck and Daniel raised his eyebrows. He and Heaton exchanged looks before returning their gaze to the drum set sitting before them in the truck.

20

ORI SMILED AS SHE came through the long line of grappling vampires. She hadn't been to see Cleos in months, and she was happy to have a legitimate excuse to do so. Despite the smile on her face, though, she had butterflies in her belly.

She and Cleos had not parted on great terms. She had basically given up seeing him in order to focus on her marriage. He had conceded to this in order to keep her happy, but he was also a little sore that she had insisted he tell her the truth regarding the actions that got him incarcerated.

His refusal to give her a reason to forgive him changed everything for her. She could have forgiven him for eating her less noticeable memories. She could have forgiven him for his crimes if it were done for any reason other than sadism. What she couldn't forgive was him purposely hiding the truth, so she wouldn't be able to forgive him.

She stepped in front of the glass wall that was Cleos's containment. The soundproof cell required that she activate an intercom that was not too dissimilar to those at apartment buildings, only you didn't have to keep pushing the button to speak.

Coming before the glass, she could see Cleos inside, reading in the dimmed light. The yellow glow outside of his cell was harsh and fluorescent. The bluish tint inside of his cell looked tranquil, almost romantic. She was always impressed that he looked at home in his cell. Whenever she visited, she felt like she was disturbing him and should apologize.

For once, his chestnut hair was actually pulled back, but only loosely. He had always looked pale and gaunt to her, but he looked more so today. She wondered if that had anything to do with her, but she decided she was just being egocentric.

Cleos put down his book and slipped over to the glass wall. He tickled his goatee as he looked her up and down, in that almost sexual way. He settled on her face and leaned against the window. At first she thought he might refuse her visit, but a smirk perked up on his lips.

She mimicked that smirk and pushed the white button on the little box. "Hi," she said, immediately wishing she had something witty to say right behind it, but she didn't.

"Hello," he said, using a deeper voice than his own. "So, the ex-lovers endure their first awkward meeting after the breakup."

Cori smiled broadly. They certainly weren't lovers, nor had that ever been a consideration, but it definitely had the feel of two former somebodies trying to break the ice enough to speak civilly. "Something like that." Cori leaned into the glass, mimicking his body, and biting her lip so she could batten down some of her oafish grin. "I've missed you."

"No, you haven't," he said wryly. "You've been too busy with work and husband to miss me."

"True, but you know how you see someone after so long, and you suddenly remember how important they were in your life? You kind of get that reverse chronological pain of loss."

He paused and let that sink in while he stared her down. "What are you here for, Cori?" he asked. "Because I know it's not to catch up."

"Ouch," she said, slipping her hands from the glass to stand normally. He did the same. "I guess that's true, but I think we both know why I haven't made the effort to come by socially."

"And we both know that nothing in that area of interest will change," he added. "What do you need?" he drawled.

"I have an issue with some fem-wolves. Apparently, I'm easy to hypnotize and I need that to stop." He stared blankly at her. "Can you do that? Stop them from being able to hypnotize me."

"Yes," he said, as if he had already said it. She saw movement below, his fingers dancing through the food slot. "You know the routine."

"Oh, right." Cori went to grab his hand, but the thought of her secret pocket trinket popped into her head. She reached and pulled back spasmodically until she found a pocket to slip her hand in to keep it still. "Listen, Cleos, I don't..."

"What now?" he growled. His curtness caught her off guard. Apparently, her perceived mistrust offended him.

"I kind of have a secret. It's just a little one, but you have to understand that it's *my* secret to keep or reveal or just forget about completely."

"You think I would tell your secret?"

"It's the only secret I have from Ethan right now. If he were to find out, that would be bad. Finding out from you, would... you know."

"I do know. He doesn't know you're down here, does he?"

"He was busy and the fem-wolves are here. I need to make sure I don't get taken advantage of by them. I also need to make sure you don't take advantage of this situation."

"You think I want revenge?"

"No, but you did tell Ethan you would not try to get between us. You knowing this secret would put you right smack in the middle. If you can't handle knowing without telling him, then I'll have to risk seeing Mezula."

"Don't you dare let that sadistic bitch touch you again," he spat. It sounded protective, but Cori got the distinct impression that it was more about competition. "I can keep your damned secret. Just give me your hand."

"Okay." She reached for his hand, but stopped again. "Since you're going to know my secret…"

"Oh, hell," he threw his head back, "no wonder he tries to keep a tight rein on you."

"Maybe you can help me find the answer I'm looking for."

"There is no plausible deniability with a mind reader, you know? Just give me your hand before I change my mind."

Cori touched his hand, and he shivered as if she had given him a good deal of pain, or a great deal of pleasure. "What's wrong?" she asked quietly, but didn't expect an answer.

"I've missed you too," he said through slitted eyes, before he leaned his head back. His eyes sorted through her mind to block out whatever loose ends were making it possible for her to be manipulated so easily by the fem-wolves.

As usual, Cleos's mind read was painless, unlike Mezula, who generally ripped open your mind to read you. Cori's experiences with Cleos were, conversely, pleasurable. He could surface the memory attached to the thrill of riding a rollercoaster, or the comfort of a warm blanket, or even the smell of her mom's homemade scones. Long gone memories could be fished up for him to share, or eat if they weren't vital.

She wasn't really clear about what it meant when he ate her memories. He insisted they were not integral, and were buried too deep for her to miss, but the fact that she could never recall that memory again seemed like stealing.

This time was a little different from the other times he read her. She kept getting flashes of things as he scanned her. At first she ignored them, but as a wave of intoxication hit her, she leaned forward and closed her eyes so the images wouldn't get confused with her real eyesight.

She saw glimpses of women, herself amongst the collage. Too many events passed before her to comprehend. She focused on one spot in the background, and a woman's image appeared before her. She was crying and kneeling before her. Though she wasn't corporeal in this place, she felt her touching her hands.

"Please!" the woman begged. "Leave me alone, Cleos! Just let me end this!" There was a pause, as if someone else was speaking, but she didn't hear anything. "You've tried that already! I've put this off long enough, now go!" Another pause. "It's my life, and my choice. You needn't guilt yourself over my death. You are not to blame for the shit my life has become." Another pause. The woman looked up and stared blankly at Cori. "You could do that?" Pause. "I don't care. There's nothing I want to keep from this life."

Cori could feel the pain from the woman, and her memories of abuse flashed through her mind, reminding her that there were indeed worse things than death. Cleos housed all of those memories, compartmentalized in his overly stuffed vault. Not because he wanted to feed off them, but because he wished to free the woman from them.

A voice louder than all the cluttered background noise spoke. "What are you doing?" It was Cleos, but in stereo in her head. She could hear him in her mind. "How the hell are you doing that? GET OUT!"

Cleos's real face and real voice were no comparison to the mental versions that were pushing her away. Her body was flung across the room, either by the will of Cleos's mind, or her desire to comply with his demand; she wasn't sure which.

She landed against the cage behind her. Hands grasped at her hair and clawed at her neck. She could see Cleos reaching out to her from his food slot. "Throw me your keys. I'll come help you."

Cori tried to reach, but her hands were tangled trying to keep the creature's claws from severing an artery. The racket that sounded down the line of cages reminded her of a bunch of drunken fraternity brothers cheering on their friend as he beat the crap out of some poor freshman who was stupid enough to endure hazing for acceptance.

Something about the noise just pissed her off. The vampire clawing at her neck was certainly scary and at any moment could be the end of her, but all she could think was, "shut up."

So she said it. "Shut up! Shut up, you deficient, puerile beings!" Her heart was racing, and her hands were making progress. She hoped her anger could give her the adrenaline rush she would need to keep her head intact. "I can't stand that damned noise!" she yelled, and she heard a loud snap.

The vampire shrieked and let go of her. She pulled away from the bars and rolled to Cleos. "Son of a bitch! Why do we even cage these things? They're like freaking rodents." Cori groped her hair, trying to figure out what was still attached, and what was just a fistful of loose flaxen surrendered upon her release.

When Cori looked back at Cleos, he was not relieved to see her freed. He looked just as concerned as when she was being held by the creature. "Cori, what just happened?" he asked gravely.

"I don't know. He just let go of me."

"No, I mean, when I was reading you."

"I don't know. *You* tell *me* what happened. I was watching you and then I started getting flashes." Cori whimpered as she pulled a big gob of hair from her head. "Crap."

"What happened, metaphorically speaking, is that you opened your eyes."

"I don't follow."

"When I go into your mind, it's like we are joined. For me, it's as easy as holding hands. For you, it's like you are there, but your eyes are closed, so you don't see me. Well, you opened your eyes. For a moment, you were linked with me. You were seeing inside my mind as I was seeing inside yours."

Cori didn't know what to do with that information. This entire trip had been a bad idea. She should have told Ethan she was coming here. She should have brought him with her. Now, with scratches all over her neck, she wouldn't be able to hide it from him.

She didn't understand what a two-way mind meld meant, but she knew it wasn't a good thing. Ethan didn't like her sharing her mind with Cleos. He certainly wouldn't like him sharing his with her.

She stood up, trying not to cry over the fear of what Ethan would do over this. "I need to go and get cleaned up before he finishes with Annette."

"Cori, we need to talk about this," Cleos said sternly.

She paused in the corridor, thinking about what she saw inside of his mind. "Why didn't you just tell me?" she asked, barely loud enough for him to hear.

"Tell you what?" he asked.

She stepped back to his cage and pressed her hands to the glass containment. She wanted to reach through and touch him, but she thought it would only spark another mind meld, and she didn't want to see anymore. "Those women... your so-called victims. Did you know them well? Friends? Lovers?"

His head cocked to one side like she was speaking a foreign language.

"Did you love them? Is that why you did what you did? To save them from themselves?" He took a step back. "Lobotomy over suicide?"

"I told you not to use that word," he hissed as he took another step back.

"She begged you to let her die. That must have been difficult to watch."

His eyes widened, and his chest bolstered. "How dare you? How *dare* you invade me?"

"Why didn't you just tell me that they were suicidal?"

"Errant, ignorant child!" he yelled, baring his teeth in his sneer.

"Cleos, I understand what you did! You saved them the only way you could! Cleos, I can forgive you for *that*!"

His fist hit the glass so hard. She jumped back, half expecting the glass to shatter. "You arrogant bitch!" Cori's mouth went slack, shocked by the audacity of his insult. "You listen to me, and you listen well. You get the hell away from me and you don't come back." His voice was low and filled with threat.

"Cleos..." she whispered, wondering what had gone wrong.

"Ever!" he added venomously.

She shook her head, trying to find something to say to calm him, but she could see that he was beyond placation. Whatever she had done was beyond apology at this point. Had she not been so shocked and frightened, her innocuous tears might have been joined by sniffles and cries. She didn't dare make a noise to irritate him further.

She backed down the corridor, and he watched her go without repentance, which only made his resolve to see her leave all the more ardent. She had preferred his reticence to his anger, but she didn't have time to fix it now and she doubted he would let her for a while.

21

E THAN WATCHED ANNETTE TAKE vial after vial of blood from the dragon's neck. For the most part, Penelope didn't seem to mind the procedure. Annette's rounds of blessings and chants had seemed to put her in a trance. "Does that hurt her—to take so much?" he asked.

She looked back at him with a smile that told him it was a stupid question, but she would never tell him so. "This is nothing more than you would lose shaving."

He crossed over to her and took the vials she had accumulated, and placed them in the box specially designed to hold them on her altar. She brought over the eighteenth vial and slipped it into the box. "Would you like to try it?"

Ethan shook his head, but he looked down at the vials. He was curious. "I don't know that Danato would approve."

"Danato has had his fair share of dragon blood. If you're anything like him, it will only increase your clarity. Don't worry, worst-case scenario, you'll be giggling through supper."

Ethan shrugged. "Okay, what do I do?"

"Just open your mouth." He didn't relish the idea of putting yet another dragon body fluid in his mouth, but he wanted to try it. Annette reopened one vial and dipped a dropper in. "Lift your tongue." He did so, and she placed a drop under his tongue. "Let it sit for a minute and then you can swallow."

After a few minutes of feeling nothing, he helped her pack up her supplies. "Well, that was disappointing."

"I'm so sorry, Ethan," Annette apologized for the lack of reaction, as if she were personally to blame for it. "Everyone reacts to the blood differently, and every dragon is different. I could bring some in for you from one of my other draws."

Ethan chuckled as he lifted her folding table and placed it against the wall to put away later. "Annette, it's alright. You don't have to cross the country just to bring me blood drugs."

She moved to him and hugged him. He was a little shocked by the sudden affection, but he wrapped his arms around her to reciprocate. "I'm going to miss you."

"We've only just met," he said, rubbing her back slightly. "Are you leaving now?" he asked, suddenly realizing this might be a goodbye hug.

"Yes, my visits are never long," she said, pulling away. "Danato is such a dear friend to me. If I stayed more than a night, I'd never leave. You understand."

"Are you and Danato...?" He let the words trail off so she could either pick them up or sweep them away.

"Oh, no, we've never been like that." Sweep away it is. "I'm *so* old, Ethan," she said, drawing out the word. "I only look young because of a perception filter, but trust me, I've got two feet in the grave. No, Danato and I just have many good memories, and many bad memories. That much history is too precious to let stagnate with long visits. It's like family. You love them, but you're secretly happy when they leave."

"You've known Danato for a very long time?" Ethan tiptoed around the *very* since it might be insulting, even though she had already disclosed her age as *old*. "Did you know his wife?"

Annette's warmth faded. A frown that overpowered the perception filter allowed the creases around her lips to show. "Anything you want to know about Danato's wife should come directly from him."

"He's very close-mouthed about it. I just thought you could tell me why."

"Romeo and Juliet have a happier ending than Danato and Olivia."

Ethan gave a grunt of understanding to cover up the fact that he had never heard the name before.

"Won't you at least stay for dinner?"

She put her hands up to his face, and the warmth returned. The glow from her blond spiky hair was almost angelic. "If I leave now, you will long for my return, and that, my dear, is the sweetest gift an old woman like me can be given."

She kissed his forehead with enough force to leave a hickey and released him abruptly. She grabbed her bag of magical paraphernalia and her box of blood. He reached to take them for her, but she shook her head as if he should not do or say another thing to disrupt her dramatic, mournful exit.

He shook his head reflectively as he headed over to coax Penelope back into her "cave." "I don't suppose you could just walk back over there without any incentive."

"*No*," the dragon said inside his head.

Ethan looked up to see if he had only imagined it. "Holy shit, did I just hear you speak inside my head?"

"*I spoke*," she said without moving her lips, "*and you understood it. Whether it is being perceived by your ears is irrelevant.*"

"Holy shit," Ethan said again, since the statement still hadn't expressed his shock.

22

Daniel and Heaton arrived at the house later than expected. They had not been expecting to babysit an entire orchestra while their musical instruments were inventoried and examined, nor had they expected the inordinate paperwork that came with such an arrival.

As they approached the front door, Heaton pulled out his pack of stink sticks, indicating that he needed to mask himself before he went inside to face Nevia. Daniel rolled his eyes. He didn't approve of the smell; he didn't approve of the health risk, and he certainly didn't approve of him hiding whatever dreadful secret he had.

Rather than fight about it, he left Heaton outside, slamming the door loudly. No one was downstairs, so he headed up to his designated guest room. On his way by Nevia's room, the door opened, and she stepped out. "Daniel, can you come in here?" she asked, looking a little flustered.

Daniel didn't bother getting excited about going into her room. It was never about sex. It would never again be about sex. Once you take the hope of that away, it was likely just going to be an errand or awkward conversation. Yay, the joy of female friends.

"Is Heaton with you?"

"Cigarette." He pointed vaguely to the front door. He stepped inside and saw Cori sitting on the edge of Nevia's bed with her head down. Her blond hair was out of its usual pony and draped over her shoulders. "Oh, Lord, please let this be a threesome," he said aloud before he understood the seriousness of the situation.

The door slammed behind him about the same time that Cori looked up with disgust on her face. "Daniel," Nevia groused from behind him.

"I can hope," he defended.

Daniel observed the scratches on Cori's neck that were bleeding into her t-shirt. Her eyes were red from crying. "What's all this? Did the fem-wolves attack you?"

"No, this is from vampires," she said, a little embarrassed. Vampires were dangerous, but given her experience, she should have known better than to get close.

"Why were you even on that level? I thought the fem-wolves were your detail today?"

"I suggested," Nevia interjected from behind, "that she see a psychic to help block their hypnotic hold on her." Daniel noticed she had shut the door and stayed by it, as if he might make a run for it.

"You mean you went to see that mind-sucker that Ethan hates," Daniel simplified, turning back to Cori.

Cori exchanged a look with Nevia before answering. "Yes, I haven't seen him in months, but I needed to get control of my shortcomings. I didn't want to interrupt Ethan, so I just went alone."

"How did you get scratched up? Did he do something?"

"No," Cori said defensively. "Look, it was an accident, but I really don't need Ethan questioning me about this right now. Nobody wants to have relationship problems with guests in the house."

"Well, he's going to notice... the scratches." Daniel let the sentence end quietly. He turned back to Nevia. "You told her I could heal her, didn't you?" She didn't respond. She probably sensed his anger. Not only was she experimenting with his powers on herself, she was pimping him out to her new friend.

"I told you he wouldn't help me." Cori stood up and headed to the door.

"Wait." Cori and Nevia eagerly anticipated his answer. "Cori, I could seriously hurt you."

"It's worth the risk," she said flatly. "You don't understand how close Ethan came to leaving me over this hot-button topic. I don't want him to think I was betraying his trust."

Daniel didn't enjoy lying to his friend, but he also understood the "better left unsaid" portion of relationships. "I'll do this, but I'm—"

"—doing it for, Ethan. I know," Cori finished, but that wasn't what he was going to say.

"I'm doing this as a favor to you, Cori. I misjudged your love for Ethan once. I won't do it again."

Cori accepted that reasoning and sat back down on the bed. He joined her and looked over her cuts. The wounds dipped below her collar line. "She needs something lower cut," he said to Nevia. "I need to see the cuts."

Nevia headed to her suitcase and pulled out a white cotton shirt. He recognized it immediately. It was the slouchy t-shirt she wore with her newspaper print drawstring pants as pajamas. The large neck left her continuously, pulling it back onto her shoulder. It was what she wore the night he took her virginity. "Not that," he said more severely than he intended.

She only looked questioningly at him a moment, before returning it to her belongings and pulling out a bronze satin nightgown with spaghetti straps. He raised an eyebrow at it, surprised she would have such a thing.

"Everything else has a high collar," Nevia defended her choice.

"Fine, but if Ethan walks in on me leering at his wife in a satin negligee, you have to tackle him before he kills me."

Nevia handed Cori the nighty and gave him the signal to turn around. He did, and she joined him, giving Cori privacy. He could feel her demanding his attention, but he didn't give it at first. "You can do this."

He glanced at her. "You need to stop doing this to me. I'm not going to go travel the world healing people." He paused and waited for her to respond. "You get that, right?"

She looked at him. He wasn't sure what he saw there: disappointment or sadness. She opened her mouth to say something, but Cori announced she was ready.

Daniel turned back around and joined Cori on the bed. Nevia came to her opposite side and took her hand. After a rapid succession of second thoughts, he removed his glasses and concentrated on the pain and hurt that came with loving someone.

23

As Danato requested, Ethan stopped by after finishing with the dragon and Annette. He gave a quick knock before opening the office door. He removed his pistol, but stood in the door, signaling his desire to get back to the house. With so many guests, Danato couldn't blame him. "Did Annette say goodbye?" he asked.

"No, she usually doesn't."

"She's interesting."

Danato smiled, knowing exactly what Ethan's first impression of her probably was. It was the second impression that mattered with Annette. "Yeah, she is that. Everything go okay?"

"Yeah." Ethan paused, chewing his lip. Danato waited for him to finish. Ethan, unlike Cori, didn't keep things from him. "She gave me some of the dragon's blood."

Danato smiled. Dragon's blood was a favorite with everyone. He didn't get the true high that people spoke of, but it always made everything seem clear and crisp. His thoughts were unobstructed, and he felt invincible. "How was that?"

"It didn't do anything for me..."

"That's too bad."

"...at first." Danato quirked an eyebrow and waited for him to regale his psychotropic experience. "Then something strange happened."

"What?"

"I could hear Penelope's thoughts."

"The dragon?"

"Yeah, it's okay. She likes the name. She said she's never had a name before. We had a big long conversation before the blood wore off."

Danato sat quietly for a moment, trying to decide how he should feel about this new development. He couldn't think of any reason to be concerned. He was actually a little envious. He was certain he should message Annette about it, since she would probably be interested in speaking with her most valued blood donors. To his knowledge, no one had ever been able to communicate with dragons. "That's new," he said finally.

"Yep." Ethan nodded as he rolled back on his heels. Danato knew there was probably something he should say to Ethan regarding this revelation. He should have asked him what the dragon said to him. He should have at least asked what Ethan had thought of the entire experience. "Well, I'm going to head back to the house." Ethan threw out before Danato could provide any solace. "You coming?"

"Ah, no, not yet. I have a few more things to do before I go. Ask Cori to save me some dinner, though."

"Like she would forget that," Ethan mumbled jokingly. "Okay, see you in a bit."

Danato nodded, and Ethan snagged his gun and shut the door before jogging away. Danato shrugged off any minor concerns about Ethan's newfound gift. He could deal with all that tomorrow or the next day. Right now, he had a party to put together.

24

W HEN DANATO FINALLY ARRIVED, everyone was in the living room drinking beers while Cori finished up the dishes. After a quick scurry of coaster-passing, everyone greeted him. Nevia seemed confused by the urgent concern for water rings, but she would catch on soon enough.

Danato joined Cori in the kitchen, and she gave him a kiss on the cheek while she continued to scrub her dishes. "You're done doing dishes," he announced. "I need you to try these on." He pulled a pile of plastic-wrapped gowns from over his shoulder and showed them to her.

She stared at them with as much confusion as he expected. He waited for her to come out with at least one question before he explained. "What are those for?"

"For tonight's ball."

"Ball?" she scoffed.

"Well, okay, it's more like a dance, but I'd like you to get dolled up for it, anyway."

Cori toweled off her hands and traced a finger along one of the gowns. He had chosen three different colors and three different styles, just in case his taste in clothing was way off. He knew they would fit, but he wasn't sure what her preference would be. He would have chosen the long crimson one, but he wasn't sure she would be comfortable in the open back and plunging neckline.

"That's sweet, Danato, but I'm not sure a dance will be much fun without music." She grimaced as if she were sullying his best laid plans with an inconvenient but obvious truth.

"The cafeteria brought in punch and snacks. I invited everyone. The guards are rotating shifts for the evening so they can all get a little two-step in. I even dimmed the gym lights for ambience." He smiled, knowing that he wasn't done, but watched her show the best fake enthusiasm she could muster. "The band I brought in specifically for the occasion can only stay for a few hours, but I'm told they are quite talented."

Cori's face blanked. "Band?" He feigned confusion. "A real live band? With instruments."

"Yes Cori, how could I throw you a ball without music?"

Her hands were around his neck so fast he had to stop himself from trying to defend his throat. She screeched in his ear and pulled back, suddenly looking fearful. "What about the music? The time bubble."

Danato put his finger to her lips. "Live music is fine. Don't worry about that. Go pick out a dress and put your good lips on." Even as he said lips, she smothered his cheeks with kisses before ripping the dresses away and running upstairs. A quiet squeal came from upstairs before her door shut behind her.

Danato stepped out of the kitchen area, facing the confused faces in the living room. Heaton and Nevia were sitting opposite each other in the chairs, Nevia in Danato's usual spot. Ethan and Daniel were on the couch. "If anyone is interested, I'm having a dance in Cori's honor tonight in the gym. It's not a fancy occasion, but it's the best I could do without making Belus's head pop off or blowing my budget. You are all welcome to attend. Casual dress is fine, except for you, Ethan. I have a suit in my room for you."

"How did you pull this off?" Ethan asked.

"Cori's gardening has left a surplus in the budget. I thought it was only fair to reward her for all her hard work."

"What about *my* hard work? I don't suppose you have enough left in that budget for a flat screen," Ethan quipped.

"No, but I did have enough left for those dresses." Danato winked at him. "I think you'll find them a good deal more fun to watch than a television."

Ethan thought about that while he swigged his beer. He glanced upstairs and back to Danato. "That suit's in your room?"

Danato nodded, and Ethan bounded off to get dressed for his date. "What about the rest of you?"

Heaton raised his hand. "I'll give it a go."

"Are you serving alcohol?" Daniel asked, holding up his beer.

"No, my men aren't allowed alcohol while on duty."

"I think I'll skip it."

Danato didn't intend to glare at him, but as Daniel tended to bring out certain emotions in him, he couldn't really help it.

Nevia kicked Daniel's foot, which was outstretched beyond reasonable leg space. "Or I could stop in for some punch. I always did like punch; and maybe a dance with the lady of the house."

Before Danato could express how he felt about Daniel openly flirting with a married woman, Nevia interrupted his thoughts. "We'd all love to go, sir. Don't mind Daniel's rudeness, he's just covering up his discomfort with dancing."

Danato laughed. He could tell this girl was going to be good for Daniel. Whether he appreciated the improvements she would bring to him was another question entirely.

25

T HERE WERE NO WORDS to describe Cori's excitement. The gym looked like an undecorated prom, and the only people remotely dressed up were her and Ethan, but there was music. The fast-paced song that was playing was probably old to the outside world, but it was new to her, so it didn't matter.

Ethan pulled her out onto the dance floor as soon as they arrived. He hadn't taken his eyes off the long crimson dress that she had donned for the occasion. The plunging neckline was more revealing than she was used to, but she hadn't dressed up since her wedding, so she thought she should make the best of it. Ethan's gray suit and purple tie just begged for a fedora, but Danato hadn't thought to add a hat to his attire.

Ethan spun her around the dance floor with prowess that she wasn't aware he had. When they settled in for a closer slow dance, he whispered his intentions for later that evening into her ear. She bit her lip and hid her blushed cheeks in his shoulder.

When they finally took a break for punch, they found Daniel, Nevia, and Heaton sitting on the sidelines, looking a bit out of place. Danato had at least found a group to converse with and she blew him a kiss, which he smiled at but didn't return. Given his position and the number of subordinates around, he could hardly be blowing her kisses across the room.

"What's with you two?" Ethan asked his friends. "You can't just leave a pretty girl on the sidelines."

Nevia didn't seem offended that neither of them had asked her to dance, but Cori knew Ethan's chivalrous side was always in overdrive. "Daniel's too chicken, and Heaton's afraid I might smell his deepest, darkest secrets." Nevia had meant it playfully, but the look of ire Heaton threw her squelched her smile.

Heaton suddenly grabbed her wrist and pulled her onto the dance floor gruffly. Both Ethan and Daniel took steps to stop the manhandling, but stopped to observe before making an unwelcomed rescue. Heaton pulled her to the dance floor and drew her in close. As they began to dance, the moment of concern died and Ethan turned back to Daniel.

"What the hell is that all about?" Ethan said loud enough to be heard over the music, but not so loud as to make him sound angry.

"I don't know," Daniel said, still staring after them. "He's..." Daniel looked at Cori and rethought his decision to speak about the topic.

"Are they an item or something?" Ethan asked, not willing to let it drop.

Daniel shook his head. "Not that I know of. He's been avoiding her ever since we were last here."

"Is that why he's smoking again?" Ethan asked.

Daniel nodded. He glanced at Cori again. Some part of the conversation would not come out while she was still there. She planned to excuse herself, but Daniel changed tactics. "You mind if I take your wife out for a spin?" He winked at her and she rolled her eyes.

Ethan looked between the two of them suspiciously. He eyed Cori's outfit, as if he were debating if he wanted to share her or not. He raised his brow to her, asking for her permission to give the consent. She shrugged.

"There's the enthusiasm I was hoping for," Daniel quipped and extended his hand. Cori took it, and he led her out onto the dance floor. He brought her in for a close but respectful slow dance.

He was taller than Ethan and his shoulders were broader. He wore a goatee now, as did Heaton. Cori barely knew either of them, but of the two she knew Daniel better, and since this afternoon was doubly indebted to him.

"Thank you," she whispered.

Daniel's attention drew down to her. She glanced back at what had been holding his attention and saw Heaton and Nevia. They were conversing, but it didn't look angry or potentially violent. "What?" he asked.

"Thank you for healing me. I know you don't like lying to Ethan."

"I don't like hurting Ethan."

"It's amazing what you do. My neck looks better than it did before."

"You haven't seen me destroy life. That part isn't pretty." He sounded bitter, like someone had foisted this power on him against his will. Perhaps they did. Or perhaps it just felt like that to him. His gaze returned to Nevia and Heaton.

"I don't know if there is anything going on between Heaton and Nevia, but there is definitely something between you and Nevia." Daniel looked back at her as if she had just ripped the mask off his façade. "You have a lot of anger toward her."

"That's because she's making me practice my healing power on her, and now you."

"You must care for her a lot."

Daniel's face scrunched. "How does scarring up someone's body translate to caring?"

"Because if you didn't care about her, then you would have just refused to do it in the first place." Daniel thought about that, but didn't comment. "She must care for you, or she wouldn't risk her own body to help you learn."

He shook his head at her somberly. "That's the sick thing. She wants nothing to do with me. She's just fascinated by my abilities. I'm like a weapon that just needs to have the sights adjusted. I'm a freakshow to everyone, but to her I'm the fecking eighth wonder of the world."

"Maybe she—"

"Can we just dance? I'm trying to make your husband severely jealous, and this conversation is ruining it for me."

Cori reluctantly agreed. He pressed her a little closer, but despite his dedication to making Ethan bristle, he kept his hands benevolently parked on her hips. When Heaton and Nevia finally left the dance floor, she expected him to rush after them, but instead, he brought his focus back to her. "Did it hurt?" Her nonplussed expression prompted him to explain. "When I healed you, how bad was it?"

"Oh." Cori had been given such a lead-up to the dangers of the procedure that the actual event deflated her fears entirely. Daniel actually seemed more affected by the experience. He left the room immediately after dosing himself with a cold shower. "It felt cold, like searing cold. Then it pinched, but that turned to a tickle... sort of. It really wasn't bad."

Daniel's feet stopped. The song had ended, but he didn't let go of her. "I didn't hurt you at all?"

Cori shrugged. "No." She was about to ask what that meant, but he quickly dipped her, which made her yelp. He kept her upside down for a moment, glancing back at Ethan to make sure he was watching, which he was.

He brought her back up and released her just as the new song started. "I'd better stop there. He's likely to start climbing the walls if I don't bring you back."

"May I?" Cori hadn't noticed Danato approach behind them.

Daniel gave a quick look to Ethan as if asking permission to give her away to someone other than him. "Far be it from me to interfere." Daniel left her with Danato and joined Ethan and Heaton on the sidelines. Nevia was no longer with them.

Cori slipped into Danato's arms for the dance. Despite his size and maladies, he danced rather well. Ethan's mother taught him to dance at an early age, but Danato danced as if he'd danced many times as an adult. "I thought you could use a break from the riff-raff."

"What's your story with him? Why do you dislike him so much?" she asked.

"I didn't think you were a fan either," he said, surveying the crowd.

"We didn't meet well, but he saved my life, so what can I do? Besides, he's Ethan's friend. I have to make an effort to at least find him humorous. What about you?"

"I suppose you could say we didn't meet well, either. Bad timing, I guess. He's changed quite a bit since I first met him. He used to have a lot of anger issues. A *lot*."

"Anger issues, huh? Not sure I've met anyone like that." Cori had meant it as a joke, but the reference to a commonality between him and Daniel hardened Danato's gaze on her. "How long ago was this?" she asked quickly, trying to cover over her conversational faux pas.

"Six years, give or take. He's just traded his anger for women and booze, if you ask me."

Cori nodded. She didn't know much about Daniel beyond what Ethan had filled her in on, but the booze and the one-night stands were a fixed description. On the other hand, she wasn't sure she was entirely off base about him and Nevia. It sounded like he might be the one chasing her, which didn't mesh with what Ethan told her. Either everyone was wrong about Daniel, or Nevia was "the who" making his heart grow three sizes.

"Where's Belus?" Cori had wanted to change the subject to something less irritating for Danato, but she chose the wrong path.

Danato scoffed. "Like he would come to this."

"Who are you looking for, then? You keep looking over the room."

"Just checking. I don't want anything to go wrong tonight."

"We're in a room full of guards, most of them still armed and technically on duty. I've got Ethan and Dr. Destruct-o on the sidelines watching my every move." Cori gestured to Ethan, but she noticed Daniel was no longer with him and Heaton. "Don't you think you could let your guard down a little?"

"I'm not going to let anything ruin your night."

Cori pushed his hands away and stepped away. She cupped her hands, so that she didn't gesture and draw attention to herself and inadvertently disrespect Danato in front of his men. "The only thing that is ruining my night is a grumpy old man who's too busy casing the room to even look at his dance partner. I need a break from your protection, Danato. I like it better when *I* take care of *you*."

"I just don't want you to get hurt," he said, looking over the room again, but for a different reason this time.

"I always get hurt, Danato. I do stupid things and I hurt myself. Granted, I've added Belus to my list of dumb luck victims, but the point is, I haven't changed. You can't keep tightening your grip on me. You have to know I'll fight against it."

He paused, taking in her words. "I know. I just don't want to lose you."

Cori slipped back into his arms and they started dancing again. "You'll never lose me, Danato. You're my family now. Nothing will ever change that, but you can certainly make me resent your attentions."

He nodded. "Is that why you didn't object to me putting Belus in charge of you?"

"I didn't object to you putting Belus in charge of me because I respect your decision and the reasons behind it. Also, I was hoping to get back to that image you had of me once upon a time."

"What's that?"

"That time when you still thought I had the ability to be warden of this prison. That time when you were the only one who did believe it." The song ended and Danato looked her over as if he were meeting her for the first time.

"I did lose sight of that, didn't I?" She nodded. "It took a good deal of strength on my part to resist protecting you during that time. I guess I'll have to start resisting the urge to kiss your boo-boos."

"Well," she said, shrugging, "I'll still need someone to kiss my boo-boos." She smiled. "Just let me get the boo-boos. I've earned the right to get my boo-boos."

Danato smiled. "Yes, you have."

"Ahem," Ethan interrupted. Danato turned to him. "Am I interrupting?"

"Not at all," Danato said. "I was just letting her go." Danato winked and gave Ethan a nod before moving on to socialize again. She knew that wouldn't be the end of Danato's overprotective side, but at least she had reminded him of who she was.

26

Daniel left Danato and Cori to dance and headed back to where Heaton and Ethan were. He resisted the urge to ask where Nevia was and leaned on Ethan as he looked back at the dance floor. "Well, lad, looks like we've got some competition."

Ethan scoffed and shook his head. "He always wins. Luckily, all he wants is a piece of her heart, though. I get everything else."

Daniel chuckled at that and feigned looking around as if he had just noticed Nevia was missing. "What happened to our bloodhound?"

"She went back to the house," Heaton said, sipping on his red punch. Daniel avoided all rainbow-colored beverages. It seemed childish to be seen with anything outside of the coffee, beer, and water spectrum. Milk could technically have been considered a childish beverage, but it reminded him of home and his mom, so he could hardly reject it entirely as a beverage.

"What was all that about before?" he tried to ask casually, but there was no way not to sound nosey.

"We were just clearing up a few things," Heaton said, sipping his drink. He probably wished it was a cigarette.

"Anything I should know about?" Daniel asked. Ethan looked between the two of them, trying to discern where the underlying tension was coming from.

"Nope," Heaton said flatly as if Daniel were some geeky kid asking to sit at the cool kids' table. He could barely suppress his anger. He wanted to punch Heaton.

Before, when Heaton rejected him, he felt hurt and displaced. After dealing with that heartache, all he felt was angry and insulted. Heaton had been his friend and partner for years. They knew everything about each other. He had no right to treat him like this. He had no right to keep secrets from him. He also had no right having private intrigues with Nevia. Granted, Daniel had slept with her twice and not told Heaton about it, but it wasn't like he had intimate conversations with her.

"Good," he finally said. "I wouldn't want to upset the balance of our friendship by staying informed." Daniel looked away. He wished he had a beer to swig on after that statement.

"Is there anything I should know about?" Ethan chimed in.

Daniel and Heaton didn't need to exchange looks to give a simultaneous answer. "No."

"Okay," Ethan mumbled.

"I think I'm going to turn in," Daniel said. "This isn't exactly my scene, you know." Ethan nodded. Daniel looked at Heaton. He looked back at Daniel. For a moment, neither balked. "We good?" Daniel finally asked.

"We're always good," Heaton said. It didn't sound sarcastic. He sounded sincere. Daniel let his irritation subside, and he gave him a nod before heading out. They probably weren't good. They were probably on the cusp of losing their friendship, but what could he do? Men don't have heart-to-hearts, least of all him. If Heaton would at least talk to him, or outright pick a fight, maybe they could fix this, but until then, the code of testosterone mandated that he get over it, or pretend it didn't happen. He was getting good at that.

27

W HEN THE OPPORTUNITY PRESENTED itself, Cori slipped out of the gym with the ever-useful bathroom excuse. She knew it was a little underhanded to take advantage of Danato's generous gift to spy on him, but this was the only opportunity in the last few months that she had to get inside his office with no one disturbing her. As easy as it may have been to slip out after hours, she usually had neither a reasonable excuse nor the energy.

Besides all that, Belus was a habitual late worker. Even with the lights out in the office, she wasn't convinced it was clear until she saw Danato's chair empty. She was certain the only reason he wasn't inside was to avoid getting roped into going to the party.

She checked the doorknob and found it unlocked. She wasn't sure they ever locked it, but she was still surprised that it turned freely. Her plans were never well thought out, so to have any part of it go smoothly was disconcerting.

She slipped inside and debated whether to leave the light off to avoid attention, or turn it on so she wouldn't look suspicious when someone inevitably walked in on her. She decided the light was better off, but left the door open just a tad, so she could hear anyone coming.

The dress she was wearing hadn't left room for her to wear a bra, let alone hide a key. She'd instead pinned it to the underside of her skirt. She pulled it out and slipped it into the lock for Danato's bottom right desk drawer. The gentle twist delivered a satisfying click.

Cori stared down at the impending revelation with as much guilt as curiosity. She had just spoken to Danato about letting her have the freedom to get herself into trouble, and here she was doing just that. She knew whatever was in the drawer was something Efrat thought would dishearten her opinion of Danato. She didn't want that, but she also didn't want to be lied to.

She reached for the drawer, hearing the clock tick louder. When the metal drawer squawked loose with a lamentably loud sound, the clock stopped ticking and Cori released the breath she had been holding.

When the contents of the drawer were revealed, her mental drum roll turned into a cliché game show "wa-wa-waaaaa." The gunmetal gray interior was empty. The base held a set of bars designed to hold hanging files, but there was nothing.

Cori relaxed all her tension and sat down in Danato's chair. The uncomfortable spring that poked all who sat on it was especially salient. She looked up at the clock and noted that, despite its lack of volume, it was ticking normally.

She rolled her eyes at her own stupidity. She wondered if there was ever something in the drawer to see, or if Efrat had only used the key as an excuse to alarm her. She wasn't entirely sure why she let herself get so drawn in by him, but it was clear that when it came to Efrat, nothing was to be trusted.

She leaned forward to shut the drawer. The new angle from her seated position offered a view into the far rear of the drawer; a file as gray as the drawer hung innocuously in the back. She pulled it out, half expecting it to be empty, but it wasn't.

Two standard manila file folders were tucked inside. Cori had always understood that the information pertaining to prisoners was free for exploration. The small and tall file cabinets were never locked and contained files for every prisoner. Though his extensive library was still where most of her education was gleaned, she had never been denied access to any prisoner files. These, however, were for some reason off limits, and she needed to know why.

One manila folder had a big red "deceased" stamped on the cover with a date and initials written in below it. The name *Olivia Nickels* was typed on the side. The name was unfamiliar to Cori.

The second manila folder had no specific designation. It was by no means thick, but it had more paperwork than the first. In no particular order, a half dozen *lawyer-fied* documents prefaced the file. She scanned them and got the rough draft of what was essentially the rental agreement for the top floor. After a double-take on the monthly payment, she moved on.

Completing the file were four stapled packets, each with the name and photo of one of the elementals. She paused, listening for footsteps or any sign that her transgression was about to be discovered. When no one came bounding in to stop her from reading the truth, she continued.

Cori gave the files a cursory read. They discussed the abilities of the elementals in great detail. She was certain that the details were necessary for their containment parameters. Although she was familiar with the elementals firsthand, she found the paperwork even more intimidating than their persons.

The documents outlined the maximum temperature of Garr's—or rather Garrett's—fire power, which was well beyond her high school science comprehension level, but she imagined it was very hot. It outlined the need for his uniforms to be made of flame-resistant fabric. The use of metal rings and zippers was suggested so that he could manipulate the clothing without touching it. Although tungsten was the recommended metal for the accessories, it was noted that tungsten was not useful as a long-term containment device such as handcuffs.

Cori found Hirem's file to be just as enlightening. Paul Hirem was apparently capable of temperatures matching liquid nitrogen. Again, she wasn't certain what that meant in the real world, but she had several images of hard-boiled eggs being frozen to the point of shattering during a grade school demonstration. The only specification for his clothing was no zippers or snaps. It didn't explain the reasoning, but she imagined that the metal, once cold, would stick to his skin.

Efrat's clothing options also suggested that he wear nothing with metal for obvious reasons. However, she had only ever seen him in jeans and a big belt buckle to boot. She wondered if he refused to comply with the suggested uniform, or if Clark had.

Cori wondered why it was necessary to go to such lengths to accommodate for their clothing needs. She understood being in close proximity to their own powers would draw the need for some attention to wardrobe, but the descriptions suggested they couldn't stop the power long enough to clothe themselves.

She went back over the less intelligible parts of the documents and tried to get more information about this. In several areas, the documents indicated that their powers had increased beyond acceptable tolerances, but there was no justification for why it had happened.

Efrat's file summoned up the report in much the same way as the others. "First Sergeant Efrat Alston has refused direct orders from his commanding officer and has attempted to abandon his post without leave. He shall hereby be indefinitely contained under the conviction of deserter and traitor to his country. Remittance to this sentence may be offered if his abilities can be subdued and utilized in commitment to the United States military. Brigadier General Maxwell Clark will oversee the containment and disciplinary actions for this prisoner."

Cori knew Efrat had been in the military, but what she hadn't realized was that he still was. He and the others were still soldiers of the United States military being held against their will by their commanding officer. General Clark was holding them based on military statutes.

She flipped back through the files for a triple check, but she didn't find any mention of crimes beyond not collaborating with whatever military plot General Clark had going on. Efrat and the others had not kicked any puppies, let alone murdered anyone. The only murders to speak of were those committed while trying to free themselves from unlawful imprisonment.

None of it made any sense to her. Danato and Belus took no exception to the laws of any country, let alone the military of that country. The unnamed contributors to the facility demanded only one allegiance: protect human life and function above all else. It was the only statement that made being a part of this chaotic place noble.

Cori touched the blue indelible ink at the end of each paper cluster. There wasn't really anything legible about it aside from the D and the date, but she knew it was Danato's signature. She could still feel the indentation where the pen had dug in to start the line of ink.

His name shouldn't have been there. Maybe the money was too good to pass up. Maybe General Clark sweet-talked him into it. What she knew for sure was that the Danato she knew and loved would not have allowed four prisoners to be held in his facility for six years under the guise of refusal to serve one's country.

Perhaps that was the piece that was missing. Maybe Danato wasn't the same man as he was then. She hoped that was the missing piece, because at this point the only other option was that she didn't know him as well as she thought she did, and that was too much to cope with.

28

DANIEL FOUND NEVIA ON the couch reading when he got back to the house. By the looks of it, she had chosen another boring volume from Danato's library. If she kept this up, she would be more knowledgeable about the creatures they hunted than he was. Then again, that was probably her goal.

He debated joining her or going upstairs. There was still a part of him that knew the only reason he came back early was to be alone with her, but the logical part of him knew Nevia didn't just say things to hear herself speak. She wasn't a gabber like most women. If she had something to say, you might want to shut up and hear it, especially since it might save your life.

The focus she had for her work seemed to come naturally to her. Motivation wasn't something that came easily to him. He had spent the majority of his young life doing manual labor, and since then, he had learned to indulge his laziness whenever he had the chance. Being a hunter was a relatively posh job, with great pay and a lot of time off, but since Nevia had joined the crew, they seemed to be working non-stop. They were bringing in criminals and deviants so fast that they even broke Ethan's record. Again, that was probably what Nevia had intended to do.

He appreciated her talents, but it just reminded him of how much of a screw-up he was. She was doing this job because she was recruited. He was doing this job because it was part of his parole.

In addition to Nevia reminding him he was just a prisoner without bars, Heaton was reminding him he was just a parole officer. Maybe they were never as good a friends as he thought.

Daniel neglected the stairs and resisted the urge to grab a beer out of the fridge. He sat down in Danato's chair and waited for Nevia to get to a stopping point in her book. She must have sensed his anticipation, because her index finger raised, as if to ask him for one more minute. After her hyperbolized minute, she put her book down on the coffee table.

She turned her attention to him, and it threw him off for a moment. He was always thinking about her, trying to decide how to be around her. Bottom line, he was uncomfortable as hell when he was around her, but she always seemed nonchalant, like nothing had ever transpired between them. It impressed him; it pissed him off, and it made him want her all the more.

"What did he say to you?" Daniel asked before his mind got too carried away.

"He just said he was tired of hiding his scent from me, so he let me... smell him."

Daniel waited, but she didn't continue. "And?" He put his hands up in surrendered apology when he realized his volume had gotten away from him.

Nevia tipped her head like she was sickened that she had to give him such awful news. "You know how you always tell me you can't talk to me about him, because that's between you and him? Well, this is between him and me."

Daniel could ignore, forget, and pretend with Heaton, because he was willing to keep his friendship on the rocks rather than lose it completely. Nevia, on the other hand, was a whole new set of rules. Either because she was new, or a woman, or because he had bared his deepest, darkest secrets to her so quickly, he couldn't stand that she would keep this from him.

He stood up abruptly. He wished he had something to throw to express his disgust, but she already sensed his anger. Her face was softening, like she felt guilty, and maybe a little scared. "Daniel," she started. He walked away, not willing to hear the rationalization of his best friend confiding in the new girl instead of him. "It's not my place to tell you."

He headed upstairs, and she followed. "Get away from me, Jordan," he said, finally remembering to use her preferred name.

"Daniel, it's private. He never would have told me if I wasn't a bloodhound. Hell, if he hasn't told you by now..."

He entered his bedroom and started to shut the door on her. "Wait!"

He waited, but he wasn't sure why. He was in no mood for sex, even if there was the remotest of possibilities for it. "We should use this. You were angry at me for making you heal Cori, and you did such a good job. We should see if—"

"Are you fecking crazy?" He gripped his hair in his fist, not entirely metaphorically pulling his hair out. He threw a finger in her face. "You need to stay the hell away from me! I am sick of this!" His front teeth were clenched so tight, he thought they might break. He lowered his voice even further, keeping control of his volume even though his hand was shaking uncontrollably. "From now on, if you come knocking on my door, it better be to use me for sex, cause I'm not putting out anything else for you anymore."

He slammed the door, feeling no satisfaction from it. He hated that things had gotten so complicated. She was to blame for all of this. He should never have agreed to let her stay. He should never have slept with her.

He sat on his bed and took his shoes off. He undid the last few buttons of his black button-down shirt. He was about to slip it off when he heard a quiet tap on the door. "Daniel." Nevia's voice was quiet and sounded nervous.

"I told you, no," he grumbled, not moving from the bed.

"We can do whatever you want. Just open the door," she said. He debated for a second before opening the door for her. She slipped inside, holding a towel to her wrist. "I'm sorry, Daniel. I just can't let you not live up to your potential."

"What did you do?" He closed the door behind her, watching the towel turn red from the blood soaking into it.

She smiled, but he could see the fear behind her eyes. "I know I came on too strong. I took advantage of your attraction to me to get what I wanted. It was wrong, but ultimately I know it's what's right."

"What did you do, Nevia?" he said, taking a step toward her.

"I know you don't see it yet. You're still angry, and bitter, and frankly, I'm not entirely sure if I'm not exacerbating that by what I'm doing, but I'd rather teach you to save lives and hate me than love me and hate yourself."

"What did you do?" he said softly. She unraveled the towel, and her wrist gushed blood from a wide gouge. "Christ, woman!" He jumped forward and put pressure on the laceration, but it was too deep to attempt to contain. "Did you do this to yourself?"

She nodded. He understood her fear now. Up to this point, all his healing had been skin-deep. She was taking a big risk hoping that he could stop the bleeding, repair the nerves and muscles. If she walked away with a gashing scar, it would still be a success.

"You stupid girl!" He pinched her chin with his free hand. "I don't know if I can heal this!"

Despite the fear in her eyes, she didn't waver on her response. "Yes, you can. I know you can. You're not just a destroyer, Daniel. You're a healer. You have to see that now."

"All I see is a suicidal girl playing with matches." He moved his hand and more blood gushed. He wrapped the towel back around her arm. He didn't know where to begin. "We should just go to the infirmary. There's no reason to risk your life over this." He started walking her to the door, but she pulled back.

"Daniel." She shook her head. "You know I'll just do it again. You might as well try."

He knew she meant it. *Tenacious* was a nice word for her. *Stubborn bitch* was a more apt turn of phrase. "I'll fix you this time. As best I can, anyway. But no more. You don't *ever* do this to me again. No more hurting yourself. You got it?" She gave a slight nod, but that wasn't good enough. He gripped her shoulder and shook her. "Promise me! No more!"

She snapped her head up like she was forcing herself to stay awake for this conversation. "I promise." She wavered, and Daniel wondered how much blood she'd lost already. She was a small woman. It wouldn't take much to make her lightheaded. At least that's what he told himself.

He picked her up easily and laid her on the bed with her wrist overhanging. He unwrapped the towel and focused everything he had on making her better. It didn't take long for the intense heat to overwhelm him. He wasn't a big fan of heat anyway, but the heat wave he got from using this aspect of his power was enough to give him heat stroke.

29

H E WOKE IN HIS bed naked with a towel draped over his better half. He could feel ice packs around him behind his knees, lower back, neck, and on his forehead. He still felt hot, but like a Saharan heat wave instead of the fiery depths of hell. "Nevia." He pushed back an ice pack so he could open his eyes. She touched his hand.

"I'm here."

"Are you okay?" He took the pack off to look for himself. She looked a little pale, and she had put a sweater on, but she wasn't bleeding.

"Yeah, I'm good."

"Let me see your wrist," he demanded with a flapping finger. She pulled up her sleeve to reveal her wrist. It was nearly completely healed. A faint pink shine marked where she had gouged herself. "It's almost gone."

"It's perfect. I can move, there's no numbness. You did it." She must have expected him to be proud. She was beaming at the revelation. Her puppet had done so well for her. The joy in her face trickled away, and they were left casting frowns at each other, his disapproving, hers penitent.

"Get out," he finally said.

Her face fell, and she put her hand on his chest. "I meant what I said before. We can do anything you want."

"That's bullocks," he said, pulling her hand away. "You're only offering because you know you've finally lost your grip on my knob. What's your plan? Throw me another shag so I'm caught up in your web again?"

She shook her head. "It's not like that, Daniel. I'm not trying to lead you on or manipulate you."

"You just said you took advantage of my attraction."

"Yes, I did, but it wasn't malicious. I want to help you." She put her hand back on his chest, but he threw it back at her harshly.

"Who said I needed your help? I was doing just fine before you came along. I was happy before you came along. Ever since you got here, I've been working non-stop; Heaton's gotten warped, and I can't get a proper lay because I'm too worried about who you're shagging. Which apparently was a waste of my time."

"I'm sorry, Daniel."

"Don't be sorry, just leave me alone. Get out of here." He motioned to the door.

She looked over to the door like she knew she would eventually have to leave, but didn't want to head that way until she absolutely had to. "I'm not leaving until your temperature goes down." She looked at him as if she needed him to agree to that, but he just rolled his eyes.

"So concerned about my welfare, when you're the reason I'm in this condition."

"And I'm the one with six ice packs, a thermometer, and a vigilant eye," she scolded. "I don't know what more I can say or do for you, Daniel. I screwed up with us, okay? I thought we could have a quick fling and move on. I didn't want to pursue anything more because I thought you would just hurt me. It didn't occur to me that I could hurt you."

"Why does everyone think I'm a sociopath?"

"The truth is, I didn't use sex to get you to use your powers. You did. I was always clear about my intentions. Your hope that I might change my mind fueled your desire to please me. Even when you knew what I was coming over for, you still let me come up."

"Is my temperature down yet?"

"Fine, you don't want to talk about us. Let's talk about you. I know you hate killing transmorphs. Even if they deserve it, you hate it. What if you could balance all that death out with life? You could do so much good."

He shrugged. "I don't give a wick about that. I just do my job. I'm not a superhero, Nevia."

She looked at him like she couldn't understand his words. "How can you say that? You have the power to save lives. You could... save burn victims months and years of recovery. You could restore function to people with spinal injuries."

"I could remove wrinkles from women's faces. I could sandblast the sun spots off of old men's foreheads," he quipped snidely. "So what? I'm not going to go into a heat coma every day just to make right something that I'm not responsible for."

The enthusiasm on her face died, and she gaped at him. "I guess I should have found out what kind of person you were before I risked my body to train your gift."

"It's not a gift, it's a curse," he griped.

"No, Daniel, it is a gift, a very powerful gift. I thought you were just too scared to use it, but I was wrong. You're too selfish to use it." She grabbed her thermometer and checked his temperature via his ear. "You're under 104, you should be fine." She tossed the device back on the bed and slipped off the bed. "I hope you don't mind, but I'm going to rescind my earlier offer. I'm not really in the mood anymore."

She stood beside the bed, looking past him into nothingness. She looked like she might cry, but no tears surfaced. "As promised, I won't ask you to use your power on me or anyone else again. I'm sorry I can't tell you what Heaton and I discussed, but I think you two will be able to work things out in time. As far as work is concerned," her toned changed to add authority to her statement, "I think six years is enough time to be a lazy, belligerent, womanizing drunk. You'll just have to step it up and be a real hard-working man for a change."

He wanted to say something in response to that, but her eyes were challenging him. She wanted to pick a fight about his lifestyle choices. She wanted to add a few more scathing remarks to her attack. She was already prepared for this battle. So, instead, he opted for the high road, which was not really familiar territory, but it was worth taking for the view of a squelched strategy. "I think you're right."

She headed to the door.

"Jordan," he called just as she opened it. "Regarding *my* earlier offer about only knocking on my door for sex, I'd also like to rescind that for the foreseeable future."

She paused in the doorway, but didn't turn around. If it hurt her, he wouldn't know. She had never shown any interest in reestablishing a relationship with him, so he assumed the only damage it would inflict would be to her ego. No one enjoyed being rejected, even if it was from someone they didn't like.

She stepped out, closing the door gently behind her. There were no clear winners tonight. They had taken their digs, but neither of them really flinched. He knew she was disappointed that he didn't want to use his powers to help people, but what she didn't understand, what no one understood, was that he didn't want to use his powers at all. He would have been just as happy to never have had them to begin with. Becoming a side-show healer was his idea of a personal hell. Whether he saved lives by killing, or saved lives by healing, he was still a freak.

30

Ethan and Cori outlasted most of the employees. With only a few stragglers, the band packed up their instruments and headed to the docks to wait for their ride back. All Ethan wanted for the last hour was to take Cori back home for a little private dancing, but aside from a lengthy bathroom trip, she hadn't missed one song and she insisted on staying for all of it. He had even suggested a tryst in the prop room, but she was appalled by the mention of it.

When it was clear there was no chance to get her to leave before she thanked every single member of the band, Ethan gave up the fight and headed back without her hoping she would take the hint and follow him.

Heaton joined him on the walk back. Once outside, Ethan expected him to light up a cigarette, but he didn't. He wasn't entirely—or in the least bit—sure what was going on between him and Daniel, but it had been developing since they last visited.

Ethan had sloughed it off as stress from the pressure of saving Cori, but no one was in danger now, and Heaton was still being indifferent and introspective. He was still Heaton, but with a monumental chip on his shoulder.

"So what's up?" Ethan asked, letting his feet slow to a snail's pace to focus on the conversation rather than the destination. "You and Daniel seem to be on the outs again, or still."

Heaton shrugged. "Daniel's Daniel." The statement stood for itself, but Ethan couldn't tell if it was said with frustration or despondence.

"Yeah, and he's always been, so what's changed?"

"Nothing. Me, maybe. It doesn't matter. I just don't know if things are going to work out with the three of us working together."

"Why? Is Nevia not working out?"

Heaton scoffed. "No, actually, she's great. She's a sniper. What's not to love? She's found dozens of vampires we would have missed, and transmorphs. We're almost too busy. Daniel hates it, of course."

"Of course, cuts into his drinking time," Ethan quipped, although it was true. "So, what's the problem? You're not feeling resentful of her, are you?"

"Resentful?" he asked, as if he needed to verify his meaning before he gave an answer.

"Nevia has her nose. Daniel has his eyes. Are you feeling a little bland by comparison?"

Heaton chuckled. "I should, I suppose. If Daniel wasn't such a complete doofus, I'm sure I would feel like a third wheel, but at this point, I think I'm relieved to share the reins on him, you know?"

"She's the go-getter she claimed to be?"

"Oh, yeah."

"I suppose my next question has to be, are you falling for her?"

Heaton scoffed again. "I think I've had this discussion with Daniel three times already. He's the only one falling for her."

Ethan perked a brow at that. "No kidding?"

"I don't know how she managed it, either. She hardly gives him the time of day outside of giving him orders on the hunt."

"Maybe that's the trick." Ethan paused. "But if it has nothing to do with her, why are you mad?"

Heaton stopped on the path. "I'm not mad."

"What then?" Ethan stopped and looked him over, but as usual, Heaton was a closed book. For the most part, Heaton was upfront and honest, so his ambiguous expressions didn't need to be deciphered. Now all Ethan could do was probe for the answers his face wasn't revealing.

"You know how sometimes you think you know somebody, but you find out something that completely changes the way you look at them? Even though it's just one tiny detail of their whole personality, you feel like you never even knew them to begin with. Sometimes it's not even something that they lied about, it's just something they didn't bring up, and since you never asked, it was never illuminated."

"You mean like when I found out Daniel had the power to kill people with his eyes?"

"Yeah, just like that." Heaton started walking again. Ethan wondered if Heaton even realized he hadn't actually answered his question.

"It took a bit of getting used to, but my image of Daniel didn't really change that much. He's still Daniel. As you said, Daniel's Daniel."

"Yes, he is."

"So, what changed your image of him?"

"My image is changing, Ethan, and I don't think that Daniel's going to like it. Even if he accepts it, we'll never be the same. He and I have something so perfect that friendship doesn't quite cut it."

"You're like brothers, so what could break brothers?"

"Not break. That's the worst of it. We would never break. We would just chip away slowly until there was nothing recognizable left. I honestly think I would rather have him hate me and not know why than to let what we have together turn into a degrading sitcom that stayed on the air one season too long."

Ethan caught the smile at the end of his thought, but Heaton was serious. "Are you seriously considering transferring?" Heaton nodded. "Why? What could be so bad?"

Heaton sighed and slapped him on the back. "Let's talk about this tomorrow. I don't want to ruin your impressions of me tonight." He walked ahead, not giving any further information. Ethan hung back, wondering what Heaton was hiding about himself. After Daniel's surprises, Ethan had assumed that there were no other bombs to drop.

31

CORI KNEW SHE WAS gushing about the evening to people who had no idea what it was like to spend the majority of two years without music, television, or computers, but she couldn't help it. She at least wanted them to understand that their trek into the unknown was not simply from the whim of a spoiled princess. The dress was probably working against her.

"There's really no need to apologize for the strange manner of our arrival," the lead songstress named Jill told her. "Mr. Calabria compensated us very well for the unusual circumstances surrounding this appearance."

Cori laughed. "I bet he did. He's pretty tight when it comes to money, but he knows how to spend it on the finer things."

Jill reached for her plastic case on the floor. Cori saw that she already had a case of microphones in her right hand, so she picked it up for her. "Let me." Jill seemed flustered by the loss of her case. "Don't let the dress fool you. I'm pretty familiar with heavy lifting."

The singer smiled warmly at her and started heading out of the gym. The guards had already escorted the other band members to the docks, so it was just her and Jill. They headed around to the elevators by the main foyer. "So, what do you do here exactly?"

Cori laughed. "In general, or me specifically?"

"Whichever is the least classified."

"I'm not sure I can answer either, but I am essentially the runner-up to the man who will eventually run this place. When I'm not having my ass kicked by my superior, I do a little gardening. When I'm not doing that, I'm usually getting myself into trouble."

"I see." Jill came to a stop before entering the hall to the docks.

"I don't mean to, of course, but I just seem to make the right choices at the wrong times."

"I'm familiar with the feeling." Jill tried to smile, but her face lost all cheerfulness for a half-second. "Was that your boyfriend you were dancing with most of the night?"

"Husband." Cori flapped her ring finger proudly.

"He loves you very much."

Cori could feel her cheeks blush. "Yeah, we've come a long way. Conflict works for us, I guess."

"Whatever it takes." Jill smiled, but her eyes still didn't meet the demand. "Well, I best get back to my group." She reached out her hand, and Cori automatically shook it.

"Thank you again." Cori could feel a tingling sensation in her hand, similar to what she had felt with Cleos. She didn't see any images this time, but she suddenly felt profoundly sorry for this woman. She wanted to hold her in her arms, and cry, pray, and scream for her.

She released her hand and backed away, not wanting to feel it anymore. The feeling slowly dissipated. Cori looked at her hand as if it had caused the strange connection. Her rings shimmered, though no particular light source was available to cause it.

Shit.

Jill cleared her throat. Cori looked back at her and her outstretched hand. "My case?"

"Huh?" Cori looked down at the plastic case. "Oh, I'm sorry." She handed it back, suddenly realizing the poor woman hadn't even intended to shake her hand. "Have a safe trip back. Maybe if all goes well, you can come back again."

Jill stared at her for a moment. She didn't even attempt to smile this time. "God willing," she said and backed away to head down the hall.

Cori made her way toward the exit. She stopped at her locker and picked up her coat. Stepping out into the cold arctic night air was somehow a relief. She didn't know what had just happened, but she got the impression that it was not entirely unrelated to the fact that her rings were made from gold medallions once worn by a wizard.

She looked at the rings sorrowfully. She didn't want to take them off, but she knew that this situation probably wasn't the first time she had experienced their special brand of power reversal. She hadn't questioned why she was able to resist Efrat's electricity, or how she was able to open her eyes to Cleos's mind, but she had no choice but to acknowledge the incidents now. The rings must possess some kind of residual magic from their former owner.

She gripped one of the rings tightly and pulled. The ring started to slip from her finger, but her hand slipped away. She tried again, but she couldn't get a grip. She tried the others, but none of the rings would let her get a grip.

Shit.

Her heart pounded, and she tried not to think of them as an entity. She had already had a sorrow demon living on her; she didn't need something else wielding power of its own over her. She took a deep breath and resigned herself to reporting the incident to Danato the minute she got home.

She made it another three steps before the images overtook her mind. At first they were all a blur, like they had been with Cleos, but she stopped and closed her eyes, and the images refocused. They collected like photographs, then like a projector the photos had movement, and finally the voices overlapped, connecting the emotions to the words, the words to the voices, and the voices to the faces.

All at once, she knew. In a split-second, she understood the pain and sorrow in Jill's eyes as if it were her own. She understood why the elementals had been brought here under General Clark's supervision. She even understood why Jill had worked so hard to get to this prison. She was here to kill someone.

THEN

32

DR. JILLIAN FRANK STARED at her clipboard. She was certain the answers to life, the universe, and everything could be determined if she could only keep proper notes. Why was there no date on the sample from September? Had she suddenly decided that dates weren't important that day?

Jill put dates on everything she did. Blood samples, tissue samples, signatures, medications, and even her lunch. How did it occur to her at one singular point in time not to do what she did every damn day, a dozen times a day?

She sighed and scratched the month and year down beside the blood sample. Was that good enough? Probably. Was it good enough for her fastidious brain? No.

Jill tossed aside her clipboard as her project guinea pigs came in the door. The lab wasn't large, but it was well stocked. Every wall held vital instrumentation and shelving for whatever she needed. On one side of the long room were hospital beds and on the other were several long metal tables that she used for microscopes, bacterial culturing, viral agents, and the one she was behind was just used for paperwork and occasionally lunch, which grossed out more than one of her staff.

"Dr. Jill," Efrat called as he shoved through the glass doors leading into the lab. "Your lab rats have arrived." Efrat Alston was one of her favorite subjects. His enthusiasm for the project had made it worth her while. He was young, handsome, and, according to General Clark, the smartest man in his unit. He had originally trained to be a Navy SEAL, but Clark had snagged him for this private project. Efrat was more than happy at the prospect of becoming a "superhero."

Paul Hirem followed Efrat in. He was one of her more interesting subjects. He was a contradiction to everything he appeared to be. His Indian lineage made him seem foreign, but his Kentucky upbringing left him with a smooth, slow drawl. He gave her a nod before finding his way to his usual bed. He hardly ever said two words to her at a time, but in recent weeks, he had opened up to her. She'd actually had the privilege of hearing him laugh in her presence.

Garrett Malone, who the others decided to nickname "Garr" for reasons that were still unclear to her, arrived with his arm around Remi Steele. Upon meeting Remi, Jill had asked if her mother was a fan of Pierce Brosnan. She got a chuckle from Efrat, but Remi's faced donned confusion.

Garr and Remi were both young and had only entered the project for the money. To her knowledge, they didn't know each other before, but that hadn't stopped them from jumping headfirst into a romantic relationship.

Jill envied their ignorant youth. She had already been married and divorced, and that was just her serious relationships. She wouldn't call herself a slut, but her work left her with few dating options: either find a man who is likely going to cheat on you when he realizes you have no time for him, or stick to the bar scene and get an honest lay when you find someone clean and safe enough to take home.

"Okay, take your places. Who wants to be first?"

"Oh, us!" Remi raised her hand. "We want to catch the matinee."

"Okay," Jill agreed, smiling at her. She grabbed a tray and started with her first. Remi squealed as she started with the blood samples. Garr dutifully held her hand through it. Jill was, of course, disgusted by the attention he paid to her. She hated weak women, especially squealing ones.

Nevertheless, she commented on how sweet Garr was. Jill may have been emotionally stunted, but she was a good actress. She knew just what everyone wanted to hear. She had even learned to flirt with her male patients so they would put on a brave front when she brought out the big needles. She hadn't quite figured out how to do that for the women.

As she was taking the blood draw, she checked Remi's scar on her forearm. She had healed well from the surgery, and for the most part, like everyone, her motor functions had not been affected. Which for known medicine was impossible, but to Jill and her underground experiments, that was a fairly normal result.

Jill had never thought of herself as an evil mad scientist, but the Dr. Moreau comparison for these experiments was not completely off base. She rationalized that first medicine must push beyond legal and moral limitations; then it can find where the line for pragmatism should be drawn. After all, most of medicine's first advancements were done on cadavers, and at the time, that was considered gruesome and barbarous.

"Ouch," Remi drew out the word, as Jill took tissue samples from internal organs. She couldn't blame the girl for that. Internal samples felt about as pleasant as a pap smear. There really wasn't any way to make that feel better. After saliva samples and a quick behind-the-curtain vaginal sample that only applied to Remi, she gave her a container and instructed her to fill it to the line with urine.

She moved onto Garr next, and he did his best not to wince at the many pokes and prods that he endured at her hands. She couldn't help but smile at how his chest puffed up when Remi re-entered the room. Men were still as much peacocks as women. It was a wonder to her how people actually managed to stay together after they realized how many lies they told each other in the early stages of their relationships.

Jill never lied to her friends, boyfriends, or one-night stands. She wasn't afraid to ask for what she wanted. It was surprising to her how often that didn't work. Men claimed that a woman looking for a one-night stand only needed to ask, but that wasn't true. Most men were put off by her forwardness. Even if she did flat-out offer sex, the men tended to stall or make excuses, as if she had offended their delicate balance of predator-prey. Honesty was never the best policy in relationships.

After Garr and Remi had bounded out for their early movie, Jill moved her rolling cart over between Efrat and Hirem. Hirem was deep into his magazine, while Efrat watched the muted television that had long since gotten stuck on the retro rerun station. "Oh goody, the kids are gone. Maybe we can have adult conversation time," she quipped. Hirem smiled from behind his magazine. His smile was almost as rare as his laugh, but he had been more liberal with that as well recently.

"What's the matter, Doc? Don't you like young love?" Efrat teased, trying to flip the channel with the remote.

"Not when I'm too old to remember what it was like."

"You're not old," Hirem mumbled behind his magazine.

"He's right," Efrat said. "You're not even thirty."

"HA!" Jill blurted out with a cackle to follow. "Please, I appreciate generosity, but you're just being foolish."

"Foolish?" Efrat mocked. "You're thirty-four, don't pretend you're forty."

"And how do you know that?"

"I have my connections." Efrat raised an eyebrow.

"Why do you keep trying to change it?" Jill pointed at the remote. "You know it doesn't work."

"Buy new batteries."

"You don't think I tried that?" She rolled her eyes. "Who's next?"

"Efrat." Hirem pointed over to Efrat.

"Okay, Efrat, put out your arm." Jill sat on the edge of the bed to take his blood. She had spent more time with these two socializing, so she was comfortable getting casual with them.

"Hirem and I are going out for drinks after this. You should join us."

Hirem shot Efrat a glare, which said he either didn't want her along, or he didn't want to admit he did.

"You know I can't, Efrat."

"Come on, Jill," Efrat said, not cringing at the large needle she inserted into his arm. "You never struck me as the shy type."

"That's why I can't go with you," she said, removing the needle and bending his elbow up on it. "A doctor is not supposed to get involved with her patients."

She distributed her blood draw into her vials and labeled them.

"Patients? Well, I was just thinking one of us, but I think that could be arranged."

Jill laughed. "Efrat, you are an impossible flirt."

"I'm just saying, Hirem and I haven't quite worked together in that capacity yet, so we may need to get a game plan together before we plan that outing."

"You can save your brain power; threesomes never work out. Someone is always left wanting more, and it's usually the woman." Jill caught a look from Hirem, but she couldn't tell what it was before he tucked himself behind the magazine again.

"Touché," Efrat said, trying the remote again. "I don't suppose you have a key to the cage," he said, referring to the plexiglass box over the television that prevented it from being manually changed.

"I did, but I think a badly timed cleaning spree has put it in the trash."

"Figures," Efrat mumbled and sat back while she finished up her tissue sampling. Despite his flirtation, Efrat showed no particular interest in her. She assumed he was just one of those guys who flirted with women in between casual conversation. It was his way of making friends, just like he teased Hirem about being a cowboy *and* an Indian, despite it being the wrong kind of Indian. Teasing was just non-sexual flirting.

Jill wondered how Efrat would handle a woman he actually wanted to sleep with. She was certain his teasing would fall short and his casual conversation would take over. He might even have better luck with it the other way around, but like rules of young love, you can never be yourself at first.

Jill gave Efrat his urine cup and moved onto Hirem. Before beginning, she rolled her neck around. "Something wrong?" he asked, putting down his magazine and offering his arm.

"Just my neck. Too much time being slumped over a microscope. Old bones." She winked at him, and his face sobered.

"You are not old," he said firmly. She wasn't sure how to take his offense to her self-deprecation, so she just proceeded with her sampling.

She wished that he didn't choose to go last so often. She preferred to have Efrat around for conversation while she was working on him. Hirem was a nice man, and far be it from her to shy away from being alone with a man with such a great body, but his verbal skills left something to be desired.

Her bedside manner failed her around him. She couldn't decide if he liked her and was shy, or he was indifferent and simply had nothing to offer in the way of small talk. Either way, she neglected the flirting that she did with Efrat, and only offered him questions relating to his condition.

When Efrat returned with his container, she instructed him to place it in the yellow bin. "I thought you and Hirem were going for drinks?" she asked when she saw Efrat was leaving before she was done with Hirem.

"We are, so don't keep him too long," Efrat said as he left.

"I guess he wants to start drinking early," Jill told Hirem. He nodded, and they continued in silence.

She sent Hirem off for his urine sample and she sat down at her "desk" to log her samples on her clipboards. Her neck kinked again, and she rolled it around to loosen it up. "May I?" She jumped at the sound of Hirem behind her. She turned to see him. He nodded to her neck. "I have a knack for necks."

She chuckled even as she realized there wasn't anything funny about what he said. "Ah, yeah, sure. I hope you washed your hands." She chuckled again.

"I am very hygienic," Hirem said, gravely serious.

"Sorry, stupid joke." She chuckled again and forced herself to stop since she sounded manic. She was nervous, and she didn't need to be. She knew Hirem was a nice man. He wouldn't hurt her, but his somberness was throwing her off. She didn't know if she should match his seriousness or override it with humor. Neither seemed right. "Please." She motioned to her neck and turned her stool away.

She heard him crack his knuckles and resisted the urge to joke about him supposed to be cracking her, not him. He placed his hands on her shoulders, where they met her neck. She expected him to crack her neck, but he didn't.

His hands gently massaged the muscles of her shoulder and neck. At first it felt awkward to receive this much pleasure from strange hands, but she reminded herself that though she didn't know him personally, she had known him professionally for months. There was no reason she couldn't allow herself to enjoy this.

She relaxed into his hands with a moan and laughed at herself for it. "I'm sorry, that sounded inappropriate, but you do have a knack for that."

"It's alright. It helps me know where to focus my pressure."

"Okay, so you're saying to moan freely." She laughed, and she actually heard him laugh too, which made her feel less like a dope.

"Yes," he answered, and she did. At one point, she laughed again because the entire scene outside of the room had probably sounded like sex.

She had expected a short massage ending with an awkward, "well, I'd better get going," but Hirem let his hands work her muscles for over ten minutes. When he finally stopped, it was only after she felt the tension in her neck completely subside.

She turned to him again with a look of amazement. "Thank you so much. That was wonderful."

"My pleasure."

She smiled, because she knew he really meant it. She could feel the moment getting weird, but she had prepared a dialogue about next week's schedule for samples and tolerance tests.

"You are beautiful."

Jill had already opened her mouth to speak. She knew it was still hanging open like a fish, but she didn't know how to respond to him. He had taken a moment on the cusp of being weird and jumped it up to uncomfortable. "I... um..."

"Your age makes no difference," he continued, unaffected by the change in her demeanor. "Your eyes are your best feature. Not just the mossy green in your irises, but your eyelashes too. I'm particularly fond of the tip of your nose. You take great pride in your hair. You rarely wear it up. I imagine you think you don't have the ears for an up-do, but you would be wrong about that as well. I might dare compliment your elegant neck, but I'm afraid if I venture any lower, you might call for security."

A moment passed before a tiny little smirk settled on his lips. He was making a joke to lighten the mood of his professed observations. She huffed what might have been a potential laugh, but it just turned into a much-needed exhale.

"I'd better get going," he said, taking a step back. "Efrat will be waiting. I'll see you next week for our tests."

She nodded, but didn't speak. She didn't know what to say, anyway. She watched him back away, still with a smirk on his face. When he finally turned and walked away, it was not fast or slow. He was not rushing to be away from her, but yet he was not lingering, hoping she would stop him.

She stared down at her samples and tried to focus on her work. For the first time since meeting Hirem, she wondered what that great body of his would feel like pressed against her.

33

THERE WAS ALWAYS TIME for romance, but never enough time for breaking down the walls of medical science. At least, that's what Jill had always told herself. She reminded herself of that again when she walked into her lab to find all four of her subjects present for their tolerance testing.

Garr and Remi were making out on one of the beds behind the curtain. She could hear their lips smacking and rolled her eyes as she passed. She nodded to Efrat and Hirem on the way by. They each said hello.

She set her files on the "desk" and glanced over at the closed curtain. She was about to holler something to make them snap out of their coquettish bliss, but she was in no hurry to deal with them. "Do you mind if we just start?" She looked at Efrat and Hirem for sympathy.

"Sure, Doc, bring on the stimuli," Efrat said as he leaned back on his bed. Jill rolled the electronic device she had designed for Efrat over. She clamped two devices that looked like pulse monitors to one finger on either hand. "Why do we have to start off at zero every time?"

"In case your tolerance fluctuates down before it goes up. Soon we may be able to test you daily. You may have slight variations in power that could be caused by stress, sleep patterns, dietary changes, or emotional influences."

"So if I get horny, I might zap somebody." He winked at her.

She resisted smiling before her comeback. "I hope not. You'll be zapping people left and right." Efrat laughed and settled in for his test. "Just let me know when it starts to bother, okay?"

"You got it, Doc."

Jillian grabbed another cart and brought it over to Hirem. She had not seen him since his complimentary massage, and she was determined to keep things business as usual. She grabbed the metal batons on her cart and handed them to him.

"How's your neck?" he asked, positioning his grasp on the batons as he liked.

"Ah, better, I think." She gave her head a subtle shake. She shouldn't have been thinking it was better, it should simply have been better. Thinking it was better implied that she might still have trouble and might need another massage. Granted, she probably wanted another massage, but that was not appropriate. "I think I'm going to start you a little higher. Most people can handle holding ice, that's not exactly a super tolerance. If you start to cramp up or if it goes numb again, tell me. The point isn't to beat the machine. It's to register when your tolerance is met."

"Numb hands make me tolerant of a lot." He smiled.

He was joking again. Good for him. Jill held his eyes for a moment before forcing herself to get back to work.

"Garr, Remi, I need to get started." Jill pulled the curtain back. She was vaguely aware that Remi paused to button her top button before leaning back in her bed.

"I don't know why I have to do this. You're not even sure your device will detect my power properly," Remi whined.

Jill hated whining, but for some reason, it came with the territory. She'd figured military trained personnel would be a little more mature, but apparently the screening process for guinea pigs was less discerning. "My device will detect moisture. That is really all we need," Jill assured her before taping the sensors to her hands.

"My power is stupid," she groused.

"It was either take a water power, or live with man-hands. You chose a water power." Jill moved on before Remi could retort. She probably gave her a searing glare, but she avoided looking at her. The greatest defense against angry looks was not letting the person see that you saw it. It was like parenting 101 with this girl.

Jill dragged a cart over to Garr that was similar to Hirem's. She placed the metal batons in his hands and set the temperature to a setting of body temperature. Most humans could tolerate heat well above that, but she didn't want to rush his temperature change. If Hirem's hands got too cold, he risked frostbite. If Garr's hands got too hot, he risked first-degree burns.

"Good there?" she asked.

"Yeah, thanks, Dr. Jill." Garr nodded appreciatively. Everything about him seemed youthful. His voice was an octave too high and his skin had a few too many pimples for an adult man. As much as she hated the display he put on with Remi, Garr was a good kid and deserved to be happy.

Jill resisted the urge to ruffle his pale blond hair and moved over to her desk. "Everybody remember to speak up when you feel anything resembling pain, and/or a loss of feeling," she added for Hirem's benefit.

At once, the entire group froze, jumped to their feet, and saluted. Jill resisted the urge to cuss and turned to face her guest. "General Clark."

"Dr. Frank." General Clark entered the lab in full dress uniform. His olive beret covered his balding head, which was buzz cut short enough that she couldn't really tell what color his hair was. His dress uniform was thick with army decals that meant more to him than anything in the world, including his own life. Jill was a workaholic by any definition, but she found that level of devotion a little scary.

General Clark had a face that was more bone structure than feature. She was entirely certain with his hat and uniform off, she would never recognize him. "What brings you by?"

"I wanted to check on your progress."

"Yes, of course, but I cced you everything so far."

"Right," he said, standing at ease with his hands crossed at the palm, "but you didn't tell me your future plans."

"I'm sorry." She tipped her head and waited for the explanation she had a feeling she didn't want.

"You keep sending me data that shows slight decreases in sensitivity, but I haven't seen anything showing how you plan to increase the rate of those decreases."

Jill looked over her subjects. "There are no plans to change the rate at which the subjects adapt to their new limbs. They are all healing well, and I expect that over the next few months, the powers will naturally accumulate."

General Clark stared blankly at her. He didn't have many expressions, so it was important to take his pauses seriously. "Doctor, there is nothing natural about transplanting body parts. Why would you think I would care to wait for the powers to naturally take hold?"

"Because the process is unnatural. I want the subjects to have time to adapt to their new hands, and to the powers they possess. The mind connection is intrinsic to controlling the power. If the mind does not accept the body part, they won't be able to control the power in it. Not to mention we need to be able to stunt the connection if it gets out of control, or reattach the original limbs if necessary."

"Doctor, I'm not one for science. This project is frankly a little strange to me, but if there is indeed a possibility that these jokers are going to be the next Ice Man and Human Torch, I want to see it happen fast so we can move on. I don't plan on wasting an entire year just to see if they can pick up hot irons and stick forks in toasters. I want potential weapons, not human anomalies."

"I can start them on steroids, but General, please understand that when dealing with human beings, we can't simply demand progress. We need to document this so it can be repaired and replicated."

"Please understand this, Dr. Jill: these men are my soldiers. They would die for their country. You can't possibly understand that commitment, but I think you do understand how important you are to our project and how much we want you to be a part of it. You want to stay with this project, don't you?"

Jill wasn't sure what kind of threat that was, but whether it was financial or mortal, she needed to take it seriously. If there was even the hint on her record that she had performed illegal transplant surgeries, she would not only lose her license, but she could go to jail. It wouldn't matter that it was the government that requested the work. They would never be held accountable for their part in these experiments, and they wouldn't hesitate to throw her under the bus if she didn't provide the loyalty they needed.

"I'm sure I can provide you with the speed that you desire while still giving my patients a safe recovery. You can recoil your fangs. I'll get on it right away."

He looked her over again, but decided to accept her sarcastic compliance. General Clark turned on his heel and left the room, giving the men and woman a belated salute back. After he was gone, everyone returned to normal. She wondered how much pride you had to take from someone to make them feel pride in being a robot.

34

R EMI WAS RIGHT. HER power was stupid.

Jill looked over the data on the strip of paper behind Remi's bed. There was virtually no way to show tolerance to water, since the human hand was not intolerant to water. At best, she could check to see how long it took her fingers to turn into raisins. Instead, she monitored the moisture already in her hands.

She pulled the sensors off Remi's palms and smiled at her. They had only shown a slight increase in moisture that could easily be sweat. "I think that's good for today, Remi."

"Anything?" she asked, hopeful.

"I think I'll start you on a dose of the steroids today. I'll try to think of a better way to detect your power." Remi's face fell, but she nodded. Jill gave her the injection and she let her go.

Not to anyone's surprise, Garr soon after mentioned his hands were hurting. Jill knew it was only so he could leave, but she wasn't about to argue with him. She could smell the heat from the metal batons. Whether or not he was being accurate, he had certainly beaten his record from last week.

She put her hot gloves on and took the batons. She gave him a dose of steroid and sent him on his way to catch up with Remi. When she turned back to the others, she saw Hirem and Efrat mouthing something to each other. "No secrets, boys. Are you feeling anything yet?"

Efrat glanced at Hirem and sighed. "I think I am."

"You think you are, or you are? I know it's boring to sit here for hours, but I do need accurate results."

"I feel a tiny tingle," he offered, like he hoped that was enough.

"Efrat," she sighed, "can't you at least lie well? You're not even up to what you were last time."

"Come on, Doc, just crank it up. The general's right, let's just get this party started or bail out while the night's still young."

"Oh, fine," Jill moved to his machine and manually raised the voltage with a press of a button. She pressed it up again and again, but Efrat saw no change.

"Come on, Doc," Efrat encouraged her. Jill looked to Hirem. She wasn't sure why she did. She was the doctor here. She supposed she just wanted permission from his friend, so that later, when his nerve endings were fried, she could say that there was a consensus. Hirem raised his eyebrows, as if he was just as curious to see how high Efrat could go as she was.

"If you can't feel your hands tomorrow, I'm not going to feel sorry," she said.

"Yes, you will," Efrat corrected, "but do it anyway."

Jill used the dial rather than the push buttons, which increased the voltage a good deal faster, and with less precision. She dialed it up slowly until she could hear a hum. She looked over Efrat, but he didn't seem affected. "Hirem, move yourself and your cart away from him. You don't want to be the one to ground him," she said, moving herself behind the machine as well.

She turned the dial up farther, but she wasn't sure it was working, because the hum stopped. "What the hell? Did it just short out?" A loud snap sounded and sparks spit out of the wall where the device was plugged in. "Holy crap!" Jill said, pulling the plug on the machine and rushing over to check Efrat.

Another snap shocked her fingers as she tried to touch him. "Shit, throw those over there." He did so. "Okay, now touch the bed frame." She heard another snap, and he brought his hands back up for her to examine.

She looked over his hands, but there was no sign of damage. She poked her pen into each of his fingers and dragged it over his hand. "Can you feel that?"

"Yeah," Efrat said, sitting up and watching her intently like she would be able to explain what had just happened to him.

"What was the monitor up to when it overloaded, do you remember?"

"The needle was pinned."

"That's 120 volts coming out of that socket. I don't know electrical stuff, but I know that's enough to electrocute someone," Jill said.

"What does that mean?"

"It means no steroids for you."

35

AFTER A LONG AND repetitious argument, Jill conceded to giving Efrat the steroids anyway. She didn't like giving any of them the medication, but when he was already showing that much resistance, it told her that he was already on his way to great things, and she was a firm believer that fast success meant even faster failure.

Efrat left as soon as he was dosed. She got the impression he had a hot date or something. That left her once again alone with Hirem. He had not been in quite the hurry to speed up his test, but by the time she was done with Efrat's log, she could see frost was forming on his hands. "Can you feel your hands?"

"Not really," he said, releasing them to her. She wore her gloves with his batons just as she did with Garr's. She was just as likely to lose a few layers of skin touching the cold batons as the hot ones.

"Do you remember the part where I told you to tell me, when you couldn't feel your hands anymore?" she said, scolding him without derision.

"I vaguely recall that, but it's hard to tell. Sometimes I just forget that my hands are even there. I think my body hasn't really accepted them yet."

"Your sensory testing is high, and your mobility is above everyone else."

"No, I mean..." He tapped his chest. "My mind may have accepted them, but my heart hasn't. You can perform all the tests you want, but until my heart believes they are my hands, I don't think they will behave the way you want them to."

Jill poked his hand with her pen, but he shook his head. "I don't want your hands to perform in any way other than to pick up objects, and to flip off bad drivers. The general is the only one with high expectations."

Jill sat down beside him and poked each finger. He shook his head again. "I think they are just cold. I know you are doing something. It just feels far away." Jill knew she could just go grab a heating pad, but she decided to just hold one of his hands between hers. "You don't like the general interfering with your work, do you?"

She rolled her eyes. "Who would? I understand his purpose. I'm just not a fan of speed over caution."

"You don't strike me as slow and cautious," he said, tipping his head as if he were reading her thoughts. "Isn't that why you're here? Medical science in the public sector is too slow. Too many rules and regulations. I think you like to change the rules."

She could feel the warmth in his hand. "Can you feel your hand now?"

"Yes." He gave her his other hand, and she let go of him.

"I'll grab a hot pack." She moved to her shelves and found a hot pack that she could warm in the microwave. She had ones with snaps inside that would be instant, but she wanted a little more time away from Hirem. She was starting to feel naked in front of him.

It was one thing for him to disarm her with clever compliments, but to have him wave around her personality traits like he had known her for years was too much. She hadn't had enough time to figure him out; how had *he* had enough time to figure *her* out?

While the microwave hummed, Jill rolled her shoulders. She hadn't realized she was doing it until she felt Hirem's hands on her shoulders. She jumped, but as soon as his thumbs drove into her tense muscles, she relaxed. She leaned her head against the shelf over her microwave.

The microwave beeped, but she knew it was pointless now. His hands were warm. He wasn't interested in a heating pad anymore. He dug his thumbs into her shoulder muscles, and she let out a half groan and half exhale. She knew she shouldn't. She knew it was only going to encourage him, but she couldn't help it. He had tremendous talent.

She couldn't help but wonder if his talent extended to other areas. With that thought in mind, she reached up to touch his hands. She intended to move them away, but all she did was touch them.

"Come lie on the bed so I can get your lower back," Hirem instructed as he steered her over by his grip on her collarbone.

She knew the bed was a bad idea. She knew lying down was a worse idea, but she didn't exactly object. Even when he crawled over her to straddle her hips, she didn't speak. She couldn't. The only thing she should have been saying was stop, but she didn't want him to, so she just shut up.

His fingers worked their magic over her muscles until she was so relaxed she was almost dazed. When he finally got off her, she was disappointed. Not so much because she wanted him to keep massaging her, but because she was pretty certain by that point that she wanted him to roll her over.

She looked up and saw him sitting on Efrat's bed. He was waiting for her to do something. Get up. Thank him. She sat up on the bed, mirroring his body.

They were similar in height, but she was certain high heels would bring her just a hair taller than him. She had only seen him shirtless once, and that was during surgery, but it was a masterpiece worth revisiting if the opportunity arose.

For a moment, they just stared at each other. They were at the impasse. One of them had to make the move. They both knew what they wanted, but someone had to act to make it happen. Avoiding it wouldn't save them from an uncomfortable meeting later, nor would it negate what had just happened. Honesty came with another fork: acknowledge the attraction and act, or acknowledge it and deny themselves.

"I'm your doctor, Hirem," was all she said. It didn't commit to anything one way or another. It was just a well-placed fact.

"None of what you're doing is condoned by the Hippocratic Oath."

She wasn't sure she agreed with that, but he had a point. This was an underground operation. So did doctor-patient relationship barriers really apply? "I'm not really sure I can do this and just go back to normal. I usually don't see my one-night stands after the night, you know?"

"I'm not offering a one-night stand," he said without flinching.

"In that case, I'm not very good at relationships. I'm kind of married to my work."

"That's very convenient, because I *am* your work. At least for the next six months. I'm sure that will be long enough for you to decide if you want to continue your work with me privately, or move on."

She looked him over. He was presenting his case logically. She had expected more of a seduction like he had offered the first night they were alone together. Perhaps he knew her even better than she suspected. She could argue with emotional flirtation, but a logical front left her nothing to defend against. All of his observations were valid.

"Besides, as I mentioned, I don't think you like following the rules, do you?"

She shook her head and stood up. She felt a little dizzy and her mouth was dry. She had had dozens of one-night stands over the years, and none of them had made her feel like this. She could have passed out just from the speed of her heart, let alone the anxiety of the anticipation.

He stood and met her in the middle. He didn't kiss her, which threw her off again. He started to undo her top. She looked down at the proven dexterity in his hands. She was fairly certain she couldn't unbutton her own shirt that fast. "I find it's easier to have second thoughts when your clothes are still on."

"I thought you were shy," she said, thinking back to what she'd thought of him a few days ago.

"I liked you from day one, Jill. I knew I wanted you from day one and a half. I've been stalking you since then."

"Stalking?" Jill asked, vaguely aware that her pants were slipping off.

"Yes, observing, listening. A man can't expect to just walk into a room and start removing a woman's clothes." Her bra was off, but she kept her eyes on him. She knew second thoughts really were out now. "A man has to know his prey. Know her weaknesses."

"What are my weaknesses?" she asked, feeling the strangeness of being totally nude in front of a fully clothed man. Except her socks. Nobody ever stopped for socks.

"Right now?" He tipped his brow. "This hand." He raised his hand to show her, but lowered it to feel her nudity. She gasped and leaned against him for balance. There was no containing anything now. She couldn't believe he hadn't even kissed her yet.

Once she was back in control of herself, she clumsily pulled his clothing off. It wasn't as graceful or sensual as how he had taken her clothes away, but he didn't object. Before she could kiss him, he moved his lips away and scooped her up and placed her on the bed.

She had the briefest guilt for being with her patient, but it subsided, and she saw his perfect bronze body crawl on top of her. She reached for his neck to draw him down for a kiss, but he resisted as he got himself in a comfortable, poised position.

When he finally consented to her kiss, he gave her a gentle, seductive first kiss that made the wait worth it. It only lasted a moment before he plunged his tongue in for a deeper kiss. At the same moment, he offered her body a deeper satisfaction as well. That was also worth the wait.

She was surprised he wasn't gentle and slow like most first-time lovers. He seemed to understand how few and far between these pleasures were for her. He didn't waste any time with pretenses of love. He just wanted to make her moan for his body the way she had moaned from his massage, which she happily, and perhaps a little too loudly, did.

36

JILL SAT AT HER overflowing desk, trying to make sense of the staggering increase in Efrat's and Garr's tolerances. They had been on the steroids nearly three weeks now and they were not only immune to electricity and heat respectively, but they were now able to exude it for short durations.

Garr had become obsessed with his abilities. He flaunted his talents by bringing cookie dough in for everyone, which he baked freshly in the palm of his hands. Everyone laughed and cheered and made jokes about where his hands had been, but Jill didn't show the enthusiasm like everyone else.

Despite her resistance to conform to mainline medicine, she didn't like fast results. Garr was young. A temper flare or fit of jealousy could lead him to use his ability to hurt someone. She reminded them all of that daily, it seemed, but everyone was too enamored with the idea of becoming Captain America to pay her much heed.

Efrat was able to keep a light bulb lit for an hour, and she wasn't unfamiliar with the pop of breaking glass when he got tired of holding it. His powers concerned her the most, because they wouldn't be limited to his hands. Electrical current could easily jump, and if Efrat was not careful, he could easily find himself arcing with anything remotely electronic.

It was nothing to say that he may never be able to use a cell phone again, but to add to that list, a computer, radio, and a microwave. She had grounded his bed, so she didn't have to keep flipping the circuit breaker during his visits.

Remi and Hirem were coming along a little slower. For Remi, it seemed to just be laziness that kept her powers from coming through. She didn't want to do the exercises that Jill suggested to induce the water power, so she struggled to make anything happen intentionally. Unintentionally, however, she had woken up in her bed freshly turned water bed three times in one week.

Hirem, on the other hand, seemed to be taking her concerns for control seriously. He spent a good deal of time meditating before and after his efforts to exude his cold. He had learned to make his hands super cold, and then warm them back up again.

In the last few weeks, they had been together after every check-up and test. At first it felt like a forbidden affair, even though neither of them was attached. Somewhere in the last week, however, it had started to feel like he was just taking advantage of her. He was just getting laid with scheduled appointments, a convenience any man could appreciate.

At the last appointment she made an excuse about a headache, which was the laziest of lies to give a man, but it was kind of true, and she wasn't really trying to hide her displeasure with being his bi-weekly hookup. As much as she wanted to be an independent woman, who freely slept with who she liked, it still felt like she was the puppet in this arrangement.

"Jill." Jill looked up from her data and saw Hirem just inside the glass doors. She hadn't heard him come in. She never heard anyone come in. The damn doors needed bells.

"Paul." She smiled as warmly as her discomfort would let her. "You don't have an appointment today."

"No, I don't," he said matter-of-factly. He stayed by the door not moving further in. She wondered if that was his way of being non-threatening or if he planned to leave right away when she refused his company again.

"What brings you in?"

"You know what brings me in." He sounded annoyed.

"I'm sorry. I'm very busy with this."

"Headache, busy; next time I'm sure you will say its cramps. Then what? How many more excuses will you give me before you admit the truth?"

"Okay." She threw down her pen and turned on her stool to face him. "This isn't working for me anymore."

"Have I not been a generous lover to you?"

She laughed, but stopped when she realized that she didn't want to imply any amusement in his lovemaking. "No, yes... you have been an excellent lover, Paul."

"So why abandon so much pleasure?" He moved forward. Now that the topic of sex had flustered her, he knew she would be thinking about said pleasure. He was a consummate hunter.

"I think this is dangerous territory for me," she said being more honest than she'd thought she could. "I think that I'm getting a little too attached to you and I don't want to get hurt when this is all over. I'm sorry if I've misled you about my tolerance for this type of relationship. I think I misled myself. I'm just not as capable of casual sex as I thought."

Hirem watched her carefully and came closer before speaking. He positioned himself in the path of her only exit. She could go around the opposite side of the table, but there were so many carts that moving them would have looked like a ridiculous effort of avoidance. "You no longer want to be my lover because you're getting attached to me. Doesn't that sound strange to you?"

"Yes, but I know you don't want a clingy love-struck girlfriend, so I'm trying to give you a way out before I turn into a slobbering pathetic blob of feminine neediness. I'm not above it, you know; it comes with the extra X chromosome," she quipped, trying to make the situation light again. It never worked with him. He was the most serious man she knew.

"Who said I don't want that?" he asked, annoyed again.

"Ah, you've kind of been implying it." She smiled and looked away when his face demanded more explanation. "Come on, don't play this off. I'm your scheduled lay. You get a quick fix after your appointments and on with your life. Look at tonight. I blew you off once, and you're here to collect. Didn't get your twice-a-week in, so re-schedule accordingly."

"That's what you think I'm doing?"

"Paul, we never do anything but have sex. There is no reason to assume that it is anything more than that."

He stepped forward and hovered his hand over her desk of ceaseless paperwork. "This is why all we do is have sex. I would love nothing more than to take you out of this dreaded work, but I see how anxious you get if I linger past my designated post-appointment slot. You are the one scheduling me into your life, not the other way around. I respect your work, and through that respect, I have kept my distance. If I had it my way, I would be with you every night: eating, talking, and making love."

Jill looked over her desk. The piles of paperwork were an endless chore. Up until recently, she was obsessed with it. Now her mind was transfixed on him. How his body felt against her. What he was thinking. When she would see him next. She hated being this way, but if she wasn't the only one that was feeling it, maybe that would be okay.

She looked up at him and saw the desire and the concern in his eyes. "It's been a long time since I've wanted something more than just sex and just work. I'm scared that you aren't going to like the emotional basket case that I keep away from civilized society."

"My heart has loved you from the moment I met you. My body has ached for you stronger every day. My mind anticipates meeting you with each new conversation and every unknown detail." Normally Jill would have gagged over this poetic nonsense, but coming from him, it made so much sense. "I'm not afraid of your inner basket case. I am only afraid of losing you. My mind is strong, my body can recover, but my heart is weak."

She didn't know why that put her at ease. Perhaps knowing that she could hurt him as much as he could hurt her made the odds more fair. Relationships were about balance. Too much power one way or another was not good, but as long as the hearts loved equally, there was no reason to worry about how often the scales tipped in one direction or the other.

Jill wasn't sure who moved first, but they were kissing and clawing at each other's clothes. They should have been whispering sweet nothings and giving each other tiny kisses, after such an expressive conversation, but that wasn't the tone.

The tone was shoving her paperwork all over the floor. The tone was him pushing her down on the desk she had been shackled to for so many months without a break.

She didn't think about how many hours it would take to reorganize it; all she thought about was him. She wanted him: his body, his mind, and his heart, and at that moment she knew she had all three. She also knew there was no turning back, because she had just given him the final piece in the triad as well.

37

THERE HADN'T BEEN MUCH point in hiding their relationship. Efrat probably knew the night it had started. Judging by how much he had reduced his flirtation with her, he must have understood how serious it was. Garr and Remi were mostly oblivious to anyone's bliss beyond their own, but Garr had given her a few coy smiles when he saw her ogling Hirem from across the lab.

The truth was, she was as lovesick as Remi and Garr. It was pathetic and unprofessional, but she didn't care. She had never been with a man like Hirem. He seemed distant and humorless, but being as close to him as she was, she understood he was reflective and unpretentious.

He did not display his love for others to see and yet with a simple look he made her smile because she saw what he felt. It wasn't for everyone else to see. It was just for her.

She did, however, have to tone down her coy smiles when General Clark started his demolition exercises. She was fairly certain that he would not be a fan of their connection. For the most part, she did her best looking like the proud teacher to all her students, rather than the proud girlfriend to one in particular.

Jill stood inside the observation room looking into a huge room that could have housed a small jet. It was filled to the brim with random walls, tanks, trucks, and dummies. This was where the real superhero potential was coming out.

Efrat took aim with the others behind him. They knew better than to stand within ten feet of him when he was working his power. He was still unskilled at his aim. Controlling an electrical current had more to do with controlling his mind than anything else, but that was the hardest part of all of it. It was the reason Jill hadn't wanted to rush their development.

Efrat took aim, placing an outstretched hand palm up toward his dummy target. He concentrated for a long moment before releasing a bolt. It was short and concise, which in and of its self was an improvement. The bolt hit his target directly in the chest.

Jill yelled and clapped her hands. She looked over at General Clark, who was not amused, impressed, or emotionally translucent in any way, except to be annoyed by her gleeful outburst. Jill shrugged his glare away with a "whatever" attitude and banged on the glass. She gave Efrat a thumbs-up and a wide grin.

He blew her a kiss in thanks and took his position at the back of the line. Hirem was up next, and Jill was nervous. She hadn't pushed him as hard as Efrat because she was too busy giving him doe eyes and making love to him. She hoped their relationship wasn't hindering his progress.

He stepped up to his target and did the same as Efrat. A freezing cold, nearly invisible trail emanated from his hand onto the dummy. Frost collected on the dummy, and it was easy to see that the freezing cold might incapacitate an enemy.

Jill applauded when he lowered his hand. He glanced over at her and she gave him a thumbs-up as well. He didn't match her enthusiasm, of course. He looked at his hand. A blob of ice had coalesced there. It was an unfamiliar branch of his abilities, as far as she knew.

He threw the blob of ice at his dummy. The rubber manikin shattered on its impact, as if it had been submerged in liquid nitrogen. Jill gasped. "Holy shit," she whispered, seeing the true depth of Hirem's cold power.

"Now *that* is impressive," General Clark said as he applauded for Hirem.

Hirem gave a nod as he went to the back of the line. They set up a new dummy, and Garr stepped to the front of the line. He took a different path. He held his hands together and grew a ball of fire within them.

Jill smiled at seeing the pleasure the young boy got from his ability. She hoped he understood what it meant to have that power. She knew Efrat and Hirem understood war, but she wasn't sure Remi or Garr really knew what the government expected from them.

The United States was a hotbed of corruption, but none was so widely accepted as the military. The specified duties of the Green Beret very clearly listed unconventional warfare as part of its duty. These four definitely counted as unconventional.

Garr's fireball reached the size of a bowling ball, but he didn't throw it. He first looked to General Clark for his approval. "Concentrate, Garr," Jill mumbled.

The comment was warranted. Garr turned back to wield his fireball, but he had lost his focus. The fire exploded in his face. "No!" Jill hit the glass as Garr's body flopped backwards. She ran out of the observation room, only slightly ahead of General Clark.

Inside the demolition room, she barked for a stretcher and a first-aid kit. She flung herself to Garr's side to assess the damage. Despite her training and her understanding of how to control one's reactions in order to put the patient at ease, she burst into tears when she reached him.

His face down to his neck was red and bloodied. It didn't look burned, but rather skinned, like a powerful corrosive had ripped off several layers of his exterior tissue. Even his eyelids were gone. "Garr..." She wanted to touch him, but there was nothing she could touch without contaminating him. "I'm going to fix this, honey, don't you worry."

Jill followed the men as they carried Garr away. She was already plotting her plan of action. Skin grafts, antibiotics, steroids, and a hyperbaric chamber. All she knew for certain was she wasn't going to let this boy walk away scarred for life.

38

J ILL SHIVERED IN HIREM'S arms. She was trying not
to, but her coat just wasn't enough insulation from his
penetrating cold. "Are you cold?" he asked.

"No," she said, teeth chattering. "I'm fine."

"Liar," he laughed as he pulled his arm from around
her. They had only been watching television, but it was
her favorite part of their evenings together. They managed
to find a happy medium between work and home, which
she hadn't achieved with any other relationship. With him,
it seemed so easy. He was far more understanding of her
work than other men had been. She found most men to
be surprisingly needy.

"I like it when you hold me," she objected.

"I don't want to give you hypothermia," he said. "The
gloves and coat are obviously not working." He pulled
off his thick gloves and rested his hands on the arm of
the couch, where they weren't touching her or him. "I'm
sorry, Jill."

"Don't be sorry. I'll figure out a way. It's a side-effect.
I'm sure we can stunt it in some way."

"The general won't approve that."

"I don't care what the general says, I want to feel your hands on me again."

He smiled mischievously. "I guess until I can, I will have to feel you with other parts of my anatomy." He licked his lips, and she laughed and buried her head shyly against his chest.

When she looked back up, he was still smiling. He was already interested in pursuing that plan. She smiled widely and stood up to slip off her coat, along with her other items of clothing. She was pleased that this handicap was barely a bump in the road for their love life. Hirem was a determined and optimistic man. He always found a way to get his prey. "I love you," she said, hoping that phrase would encompass everything she wanted to say.

"I love you," he said as he leaned forward to kiss and bite her stomach playfully. "I will always love you," he added before he explored her as promised.

39

"WHAT DO YOU MEAN we can't reverse this?" Jill yelled at General Clark. They were alone in the lab. She had asked him down to discuss the treatment options to reduce the group's capacity to use their powers.

Garr had healed from his burn incident, but he, like the others, had developed an inability to touch anyone or anything without inducing the powers. Efrat's frustration with shorting out small appliances had become a bitter awakening when he realized he couldn't touch his girlfriends without shocking them. He couldn't even sit next to them without making their hair stand on end.

Hirem, for the most part, had handled his inability to touch her, but making love was becoming increasingly more difficult because the more excited he was, the colder the bed got. His hands were now so cold that touching her would burn her like liquid nitrogen. He had, for some time, been keeping a strict distance from her. They were trying to pretend it was okay, but it wasn't.

Garr's hands were so super-heated that touching anything remotely flammable would set it on fire. She wasn't sure what pressure his relationship with Remi was under, but he was growing distant from everyone. He was becoming dangerously introverted and, unfortunately, was still obsessed with his powers.

Remi probably should have been the least affected by her powers, but she had a surprisingly horrific skill. The extension of her powers was only visible as a directed water laser. In close quarters, she could propel water in a laser thin burst that could rip flesh from bone, and with enough concentration, could actually cut *through* flesh and bone.

Aside from constantly dripping wet hands, Jill had thought that Remi would be able to tolerate touching people, albeit wetly. It wasn't until Remi reported her incident with her friend that Jill truly understood what Remi's affliction would be.

Her friend was trying to console her with regard to Garr's accident, so they hugged. Remi thought nothing of placing her hands on her friend's back. And her friend thought nothing of the moisture that she no doubt assumed was from her tears.

Remi didn't understand the dangers of osmosis at the hands of a water power. Her friend gasped, coughed, and sputtered. When she drew her friend back, she saw water draining from her mouth and nose, like a faucet. Remi had got an ambulance there in time to save her, but she almost drowned her friend because of a hug. That was not something you just got over.

It was that incident that finally put the brakes on the operation. Jill put in the request for emergency surgery.

She was going to remove the new hands and replace them with the old ones. The response she got from General Clark was, "We can't put their original hands back."

"Garr can't even sleep on a mattress or he'll burn to death. Efrat fries every electrical device he holds. I can't even measure his voltage because it's too high. Hirem can't eat with his hands—for God's sake, the men can't even use the restroom properly without risking their manhood!"

"I understand your concern, but the men knew the risks."

"No, they didn't! They knew the risks of lobbing off their hands in exchange for new ones. They knew about nerve damage and possible amputation. They were prepared for that. There was no discussion about the risk of the powers associated with those hands, because we had no idea if the powers would truly be transferred in that flesh, or if it was only the mind that carried the ability.

"These men took a risk. The danger has now outweighed the potential for a safe, human-contained weapon. Let's be done with this. Let me remove the hands and put back the old ones."

"We can't reattach the old ones."

"I know the nerve damage will be extensive with the procedure, but at this point, these people are better off as amputees than as a menace to themselves and others."

"You don't understand. We don't have their hands anymore."

"What?" Jill clenched her fists, not understanding and not wanting to. "Just get me the patients that you switched their hands with. We can switch again. If you don't want those patients to have their powers back, then we can leave them as amputees, but let our people have their hands back, at least."

General Clark looked her over as if he couldn't believe he had to explain this to her like she was a simpleton. "Dr. Frank, do you really think that we surgically switched their hands? The hands you received were the only thing left living from those patients."

Jill shook her head. "No, I packaged their hands for transfer back to the facility for that purpose. The helicopter..." she trailed off, hoping that he was lying, or had been misinformed.

"We all have to do our best to give the civilians what they want. Your talent was essential for this project. I couldn't have told you we were going to kill the donor patients after the removal. We had no way to store the live tissue after it was removed. We threw away their hands, Dr. Frank."

"You son of a bitch!" She couldn't comprehend the callous way he suggested that he threw away body parts like they weren't of any value to him.

"Let's not get personal about this, Dr. Frank. I am still commanding this project. I expect to use these men as weapons, and that is not contingent on whether they can hold their dicks to piss."

"Oh my God, your arrogance... you presume that this project is all that is going to matter to them. They can't touch anyone!" She shook her fists at him, engaging as much anger as she could without just outright bawling or screaming. "They will never lead a normal life. They can't even touch their own body to wash themselves."

Jill turned away, thinking of the handicaps that Hirem had been enduring, and the humiliation he had felt at having to ask her to do so many personal things for him. She loved him so much, and thought nothing of supporting him, but a man could only endure so much before he started to resent her for her compassion. Eventually, he would turn her away despite needing so much help.

Now that she knew she could never undo what she had done to him and the others, she was so grieved by it. She was ashamed of her part in this debauchery of medical advancement. She felt guilty for Garr's slowly diminishing grasp on reality, Remi's fear of getting close to her friends and family, and Efrat's once jovial flirtatious spirit that was turning acerbic and indifferent. Mostly, though, she felt guilty that the man she loved more than anything was pulling away from her because he loved her too much to stay with her.

Jill whipped around with her hand ready to slap General Clark, but he was ready for it. The pinching hold that he put on her wrist was painful, but it didn't matter.

She was already crying. "You bastard, how could you do this? How could you watch them go through this?"

"I don't let myself get personally involved, Dr. Frank. You should have maintained your objectivity with this case." He threw her hand down. "These men will perform the duties they were hired for or they will be considered deserters and will be dealt with accordingly." He turned and walked out. The discussion was over. The hope was gone.

40

J ILL SAT AT THE candle-lit table with soup that she had pureed and placed a straw in for Hirem. She had learned to make food that he could eat without hands, or with little assistance. Feeding one's lover was fine for the first few bites, but it lost romanticism when your lover was actually incapable of doing it themselves.

Hirem walked in and looked over the dinner. He might have found it romantic at first, but the gun sitting in her lap and the vacant stare she gave it probably ruined that. "Jill, what are you doing with that?"

She looked up at him. It was obvious she had been crying—her face never hid it well—but the tears had since dried and her logical side had taken over. "I was thinking that we could be like Romeo and Juliet. We could die just on the cusp of our love. I thought it sounded romantic, but the gun seems so emotionless. I thought about poison, but they are rarely as quick as they say."

She looked back down at the gun. "And then I thought, maybe I was wrong, maybe we could do this. I thought maybe you might want to live with this. Maybe this life is possible. Maybe you won't resent me for staying with you beyond reasonable constraints on our relationship. In the end, I just realized that I couldn't sit across from you at a beautiful dinner, and then shoot you in the face like a coward." Her tears started again. "I want a better life for us, and I'm so selfish that I want to kill us both to get it, but I'm too much of a coward to actually do it."

"I wish you had done it," he said.

She looked up at him. He was serious.

"I don't know how romantic a gun is, but I definitely don't want this life for us, either. I don't want you dead, but if you won't leave me, then we should do something to end this madness. This is no life for a human. I am not handicapped or feeble. I am of sound mind, and I am dangerous to myself and you." He moved to her and pulled the gun away. It frosted as he moved it to the table. He kneeled before her, not touching her, not holding her. "I have found everything I ever wanted in you, Jillian. I need nothing more from this life. If I can't hold you and make love to you, then let us be rid of these bodies. If nothing else, our souls can hold each other."

Jill remembered a time in her past when those words might have sounded tawdry, but from him they were beautiful. All the more potent to her, because she knew he meant it. He had just given her permission to kill him and invited her to join him in that death. Gun or poison, it made no difference. The idea of releasing this misery was a relief.

Jill leaned forward and kissed him. She leaned him back against the floor and made love to him. He cupped his hands together over his head, not daring to touch her or the floor. In addition to touching him, she touched herself. She caressed her own body in the way that she knew he so desperately wanted to. He watched and smiled at her. He loved her, and loved that she met his shortcomings with as much inventiveness as he had.

She lay on his chest after and he lowered his biceps to hug her as much as he could without letting his hands touch her skin. They exchanged, "I love you," and she promised to kill him tomorrow.

41

TOMORROW NEVER CAME. OR at least Hirem didn't return to her that next night. She searched for him and the others, but General Clark informed her that they would not be returning to her facility.

She demanded to know where he had taken them. She fought for weeks on the phone with high-ranking officials to get their location released to her. No one would tell her or no one knew.

It was years before she got a lead.

It was several more years before she found a way to get to them.

It was strange. Despite her talent for it, she had never really liked singing.

NOW

42

C ORI KNEW SHE HAD no time to get Danato or Ethan. She had to stop Jill. She had to prevent a murder-suicide. She ran back to the prison, cursing her heels the whole way. Once inside the warmed facility, she ripped them off her feet and headed to the elevators. Not trusting the slow machines, and assuming that Jill was already ascending slowly in one, she chose the stairs.

It was a calculated risk to assume that she could run up six flights of stairs before the elevator made it to the top, even with a few minutes' head start, but the elevators really were that slow.

Halfway up, she realized she was thankful for Belus's persistent training. She still wasn't as fast as Ethan, but she was making good time. She reached the top floor and shot out of the stairwell, prepared for a fight.

She only caught a glimpse of the two guards Danato had posted outside of the elemental level before heading to the entrance. She could see blood pooling beneath both of them, and they didn't appear to be breathing. She shoved that concern into the back of her mind. She couldn't save them now.

The keypad by the door had a hole in it. It was still smoking. She might have arrived just in time, or a few seconds too late. The door was barely open. She pushed through and scanned the scene to find Jill.

The guards were all at their posts on the main stage observatory. They were only beginning to notice the danger in the room. Cori could see the back of Jill's head. She had her weapon of choice in hand with a shiny silencer.

At the end of her muzzle was the beautifully built Paul Hirem. His eyes were locked on her with a proud sadness. He was a soldier and understood what a good death was, and this would be a good death. A relief from this existence. An extinguishing of pain.

Cori couldn't allow it. She understood the pain and sorrow that brought this woman to brandish her weapon at her lover, but she couldn't let it happen. There was always a way. If there was a will, there was a way, and Cori was never without will.

Efrat was nearby, observing the meeting. He made no attempts to stop the interaction. He seemed sad and proud to see Jill there. He gave her a nod, as if he approved of her noble act.

Cori knew this was what Jill wanted. She knew it was what Hirem wanted. She could feel everything Jill felt for Hirem. The love inside of her was as deep as her love for Ethan.

At that moment, Cori couldn't tell the difference between her lover and Jill's. Hirem may as well have been Ethan standing there with a gun in his face. All of her instincts screamed at her to stop it. Don't let him die. Save him.

So she did just that.

Cori barreled into Jill as ungracefully as a drunken epileptic, but it did the trick. She dove forward. The gun went off, but it missed Hirem completely. As they landed, the gun slid from Jill's hand. The room erupted in orders, being yelled back and forth between the soldiers and feet, trampling to get into position.

Jill lay sprawled beneath her, reaching after the gun. She screamed in agony. Hirem looked down at the gun. The pride was gone and only sadness remained.

Jill looked up at Cori as she gained her footing enough to lift her weight off the woman. She was angry, but Cori was still glad she had stopped her from doing it. "You stupid bitch!" Jill yelled.

"I'm so sorry I couldn't let you—" Jill's head whipped back and Cori flinched at the feeling of liquid splattering her face. She barely registered the ringing in her ears over the sound of Hirem's mournful bellow as he dropped to his knees.

Cori looked back at Jill and saw blood pooling beneath her head from an unseen hole. The tiny dot on her forehead seemed to grow in severity the more Cori stared down at it.

Cori wiped her mouth and found blood there. Jill's blood.

"Jill?" She said her name like she imagined the woman might just rise up and shake off the wound. The vacant eyes looking back at her told her it wouldn't happen, but her mind wouldn't accept it yet.

Her hands matched her flummoxed mind. She reached out to scoop up Jill's head and cradle it, but she stopped for fear that it might cause her pain to be moved. She wanted to clasp the wound to prevent blood loss, but the little part of her that was still demanding to hang onto hope knew what she would feel if she did. There would be no question then.

Cori pushed her anger in front of her pain and turned to face the cause of it. General Clark was still holding out his pistol as if he intended to take a second shot if necessary. His men were at ease behind him. They were no more shocked by this than if he had stepped on a bug. Clark was no less pleased than if he had shot a ten-point buck.

Cori felt her mouth open, but it took a moment to understand the many levels of objection. "I stopped her!" She felt herself trying to yell, but her anger was adding more depth and enunciation to her vocal cords than volume. "She was unarmed! You didn't have to shoot her!" She saw movement from the corner of her eye.

"You son of a bitch!" Hirem hadn't bothered to use his ice magic on the general. He picked up the gun that had slid from Jill's hands and stood tall. "I hope you burn in hell for what you've done." He raised the gun, though it was too frozen to function, and charged at the general.

"Paul, no!" Cori screamed at him, but he knew what he was doing. He knew what he wanted to come from his attack.

The shot was loud. Cori hadn't remembered hearing the shot that killed Jill.

Hirem bucked backwards and landed with a sickening thud on the floor. The shot to his chest left him, at most, a few labored last breaths. "Hirem!" Cori scrambled to his side. She knew that this wasn't Ethan. She knew this wasn't her lover, but it didn't matter. She felt what Jill had felt for him. She felt the pain of his loss as she would have felt it.

She took his hand in hers. A layer of frost developed, encasing their hands. She was crying, but the tears froze to her cheeks before they could slide off. "Paul," she whimpered. "She loved you so much. She had to free you."

Hirem may not have understood how she knew that, or why she was so emotionally invested, but he gave her the slightest of nods before his eyes rolled back. Cori felt the cold diminish and the frost and ice melted. She fell on his chest and wept. It took several moments of sheer strength to remind herself that she didn't want to die with him.

Cori raised her head and screamed. It wasn't so much anger and pain as it was a war cry—a promise of revenge. Including Efrat in a previous timeline, she had now seen General Clark kill three people, and she wouldn't allow it to go unchecked.

She was up and turning toward him almost before she could walk, but it didn't matter. She intended a full-on fist fight with the murderous bastard. She was going to use every last bit of Belus's tutelage against this one man. She wanted to strangle him with her bare hands. She wanted him dead.

She hadn't anticipated Efrat's interception. She barely made it three steps before his arm wrapped around her waist, stopping her advance. She fought against him as he dragged her back. She could see General Clark's smile mocking her as he holstered his gun and crossed his arms. He waited patiently for her to regain her freedom and attack.

Efrat struggled to hold her at first, but eventually he wrenched her arm behind her back and pressed her to a wall with his hip. She ground her teeth and screamed at the audacity of him, stopping her from avenging his friend's death.

"Let me go!" Her throat was feeling the pain of too much emotion being voiced, so she let her words out slowly with as much threat as she could throw at a man that didn't fear her in the least. "Let me kill him!"

"No." She could feel his breath on her neck, and the prickling in his fingers. "He will kill you. Without a second thought."

"Danato—"

Efrat pressed up against her so hard she could feel his hip bone in her back. "He isn't here to save you! I am, so shut up and trust me." She gave up her resistance, and he relaxed against her. "You listen to me before they break this up. Clark is too dangerous for you to take on, so just hoist up your pretty skirt and leave. Don't say anything, just walk out."

"Do you need some assistance?" Clark called over to Cori.

"Revenge is best served cold." He brushed his lips against her ear.

Efrat moved away from her before the guards could pull him off her. She resituated herself before she turned to face him. "No," she said simply, before walking toward the door.

When the guards didn't move from her path, she didn't look at Clark. She continued to face the direction she wanted to go in hopes that they would part eventually, but they didn't.

In her rush to satisfy her retaliation, it hadn't really occurred to her that Clark might kill her for it. Nor did it occur to her that he might kill her, even if she didn't retaliate.

"Mrs. Pierce, is it?" Clark chimed. His steps were slow, but threatening simply by their approach. "We should probably talk about what just happened here, don't you think?"

Cori turned to him, glancing at Efrat. He was watching carefully, but keeping his distance. "General, I don't think I'm in any condition to talk. I'm tired, stressed, and frankly, I'm wearing an evening gown. Perhaps we should take this up later with Danato."

"Yes, I imagine he will be getting involved, but my concern right now is for you."

Cori's eyes danced between his. She had faced every manner of being in the prison, but she had never felt so threatened as she did in front of this human. "I assume you aren't concerned about my emotional wellbeing."

"No, your physical wellbeing."

"Am I in some sort of danger, General Clark?"

Clark's twisted smile let her know that he knew she knew what he knew—which was essentially that veiled threats are fun. "My concern lies with your hands."

Cori looked down at her blood-soaked hands. She could only imagine what her face looked like. "This isn't my blood," she said without the ire she felt.

"No, that isn't where my concern lies, either. You have now been touched by two of my elementals, and you don't seem to be in any pain. Your hand should be dropping fingers as we speak."

Cori didn't know what to say to that. She hadn't taken any care to hide her newly discovered abilities. She should have known Clark might be interested in that power. Given his obsession with finding new weapons, she imagined that mistake might have graver consequences than attacking him.

She shrugged. "I guess we'll have to run some tests or something. I'll let Danato know." Clark smirked again at the mention of Danato. He liked this game. "It's not like I can give you any answers now. I'm overwrought by witnessing two attempted murders and two... executions. I'm not used to seeing so much blood. In fact, I really think a may need to vomit. So, if I may, General, I would like to postpone this discussion until tomorrow."

Clark didn't like the sound of that, but he was at least considering it. He must have been weighing the consequences of dealing with Danato on her death, versus dealing with Danato on the other two deaths.

She, on the other hand, was considering fighting versus sobbing like a baby to get out of there.

Cori had always thought of herself as tough. Strong-willed may have been more apt, but definitely someone resilient enough to fight for what she believed in. At that moment, she believed that General Clark should die a painful death—preferably at her hands, but she had no way of accomplishing it. Even if she could summon Efrat or Hirem's powers on command through the rings, she was still vastly outnumbered.

It wasn't often that she gave in to her logic over her emotion, but Efrat was right. She needed to get out of there. What happened after that was still being debated in her unconscious mind, but survival was the only concern she had at this moment. "I should probably go tell the dock supervisor that Jill won't be making it out tonight. He gets so irritated when his empty boxes go out late."

Clark eyed her, sensing the underlying suggestion that someone might be looking for Jill or herself. He stepped forward. It wasn't a threatening move, but she saw the soldiers tense and raise their guns at a target behind her. She assumed Efrat had repositioned. At least he was still playing the part of the good bad guy for now.

Clark shot back a confused look at him before speaking. "It's a shame what's happened here tonight." He sighed, giving her a somber expression. "Jill was an intruder. I have very clear instructions on how to deal with intruders."

"We could have wiped her mind," Cori declared boldly, but her bravado immediately shrank as she realized the stupidity of arguing with a man that already had a body count of two. "Couldn't we have?" She looked at the general, pleading for her answer to be right. Her eyes were watering from fear, but she let her face show sadness. A tearful woman can't be nearly as much a menace to him as an angry, vengeful one.

"I'm afraid not. She knew Hirem. She was here to kill him. You saw that with your own eyes. This was no accidental hiker. This was a planned murder. It was a necessary death."

"I just hate to see..." Cori gagged somewhat unintentionally, but she let it work for her. "...the blood."

Clark looked her over. He knew enough of what he saw not to trust her, but she must have looked as blanched as she felt. "I'm sorry about that. I wasn't aware that you were so close with *Paul*, or was that just the blood?"

Cori glanced back at his body. "I just..." She couldn't take back the degree of sympathy she'd directed at Hirem.

"You saw him attack me. It was a legitimate reason to kill him. You can vouch for that, can't you? That's what we can tell Danato tomorrow, right?"

Cori nodded. She just needed him to trust her until the door.

"Unless you think that I'm a monster that just randomly kills people who are in my way?" Clark pulled his gun, but left it at his side. Efrat must have moved again because the men in front of her moved forward, directing their weapons more obviously at their target.

She glanced down at the gun. She was really starting to hate the efficacy of bullets. "No, of course not. I will vouch for what I witnessed: self-defense and the security of the prison. I understand you now... fully." Cori hated pandering for her life, but what was the alternative?

Clark smiled. "You're a very smart young woman, Cori. You've come a long way since you first started here. You aren't the little hothead you once were, are you?"

"No, sir." She knew he loved her groveling, but fortunately, the last of her anger had been replaced by cowardice. Little metal bobbles were an excellent anger management device. "I have my moments, but in the end, I try to do as I'm told."

He smiled again and looked her over. He clucked his tongue and shook his head. "That was such a pretty dress. I hope it's not ruined." She looked down at the gown and found the red blood was meshing well with the scarlet. The drops and smatters of blood dotting her skin were more alarming. "You know going home covered in blood might alarm, Danato. We don't want to do that, do we?"

Clark brushed back a tendril of her hair. She wasn't entirely sure what he was getting at. She naturally feared any suggestion that might involve her losing her clothing, but she got the impression from his glance behind her that he did it to make Efrat flinch again. "Maybe you could clean yourself up and slip on a jacket before you went home. Wouldn't that be better than walking in covered in blood?"

"Yes, I think so. I can do that."

"That way by tomorrow I can have a report prepared for Danato about Jill and Hirem. All you have to do is nod your pretty head convincingly and the paperwork will be a breeze. That's what you want, isn't it? For this all to be done with?"

"Yes." She barely spoke it.

"Now, Mrs. Pierce." He pulled her shoulder, so she was facing him straight on. "I know you aren't that hothead anymore, but I have to make sure I have your full compliance. If I have to be investigated, I won't be happy. If I'm not happy, I might misinterpret the intentions of my prisoners." Clark raised his pistol, aiming it behind her. She looked back and verified the target was Efrat.

She was surprised he had moved so close to them. He didn't quail at Clark's threat, but she did. She couldn't bear to watch Efrat or anyone else be shot. "No." She pressed her hands to Clark's chest. She could see she was shaking. "Please don't kill anyone else. I'll do everything you've asked. Please."

With his gun still trained on Efrat, he grabbed her face, pinching her cheeks until her lips looked like an open-mouthed fish. "Let me make this perfectly clear, you conniving little brat. If my rental agreement is compromised, or if I get even the slightest hint that Danato is investigating me or my prisoners, then... BAM! BAM! BAM!" She recoiled at his volume. "The remaining three are dead, and trust me, close-range bullets will kill them, as you saw with Hirem. Have I made myself perfectly clear, Mrs. Pierce?" He threw her back with his release and pointed the gun at her.

"Yes, sir, I won't tell Danato anything until after you've spoken with him. I promise. I'll clean up and go home and leave you alone. I don't want to be a part of this any more than I have to," she said, backing away slightly. She glanced at Efrat. "I'm sorry I even got involved in the first place. I *wish* I had never come here." She said the last statement like it should cause the floors to shake and the walls to cave in.

Efrat's interest heightened, but the lack of change caused him to perk his brow. Their mutual confusion waned, replaced by disappointment. Cori looked at her rings and wondered if they were preventing the wish from transpiring.

"Good." If Clark noticed their momentary hope of survival, he didn't mention it. "Now get out!"

The guards started pushing her along. She kept looking back at Efrat for an answer. She wanted to get out of there, but she didn't want to leave him in the hands of a madman. She finally understood. Maybe the gray areas were stretched a little too far to make the elementals good guys, but they certainly weren't malicious. Bitter, traumatized, and mad as hell, with an imbalanced sense of morality, but six years was a long time to play the part of Frankenstein's monster. After so many brandished pitchforks and torches, it was no surprise they resembled the monsters everyone accused them of being.

Efrat shook his head. He wanted her to go. He wanted to save her. She appreciated the gesture, especially since he still had several more attempted murders to make up for. Somehow she knew, though, that she had disappointed him. He had given her the key so she could discover the truth and help him. After tonight, she was going to be just as trapped as he was. She couldn't fight to get him out, and now, with Clark on hyper-alert, she couldn't even manipulate the system to negotiate for his freedom. She was turning out to be a pretty useless heroine.

43

C ORI SHOULD HAVE GONE home. She had already cleaned herself up. The blood on the dress could have passed for punch, but she put on her jacket just to be sure. She had already informed the dock manager that the truck could leave. It took a stern look to keep him from calling Danato about it, but he seemed to sense the stress she was under and let it go.

She was done with her necessary cover-ups, and it was time to go home, but she was standing in the front foyer at a crossroads without a plan. Door one was simply to go home and try not to let the guilt and anger get the better of her. She already knew she couldn't go home without tattling on Clark.

She knew if anyone was capable of getting her out of this mess, it was Danato, but her concern was not with his ability, but rather his desire. If he had signed those files six years ago, then he already knew the elementals were innocent victims of a government agenda, and he was apparently okay with that. As much as she wanted to run to Danato for help, she suspected he wouldn't give her the type of help she wanted.

Cori wanted to free the elementals, and she knew Danato hated them too much to do that. Even if she could convince him they weren't deserving of their imprisonment, Belus would demand that they follow protocol to release them. A slew of paperwork would only result in Clark killing them and abandoning his rental agreement. She couldn't play by the rules if she wanted to keep them alive.

Violence at this point was futile. Without recruiting the entire staff to back her up, she had no chance of freeing them. Even if she did miraculously find a way to get them out, what would she do with them? Her only option would be to let them go. She wasn't sure how well that option would work, but she was very sure that it would involve a good deal of yelling from several men.

Her irritation with her lack of options led her to the prop room. She let the door slam open. She huffed and stalked into the fluorescent-lit room. The buzzing lights barely provided enough light to walk, let alone find what she needed. The blinking, dying bulbs desperately needed changing, but since no one was supposed to be in here, she doubted anyone would be concerned whether the trespassers could see well.

"Where the hell are you? I was supposed to have wishes, wasn't I? I wished for normalcy and you didn't deliver." Cori backtracked three times before she found anything remotely familiar. She knew the prop room was disorganized, but she couldn't even find the blob of mess she had previously bumped her lamp from. "I need to save lives, damn it."

Cori picked up the snow globe that had fallen in her lap during her time-warped day. The lamp should have been near it, but she couldn't see it anywhere. "Shit," she whispered, feeling her last-ditch effort hit a speed bump. It was probably just as reckless to use her wish to free the elementals as it was to break them out with weapons, but she owed Efrat for saving Belus, and he had taken a bullet for her.

She rolled the snow globe around in her hands as she made her way back to the door. When she made it into better light, she looked it over to see what exactly it was. There were probably thousands of dangerous and useless trinkets in that room, but so far as she could see, this was just a snow globe.

She flipped it over to see if there was any reason the decoration was even in the prop room. The base of the globe was covered in duct tape and a handwritten index card. The card read: *Spirit of Pamola: Do not break, causes winterized conditions detrimental to human tolerances. If broken evacuate area immediately.*

Cori looked deeper into the glass ball and found the figurine of a bird inside. She felt the weight of the snow globe in her hand. It was heavy, but no heavier than her guilt, and a good deal lighter than her desire for revenge.

As she stared at the tiny bird, the glass frosted over, obscuring her view. She wasn't sure if this was a natural consequence of the power it contained or something she had done. She withdrew her hand and focused on it. She tried to remember what had set her off when she had experienced a spark from her hands. Most recently, it was the damn vampires. They were disgusting parasites, and they deserved to be...

Snap!

Cori stared at her fingertips and the faint ripple of blue that covered them. "This can't be good," she murmured to herself before attempting to make the energy circulating between her fingers stronger.

44

DANATO COULDN'T HELP BUT wait up for everyone to get back. He didn't mind having houseguests, but keeping track of so many bodies kept him on high alert. When Heaton and Ethan walked through the door, he felt his parental relief set in. When Ethan shut the door behind him, he felt his leg cramp with tension.

"Cori not with you?" He tried to sound casual, but Ethan knew him too well for that.

"She's just saying goodbye to the band. They impressed her. She wanted to thank them."

Danato grunted some kind of response and Ethan took it for what it was: a discontented retreat. Heaton and Ethan headed straight for the fridge to grab a beer. Danato rarely dipped into his private stash of alcohol, and he abhorred daily drinking, but he knew that Ethan only drank this much when he was around his friends. He could hardly criticize him for wanting to indulge the social scarcity.

Daniel came downstairs just as Heaton and Ethan settled in on the couch. "Daniel, grab a beer and join us."

He glanced at the fridge and shook his head.

"Nah, but I'll take the company."

Heaton and Ethan exchanged looks. "Dude, are you sick?" Heaton asked, legitimately concerned. Daniel shook his head and sat down in the chair across from Danato. He started to put his foot on the coffee table, but corrected the offense immediately. "Seriously, what's wrong?"

Daniel looked across at Danato like he wasn't sure he should speak in front of him. He leaned back in his chair, indicating he wasn't leaving. "Can't I choose to end this night soberly?"

Ethan and Heaton looked at each other and answered in unison. "No."

"Speaking of sobriety," Daniel leaned forward and looked at Danato, "Annette usually leaves us a tip for accompanying her up here. Did she leave it with you?"

Danato dipped his brow in feigned confusion and watched Daniel's face melt like a child getting socks for Christmas. He chuckled and Daniel wiggled his finger at him. "That's just cruel, big man. You know how much we look forward to our tip."

"I'll give it to you just before you leave. The last thing I need is you two giggling like schoolgirls on my couch."

Daniel and Heaton snorted at even the thought of the dragon's blood high. He noted a look of disappointment from Ethan; he must have coveted the experience himself. Danato remembered being disheartened by his experience at first, but now he was glad for the clear mind he got from the blood. If Ethan's experience with the dragon was legitimate, he may find that being able to communicate with dragons is a far superior experience to a psychedelic twitterfest.

45

C ORI FOUGHT THE URGE to use her bolt on the first soldier that stuck his gun in her face. Clark already had an inkling that she was resistant to the elementals' powers. She didn't need to announce that she could absorb it and reverse it as well.

When Clark came ripping out of the control booth, she knew she had used up his last smidgen of patience. She wanted to be sassy and sarcastic in the face of his bluster, but the truth was, she was treading on thin ice. Hopefully, she could make some new ice to keep her afloat.

"What the hell are you doing back here?"

Cori pushed through the guards toward the center of the room before Clark could reach her. Efrat shook his head at her like he couldn't believe how stupid she was. There was a fine line between tenacity and stupidity, and she definitely skirted the edge of it... repeatedly.

"You didn't think I would be that easy to get rid of, did you, General?" Cori pulled the globe from the crook of her arm. Clark analyzed it, stopping his approach.

"What's that?"

"You've put me in an awful position, General. I can't let two murders go unanswered for. Even if I could rationalize your motives for that, I can't allow three innocent people to stay in your custody just because you don't like the results of Jill's project."

Clark's eyes flared with anger. "How the hell do you know about that?"

She backed away, feeling the error in revealing the information. She was 0 for 3 at this point in the enemy banter category. "These men shouldn't be here," she continued her rant, but Clark pulled his gun before she could wrap her head around the fact that she was about to die.

Just as when he shot Efrat in her skewed timeline, there was no lead-up or fancy cliché dialogue. It was just point, click,—BOOM. She turned away—to run, duck, or just avoid a face shot.

Her progress in surrender was stopped when her face hit up against Efrat's chest. She heard the gunfire, and she winced. Her expectations for death fell away as she felt her hair lifting from static. She looked at the concentration on Efrat's face. She looked back and saw the magnetic field he used to stop bullets. His normally tumultuous electric rivulets had coalesced into a swirling shield that resembled a wall of water.

She looked up at him with honest gratitude. Had she not been in such a dire circumstance, she might have been compelled to hug him. The indignation on his face helped deter that instinct as well. He was looking at her the same way Danato did when he disapproved of her actions.

"You can't stop all of them, Efrat," Clark announced.

Cori turned back to Clark, but kept her back firmly pressed into Efrat's chest. She had overestimated Clark's tolerance for her witty repartee. She had also underestimated his willingness to kill her. Danato's wrath was apparently no concern to him. "He doesn't have to. We can end this with a simple exchange. You give me the elementals, and I won't let Danato kill you when he finds out what's been going on here."

Clark shot three more times. Cori cowered against Efrat, but his shield held. "Shit, shit, shit," she squealed a belated response to the effort.

"He's right. I can't keep this up forever. I will wear down eventually."

"Okay, I'll jump forward in the speech," she mumbled, pushing back against him. He took the hint and stepped back, giving the soldiers a wide berth. "General, I'm taking the elementals, whether you want to—"

"You arrogant little pain the ass. I am personally going to slap that out of you before I finish you off. What makes you think that you can take them? I am armed to the teeth and you have a Christmas decoration."

Cori looked down at her snow globe. She was clutching it like a child would a teddy bear in the middle of a thunderstorm. "It's not a decoration. It's a little birdie." She smiled broadly, just to see him grimace at her enthusiasm.

"Somebody get him the hell off of her so I can kill this bitch," Clark growled.

The soldiers surrounded them slowly. They seemed to be reluctant to use their firearms unless it was necessary. The soldiers kept glancing behind them. Cori suspected that Remi and Garr might be threatening to join the fight.

"Time's up, kitten; what you got?" Efrat said, dancing to avoid having anyone directly behind him.

"It's going to get cold," she whispered. "Stick with Garr."

"Are you sure about this?" he whispered, shifting them in Garr's direction.

"No, but do you have any other ideas?"

He dipped in closer to her ear. "I can kill them."

"All of them?" she mocked.

"Yes." His voice was breathy, like he didn't even want her to hear him. She could feel his heart pounding in his chest, like he was as scared as she was, or perhaps he was just anxious. "Every last one. One bolt. Just say the word."

Cori sensed that he wanted to do it, but his morality was too skewed for him to make the decision on his own. If he was telling the truth—and she had no reason to doubt him—all she had to do was say yes, and he would have laid waste to the entire room for her. It was a dangerous position to be in, particularly because she was scared out of her mind.

For a moment, she wanted him to do it, but it occurred to her that even Remi and Garr would not be safe from this type of attack. She wasn't entirely opposed to the eye-for-an-eye theory when it came to Clark, and she accepted that some of his men might have to be taken down to get through this, but Remi and Garr were still innocent as far as she was concerned. "That's a great Plan B, but let's try Plan A first. More destruction, but less death."

He let out a breath that she hoped was relief and not lamentation.

Cori let out a wail that was supposed to be a war cry before she threw the snow globe to the floor. The heavy containment device for the spirit of Pamola bounced around on the floor without breaking. The snowy interior remained on the interior.

Cori's mouth dropped open, and she huffed in disbelief at her unending bad night. The soldiers stared at the decoration, then looked back at her for an explanation. She smiled and shrugged, hoping that a little humor might keep them from breaking her nose with the butt of a gun.

She opened her mouth to speak, but Efrat pulled her to one side as he bolted the glass containment. It shattered, whipping glass splinters everywhere. Efrat took most of the shrapnel for her, intentionally or otherwise.

A gust of wind immediately filled the room as a translucent bird that might have been confused for a phoenix floated up from the debris. Efrat continued to push her back as a hail of gunfire, electricity, flame bursts, and laser water sprays erupted in the room.

The cool torrent of wind increased, but her focus of concern was still the onslaught of battle that was barely more than a barroom brawl. She had no choice but to rely on Efrat for protection.

"Cori!" Efrat yelled over the melee. "What the hell did you just do?"

She happily stayed behind him, but she peeked around him to see for herself what, in fact, she had done. A tornado was developing in the center of the room. The rotation started from the globe's wreckage and grew upward to the ceiling. The funnel puffed out billowing clouds into the rafters, like a steam engine. Lightning was even developing, which, considering the occupants of the room, might have been just a little too much energy.

"It's supposed to make it cold," she yelled back. "Freezing cold."

In the midst of blowing winds and gunfire, Cori couldn't hear much, and seeing depended on how fast she blinked. It was no surprise that Clark got behind them without them noticing, but she was nonetheless shocked to see him charging her.

She shrieked and hit the floor with him weighing on top of her like a sack of potatoes—and the truck they came in on. Efrat whipped around to help her, but two men tackled him. While he struggled to get his hands on or near the men, Cori struggled to get Clark's hands off and away from her neck.

She sputtered and gasped under his incredible pressure. Her head felt like it might explode if his hands didn't release her neck soon. She clawed at them, but he didn't seem to feel it even when she struck blood. He was determined to kill her, and a little storm from her snow globe was no deterrent.

She couldn't believe how many attempts had been made on her life in one short night. She hated giving Clark the satisfaction of killing her, but she wasn't in a position to stop it. Efrat, her would-be heroic bad guy, was saving his own butt. The others were fighting amongst themselves and her stupid globe wasn't doing anything but messing up everyone's hair.

If she wanted to survive this, she had to use her only other weapon. Calculated risk wasn't the right word for revealing your best-kept secret to your enemy. Shooting yourself in the foot was a better idiom, but a bloody foot was still better than a broken neck.

Cori closed her eyes and focused on the pain and anger she'd felt seeing Hirem and Jill dead. She wanted revenge. She wanted to show Clark that she was indeed a pain in his ass. She wanted *him* dead.

The cold was tangible. She wasn't sure why Hirem's power overtook Efrat's, but the slow decrease in temperature in her hands made her feel in control. It took Clark a moment before he realized his fingers were numb with cold, and he no longer had the strength to grip her neck.

She pulled his hands away with an uneven smile and coughed through her next breaths. His face was in shock. Her parlor trick had been revealed, but he didn't understand it any more than she did.

A wave of cold hit them both, and her rings glowed brightly. She looked at the tornado and saw the men closest to it covered in frost. Everyone was now being impacted by the cold it produced, including her.

She pushed Clark off her while he was distracted and crab-walked closer to the cold. He followed, still determined to end her existence, but the powerful cold that was icing his breath and frosting his hair was too much.

He tucked his arms and sounded a retreat. The men tried to comply, but they had slowed down. The cold had frozen the triggers on their weapons, and they were doing all they could to keep their fingers warm. A few of them made it to the door, but it was frozen shut.

Cori could feel her rings burning. They were trying to protect her, but she was too close to the storm. Frostbite was the least of her concerns at this point. She was frozen to the floor by her dress, and she couldn't even shiver because she was so stiff.

Clark and his men huddled together as far away from the storm as they could. They were alive, and might stay alive with that much body heat, but soon they would fall asleep and if they didn't get help, they wouldn't wake up.

She didn't mind the idea of sleep either. She closed her eyes just for a moment, but she could feel how easy it would be to just let go. When she opened her eyes, she saw another vision of a bird. The wavering, flaming wings of the phoenix approached her.

It took her a moment to realize that it was a person with the flames, not a bird. Garr's arms were outstretched and the outline of liquid heat surrounding him was beautiful, like an angel. Remi and Efrat were at his back, tucking into the warmth.

"You look chilly, kitten," Efrat quipped behind wavy heat.

She nodded. Her brain was too tired to think of a smartass remark. When she didn't move to get up, he came around Garr and pulled her from the floor. She winced as part of her leg that was exposed to the floor ripped free, minus a few layers of skin.

"Sorry." Efrat grimaced when he realized what happened. He tucked back into Garr's heat and headed to the door, which Garr had no trouble opening.

46

F OR A MOMENT, CORI thought she might be back at the house roasting comfortably by the fire. The hand that pushed back her hair and caressed her face didn't discomfort her, but the unfamiliar touch did.

When her eyes fluttered open, Garr was holding a giant fireball above her. She gasped and pulled away. "Easy," Remi said, pressing her hand to her chest to keep her still while she continued to brush back her hair.

Garr let the fireball burn out. "All warmed up?" he asked.

"Yeah, thanks," she said, wondering if this was the first time they had ever spoken.

"Can you move?" Efrat asked from behind her. She wrenched her neck to see him.

"I think so." She stood up with Remi's help. Whether she needed it or not, Remi seemed to want to offer it. She also wanted to keep touching her. "How long was I out?" Cori said, suddenly concerned that hours might have passed.

"A few minutes," Efrat said, staring through her as much as at her. "What now?"

Cori looked back at the frozen door leading to the soldier popsicles. "They won't last long in there. We should at least prop that door open to let some heat in. Maybe we can start a fire." Remi and Garr joined Efrat in the blank stare.

"What the hell would we do that for?" Garr asked, looking back at Efrat.

"Because I didn't come here to kill a dozen men," Cori clarified sternly before they rationalized letting the soldiers die.

"They aren't worth saving." Garr's muted expression made him look cold, but the statement sounded informative, more than vindictive.

"They're soldiers, Garr, just like you three. They are just following orders."

"You read the file?" Efrat tipped his chin.

"Yes, but I also know about Dr. Jill's experimental procedure. I know how you obtained your powers, and I know the burden it is to all of you."

"How do you know that?" Efrat asked, narrowing his eyes back to suspicion.

"I read Jill's mind just before she came up here. That's how I knew she had come to kill Hirem."

"Since when are you psychic?" Efrat strode over to her.

Cori looked at the other two. They were eager to hear that answer as well. She wasn't sure she wanted to share her secret with any of them, but she knew Efrat wasn't the type of man to be satisfied with, *I'll tell you later*. He was still waiting for an explanation about her being able to touch him and she had only staved off his insistence on that, because at the time she really didn't know. "It has something to do with the rings."

"Is that why we're able to touch you?" Remi said, drawing closer to touch her face. Cori let her, but pulled her hand away with a gentle squeeze before reestablishing her preferred boundaries.

"I don't really understand it yet, and I don't have time to figure it out tonight. I need to get back home before Danato sends out a search party. If Ethan didn't have guests, he would already be here. My guess is you have an hour or so before the next shift shows up and finds Clark and his men."

"An hour to do what exactly?" Efrat asked.

Cori perked an eyebrow. "Escape, of course." To her surprise, Efrat and Garr chuckled. Remi turned away and added a distance of her own. "What am I missing?"

"You're still stuck in that fairy-tale world, kitten," Efrat said flatly.

It was Cori's turn to laugh, but her voice hardened, unable to resist her irritation at his condescension. "I just threw my fairy-tale world out the window for you, you son of a bitch! Do you think any of this is going to end well for me?"

"I never asked you to do this!" Efrat's voice pitched with frustration more than anger. She'd thought that he would be grateful to her, but he wasn't. He was scolding her. It was familiar territory, to say the least, but she didn't expect it from him.

"Then why did you give me that key? What did you expect me to do?"

"I expected that you would have a good long talk with Danato and he would see the error of his ways. I thought maybe you could convince him to give us asylum."

"Asylum?" Cori blanched.

"Yes, Cori. I knew Danato would never agree to release us. I was hoping to get a less oppressive cage."

"Once again, my life is made ever more complicated by inscrutable men," Cori mumbled. "You don't want to leave."

Garr scoffed. "We can leave anytime we want, you stupid bitch!"

"What?" Cori screeched, not sure which to address first, her confusion or her indignation.

Efrat pulled her off to the side by her arm. "Listen—"

"I'm trying to help!" she yelled back to Garr. Efrat drew her face back to him with his hand. She brushed him away. "Personal space, people! I am not your designated hand-warmer."

"Corinthia," he whispered. Had he yelled it, she might have slapped him, but the quiet urgency in his voice reminded her that they were in very dangerous waters, and the life-preserver was already floating away. "I know you're trying to help, but you have to understand something. By definition, we are supernatural beings. Danato can send the collectors after us the minute he hears we've escaped, and he will. Even if we steal a truck, we can't outrun them. They have our scents. Cori, escape has never been an option. Been there, done that."

Cori winced at that realization. She had focused so much on the threat Clark posed; she hadn't considered that Danato was just as much a threat.

If the collectors were capable of bringing in werewolves, they would have no trouble with the elementals. Despite their powers, Efrat and the others were still vulnerable to the same things humans were. The collectors were pack animals and would have no trouble distracting them while another knocked them out from behind.

"Why do you keep trying to break out, then?" He didn't give an answer, and she didn't have time to probe for one, but she got the sense that he didn't really have a good reason. "Maybe I can convince Danato not to send them out right away. If I can get you a few hours..."

Efrat shook his head. "You know better than that." He put his hand to her mouth before she could object further. "I'm sorry, kitten. I didn't mean for you to... I had no idea you were this—"

"Stupid," she suggested.

He smiled. "Pig-headed, disillusioned... noble... brave."

"So... stupid," she suggested again. He chuckled, but didn't agree. "Shit." Cori lowered her head into her hands. Without escape as an option, she had brought her quagmire full circle and parked it in a cul-de-sac. "I've just signed your death warrants. Run, hide, or stay. Now it doesn't matter. He'll kill all of you, won't he?" She looked at Efrat for the answer. He didn't offer any contention. "Why do I always screw things up?" she mumbled.

She sank back against the wall and tapped her head against it. "Maybe I can convince Danato in an hour not to turn you over to Clark." Even as she said it, she heard how insane it sounded. Besides the difficulty of convincing Danato to change his mind about the banes of his prison, the fact that she had already freed them would drive a wall up on any negotiations.

"What do you suppose has changed since his signature condemned us here six years ago?" Efrat sounded defeated. She wasn't sure that the empty expression he held matched the upbeat, incorrigible flirt from Jill's memories, but it reminded her of when she first encountered him.

"A lot, I hope," Cori said, losing a tinge of her own defiant optimism.

"I'm open to suggestions, but I'm reluctant to believe you showing up after snowballing Clark's men is going to win us any sympathy with him."

Cori nodded in agreement. She had already pictured Danato hitting the roof when he found out she let loose a spiritual entity on the upper level to help the elementals. "Clark's going to kill you, and Danato's going to kill me. I just keep disappointing him." Cori pinched her brow, contemplating the clarity of Danato's reaction again. She knew him well enough to know that his anger would blind him to any rationale beyond the parameters of his job. "They will both be so pissed."

"Yes, I think that goes without saying."

"No, you don't understand. I'm a screw-up. I'm irrational and emotional. I came up here with piss and vinegar and not an ounce of forethought."

"I'm sorry that *my* dying is going to be such a burden on *your* conscience."

Cori grinned. The more she thought about it, the more obvious it was. "Efrat, even if I don't let you go, it doesn't mean that I wasn't stupid enough to try it. Hell, I *was* stupid enough to try. Luckily, one of us isn't so pig-headed. The point is, they'll have no trouble believing that I let you go." Cori stood back up, reveling in her new anti-plan. Remi and Garr were closing in to hear her, but they still held the same glare of mistrust that had taken up residency on Efrat's face in place of his resignation to die.

"We can't just hide out until you have a chance to sway Danato's opinion," Efrat said.

"Yes, you can, because no one will ever look for you. They'll be so irate about my betrayal that they'll be fighting over who gets to bitch me out first. Even if Danato sends out the collectors, they'll release them outside the prison walls. They won't think to look inside, and if by some strange luck they do think of that, there is one place you can hide that they won't smell you."

Garr and Remi weren't as excited about her rant as she was, but Efrat was sensing her enthusiasm was justified. "You do realize if they think you've let us go, you may lose your title as Ethan's second?"

Cori felt her breath catch in her throat. She hadn't expected that. She cleared her throat, trying not to think of the worst-case scenarios. She looked Efrat over. "You've earned the right to call in some favors. What are we up to now, one for Belus, and a whole gun clip for me?" She smiled, even though she could feel her eyes well up. "I hope you're worth it. You're not the same man you were six years ago, either."

Efrat raised his chin, taking in her statement. "I may not be, but I can only get worse if something doesn't change. No matter how this goes down, I want you to know I appreciate the effort."

"Come on. Let's go punch out the dock manager," Cori proposed with a little more enthusiasm than she probably should have.

47

THERE WAS SOMETHING DREAMLIKE about standing in an elevator with three people that a year prior were trying to kill her. Like Batman joining the Joker, the Sandman, and Catwoman for a leisurely stroll. The fact that she was still alive was comforting, but the awkward silence that ensued once they were in the elevator was agonizing. Despite her fervent push of the button, the elevator was in no more of a hurry than usual.

Cori stood next to the button panel with her back to the side wall of the elevator. Efrat was beside her to the rear. Remi and Garr took the other corners, with Garr right in front of her. His expression, though muted, was clearly one of careful examination. He still didn't trust her, but she couldn't really say she trusted him. This agreement wasn't about trust; it was about lack of available options.

When Garr lunged at her, she jumped out of his way, landing against Efrat. He wrapped his arm around her, which at first seemed comforting, but she soon realized he was holding her still as Garr turned to her new location. She struggled against her captivity, irrational fear taking the driver's seat.

Efrat gripped her tighter and leaned into her ear. "Easy, kitten. He just wants to pet you." Cori kicked her foot back at him, but he took advantage of the movement, and locked her ankle between his legs, further incapacitating her.

"Efrat!" She tried to sound angry, but it came off exactly like she felt. *Petrified*.

"I know, I know, you don't like boys. He isn't going to hurt you." He let his lips dip even closer to her ear. "Quid pro quo."

"I think there's a lot more quid than quo going on here tonight."

Garr raised his hands to touch her face. She flinched, but even as she did, she noticed his hand was shaking. She held still as his fingers dallied on her cheek. She could feel the heat from his hands, and the burning of her rings, but there was no pain.

His eyes softened as he continued to explore her features: her hair, her ears, her lips, and her neck. Her fear that he might continue further down her body was availed when he reached for her hands, which were still latched onto Efrat's arm, imbedding stubby nail prints in his flesh.

She released her grip, and Garr explored her fingers. The fascination he had with them was indescribable. At last, he linked his hand with hers, like they might take a leisurely turn around the elevator. The sadness that darkened his face made her squeeze his hand back.

The soft porcelain face that stared down at their hands transformed. Cori pulled her hand away when his tension on her released. The once-fascinated eyes were now angry.

His face, not fully able to articulate the emotion, made him look like a man in a ski mask. The growl he exuded was nothing compared to the punches he planted into the metal elevator. Three and four punches later, his fist was bleeding, but he didn't stop.

Cori gripped back onto Efrat's arm for new reasons. He reflexively pulled her back with him as he got a little distance from Garr's tantrum.

It wasn't until Remi came to console him that Garr finally stopped hitting the wall. Cori watched the couple awkwardly embrace, first her torso pressed to his back, and then their torsos together with necks locked, and hands carefully positioned in prayer behind each other's backs.

Cori looked up at Efrat to see what he thought of this scene. His face was passive, like he had seen it all before. He glanced down at her, trying to glean her thoughts as well. Her eyes welled with tears as the burden of Jill's actions was too hard to ignore in her mind.

"I'm so sorry, Efrat. I'm sorry for everything I've done to you." His face donned confusion. "I should have stood up to Clark. I should have given you placebos. That fat fuck wouldn't have known the difference. I'm a doctor, for Christ's sake. I should have known better!"

Efrat's eyes widened, and he loosened his grip to turn her toward him. "You didn't do this."

"Of course I did! All because I wanted to break through the boundaries of medicine. I ruined your lives!" Efrat shushed her gently, petted her hair back. He glanced back at the others, who no doubt were observing this out-of-mind experience. "Poor Paul. My poor, sweet Paul. How could I... I'm such a coward."

Efrat's brow furrowed, and he bent his knees to look at her. "Cori, you didn't do this. Jill is gone."

"I killed—"

"No, you didn't kill anyone, Cori. Clark killed Jill, Clark killed Hirem. No one died on your watch, remember?" He brushed a tear from under her eye despite it being replaced immediately. "Are you with me, kitten?"

Cori could feel the pain of the memories release her mind like the tentacles of an octopus. She took in a deep breath and looked around as if the elevator would somehow give her the answer she needed to explain what had happened. The concern on the faces around her made her chuckle.

"Shit, if you guys are worried about me, I must really be off my rocker. I guess reading minds isn't for amateurs." The elevator mercifully *ponked*.

Garr and Remi shuffled out. Cori attempted to follow, but Efrat pulled her back. He looked her over like he was looking for evidence of Jill in her face. "What was that?"

"I don't know. Leftovers from reading Jill's mind, I guess."

"Time jumps, genies, magic jewelry—you really are accident-prone, aren't you?"

"All in a day's work."

48

ORI CHECKED THE AREA before she came back to the stairwell to retrieve her pseudo-escapees. They snaked their way outside into the harsh evening cold. Garr and Remi stayed behind to watch the rear while Efrat stayed with her, watching for any hint of a witness. He was just as surprised as she was that they could simply walk out of the building without sirens, flashing lights, and barking dogs.

When it was clear that no one was around, he settled down and started walking in time with her. She wondered if that was coincidental or an innate talent for a military man. When she glanced over at him, she caught him staring down at her hands. "What is it?"

"The rings..." He looked away, suddenly interested if Garr and Remi were keeping up. "They allow you to touch us. I wonder if they would work on us. Allow us to touch others." He was trying to make the statement casual, like he had just thought of it, but it was too important a question to be chit-chat.

"I'd be curious myself," she said. His eyes pinned her with visions of Christmas morning exuding from behind them. "If I can ever figure out how to get them off, and assuming this plan works, we'll have to try it out."

His eyes sobered of their sugar plums, and he looked at her hands, confused. "Get them off?"

"They're stuck."

"I take it you don't mean vegetable oil, soapy water stuck."

"No, like parasitic jewelry stuck." When he still seemed baffled, or at least disbelieving, she stopped and showed her right hand to him. He pinched one of the rings and yanked on it. His fingers slipped off of it. As with the carrot-driven turtle, Efrat tried again and again, until he finally understood that his inability to remove the rings had nothing to do with his strength or the thickness of her fingers. "See?"

His deflated expression returned with a big helping of interminable irritation for his bad luck. She shrugged apologetically. He looked away and walked again. This time she kept in time with his pace, which was decidedly harder with shorter legs.

She looked over at him with the intention of breaking the silence. His eyes were once again pinned on her rings. She understood his fascination, but she didn't like the malicious look on his face. His mind was plotting how he might get the rings. She wanted to believe that plan didn't involve causing her harm, but she doubted she was misinterpreting his intentions.

"You know, Efrat"—his face jerked up to hers—"at some point you are going to have to figure out whether you're a good guy, or a bad guy."

His face relaxed into guilt and then quickly went to anger, which he directed away from her at nothing in particular in the landscape. "It's been a long six years."

"I don't doubt that." Cori looked back at Garr. He at least had Remi to keep him sane, and vice versa. Hirem probably stayed strong through the hope of seeing Jill again. Efrat only had his anger to keep his pain in stasis, and she knew as well as anyone that anger only worked for so long. Eventually, sorrow will wear you down.

"I'm not going to pretend to understand your plights, but I know what Jill knew, and that's enough to warrant me risking my future to get you away from Clark." Efrat refused to look at her even though the mention of Jill's name made his jaw clench. "I'm not sure how these things work," Cori looked at her hands, "but give me time to figure it out before you start plotting against me. One thing at a time, Efrat."

"Part of me wants to rip your fingers off to get those rings," he said coldly, still facing away from her.

"I can see that." Cori instinctively tucked her fingers. "I hope there's a 'but' in there somewhere."

He looked over at her finally, letting his cool blue eyes settle on hers. He looked stern, and he spoke disciplined. "Part of me doesn't," he said proudly, like that was the part of him that was still winning his mental debates.

Cori nodded, relieved to hear it.

A smirk grew on his lips, and for a moment, she thought she might be in danger. "There's also a part of me that just wants to take off one." Efrat reached over and wiggled her left ring finger. She looked down at her diamond-studded ring. "So we can try that kiss again without you feeling too guilty."

She opened her mouth to speak a scathing retribution, but she saw his smile widen and he winked at her. She clamped her mouth shut and glared instead. She wasn't entirely comfortable with any advances from Efrat, but she decided his ornery humor was better than his relentless ire. "You'd better be careful." Cori stopped at the door to the greenhouse. "My husband is the jealous type."

"Mmm." Efrat nodded, looking over the obscure building with his grin still plastered to his face. "I gathered that from our short meeting." He chuckled like he was remembering something funny. "Don't worry, kitten, I know better than to stick my hand in that can of worms. No matter how conveniently touchable you are." Efrat opened the door for her.

Cori scoffed. "Conveniently touchable, oh, the flattery. I might just blush, Mr. Alston." She went inside, with him quickly behind her.

"Then again, maybe the ring is just a problem for you." Efrat pulled her back and dropped her down into a cliché Hollywood kiss.

Her arms flailed, searching for purchase, while her legs became virtually useless since she was technically not being held up by anything but Efrat's arms. She gripped the back of his neck, trying to pull his probing mouth from hers.

Panic-stricken, she feared Ethan walking in on her at that moment in another man's arms. She had already almost lost him by choosing to continue seeing Cleos. She couldn't imagine what he would think of her once again helping Efrat, and once again with his tongue in her mouth. She couldn't bear causing him any more grief than she already was with this stunt.

Before Cori had a chance to bite Efrat's tongue, he pulled away, simultaneously raising her up. The hiss between his clenched teeth was unmistakably pain. Once he had righted her, he pulled her hand from behind his neck. "Damn, kitten," he seethed, feeling the back of his neck. "Couldn't you just smack me like all the other girls?"

Cori looked at her hand, confused. Efrat showed her the back of his neck. A red hand mark puckered there, already starting to blister. Cori stared at the wound with surprise, but then she puffed her chest with satisfaction. "That's what you get for kissing a married woman."

He shrugged, letting his smirk return. "What can I say? I chose bad guy."

She rolled her eyes. "Come on, I have an aloe plant."

49

When Cori finally made it home, without so much as an alarm sounding, she was in awe. In a moment of pure panic, she had considered confessing everything to Danato, so she didn't have to endure the agony of being blamed for something she technically didn't do. She had been willing to do it, though, and that was enough guilt for her to proudly withstand a healthy dose of Danato's rage.

Unfortunately, Cori knew that if Danato wouldn't listen to her beyond, "the elementals are out," the alarms would sound, and she would be lucky to get even a fraction of her concerns across to him before he sent every guard in the building out on a rampage to find them and, with Clark's blessing, kill them.

It wasn't just the elementals she was protecting. No matter what misplaced trust she had in Efrat, he was still dangerous. If pushed into a corner, he would fight, and as the past has shown, he would win. The morality behind self-defense was already sketchy, especially when both sides are claiming it. She didn't want her faith in Danato to be so short-sighted that she ended up turning this night into a bloodbath for everyone, instead of just a really bad night for her.

When she came in, she found the men drinking in the living room—it was probably the only reason no one had tried to track her down already. Danato wasn't indulging since his palate was too sophisticated for beer, and he could hardly reveal his hidden stash to anyone. Cori wondered what he would think if he knew she and Belus had been siphoning from that stash.

They all gave her a "hey" when she came in, like she was part of the drinking game they were playing. Danato left the party and joined her in the kitchen as she searched for a snack. Betrayal always left her stomach empty. "Well, how was it?" She looked at him, trying to decide what he meant. "Was the party any good?"

"Oh." She chuckled, thinking how many years had passed in her mind since that little soiree. "It was wonderful. Thank you so much." She hugged him, remembering how fun the first half of her night had been—and the worst of it was still to come.

"What took you so long?" he said, pulling her back to eye her carefully for any signs of trouble. Luckily, the immediate frosting of her body kept her neck from bruising. The skin that had ripped off her leg was hidden by her dress.

"I had to take care of a few things. About a gazillion 'thank yous' for the band and some small talk with the lead singer turned into some large talk." Danato's eyes searched her face. He could probably see it already: the shame and sadness that lurked behind her eyes. It prevented her from smiling as big as she should have, considering she had just had a night of music and dance.

She wanted to beg him for the asylum now, but timing was the key. She had to let everyone assume the worst. Once she was clear of the initial reactions, she could start to explain things. Of course, the longer she hid the truth, the worse she would feel, and the harder her punishment would be. Not to mention she was going to break Danato's heart, again.

"What's wrong?" he asked, squeezing her shoulders gently.

"Nothing, I just need to get to into some comfortable clothes. I'll come back down for a little bit before I go to bed." Cori kissed him, thanked him again, and walked away. Her stomach was roiling even more for a snack, but it would have to wait until later, if there was time.

She went upstairs and showered. She slipped into some clean clothes that she thought would be comfortable enough to wear in a jail cell. She slipped on her Abalone and Fish t-shirt, a parody of the Abercrombie and Fitch name brand, and a pair of jeans.

She wrote a quick note to Ethan and tucked it under his pillow. It didn't say much, just that she was sorry and that she hoped he could forgive her for putting him through this. Love wasn't mentioned, but that was the reason behind the apology.

Instead of returning to the party, Cori stood on the balcony overlooking the downstairs. She watched her husband interacting with his friends. They laughed and playfully fought. Danato even found enough humor in their ruckus to chuckle once or twice.

She wasn't sure how long she watched. All she knew was that it wasn't long enough. The banging knock on the door seemed to shake the whole house. The men stopped and looked at one another, shocked by the late-hour visit. Nothing was spoken, but everyone shared the same expression: "this can't be good."

"Who the hell is that?" Danato groused as he got up to answer the door. Cori left the balcony and began her descent to the main floor. "Clark, what are you—?" Danato said after he opened the door.

"Danato, where is she?" Clark barked, out of sight behind Danato.

"Who?" Before Danato could get an answer from him, he barged in without admittance. She had hoped that he would need an invitation, like Belus, but apparently arrest warrants transcended the house etiquette. She wouldn't have time to explain before Clark took her.

"What's going on?" Danato shuffled back as Clark and six of his men entered the house. Cori continued to the main level, where Clark caught sight of her. He may as well have had cartoon devil horns, for as menacing as he looked at her. He looked burned, but she knew it was the frostbite that had done it.

"Take her into custody," he commanded with satisfaction.

As soon as Clark barked the order and pointed at her, the room erupted into organized mayhem. Three men charged her and grabbed her. Ethan hopped the back of the couch with Heaton and Daniel flanking it to join the defense. Danato slammed the door with his cane and went head to head with Clark, which was a losing battle for Clark since Danato overshadowed him in more ways than height. "What's this about?"

Ethan reached her and stood in front of her and her apprehenders. The two men flanking her held her arms tightly, while the third remained backup, aptly at her back, shoving a gun into her spine. "Release my wife," he said with smooth, sadistic intent.

The two flanking soldiers each gave their resistant statements. "Not a chance." and "Back off."

"She is being detained for her crimes!" Clark shouted above the din of flared tempers. Everyone paused, waiting for the remainder of his explanation. It was probably only to keep things civil that Danato even listened, but it might have been her history catching up with her. Or it might have just been the fact that she wasn't defending herself in the least.

"The elementals have escaped. *She* assisted them in that escape." Clark pointed a crooked index finger at her.

"Don't be ridiculous," Danato growled. "She hates them. She wouldn't help them."

She was surprised to see that Ethan didn't react to the statement. He either didn't believe it, or he was so intent on hurting the men holding her that he hadn't registered it yet.

"She attacked me and my men," Clark was trying to yell, but his vocal cords were muted from his recent bout of cold weather. She resisted the urge to smile when he croaked into silence and had to clear his throat to continue. "She assisted all three of them in their escape. Ask her yourself."

Danato looked over at her. She could see him over Ethan's shoulder. Ethan didn't make any changes to his stance, but his glare softened, as if he was waiting to hear from her as well. "Ask him why it was only three of the elementals."

Danato donned disillusionment along with his suspicion. He probably had hoped that this was all just a horrible mistake and not what it really was: disloyalty to him. Still, he turned his attention back to Clark. "Why only three?"

Clark's maniacal smirk shifted into a grimace. "That has nothing to do with this!" Clark's voice went hoarse again, but his attempt at volume was enough to incite her own voice to rise.

"That has *everything* to do this!" she chided, baring her teeth even after the statement was done. Clark eyed her, not willing to justify himself. "Tell him, or I will."

"Go ahead, he won't care," Clark said, allowing his voice to calm back to conversational level. Danato looked between them, but said nothing. He was still evaluating whom his anger should be directed toward. At the moment, it was everyone.

"General Clark shot Hirem."

Danato looked to Clark for answers for this new accusation.

Clark raised his chin as if he were proud to admit it out loud. "Hirem charged me with a weapon. It was self-defense, not to mention strictly within the guidelines of irrepressible insurgence."

Cori didn't know what that meant, but she could see Danato's eyes soften, like he was unhappy that he could no longer direct his rage at Clark, and would have to go back to her. She waited for him to fix his eyes on her before she spoke. The buck in her chin paused his scolding expression for a moment. He was expecting her to try to mollify his temper with long-winded explanations, teary eyes, and pleading. She wasn't going to do that—at least not yet.

"Hirem only attacked him after he shot his lover, Dr. Jillian Frank, in cold blood."

Clark's head snapped to her. The shock in his eyes made her mouth tip with pleasure. He narrowed his eyes at her. He hadn't presumed Cori had any idea who the woman was. He had no doubt hoped to keep that secret with the bullet in her brain. "How...?" The word got caught in his throat, but he didn't continue the statement.

"Who's Jillian Frank?" Danato asked, sensing the tension developing between them.

"Our singer for the evening," Cori said, not taking her eyes off Clark. She wanted to watch him squirm at the knowledge she had. "She was Hirem's lover. She came here to relieve Hirem of his miserable existence. She was the doctor responsible for creating the elementals."

Clark's narrowed eyes widened at the extent of her knowledge, and she dared to let her mouth show her amusement. The insult to injury spurred him to dash toward her with his hand dangerously rising in a fist.

She expected Danato would come to her rescue, and he was on his way, but his stunned cognizance gave him a belated response. Though she wasn't in any danger with Ethan right in front of her, the opening left room for a savior she hadn't expected.

Before Clark could reach her, Daniel had him in his grip, crumpling his manicured uniform. They were face to face, and Clark's wrath slowly faded in the face of Daniel's vacuous chasms that only pretended to be his eyes. "What the fuck *are* you?" he asked, drawing his head back as far as he could.

"Don't you even try to hurt her." His voice was so quiet Cori almost couldn't hear him. Ethan lost his militant façade and glanced back at his friend to see what had transpired behind his back.

For a moment, all the interest and concern in the room were off of her. The soldiers holding her eased slightly, as if preparing to aid their senior officer. Danato approached Daniel instead of Clark. He kept his movements slow and steady, like Daniel might go off like a bomb if he jarred him. Even Ethan took a step away from her.

She was aware of Daniel's power per Ethan's description, but she didn't understand the grave concern that everyone had. Perhaps her perception had been skewed by seeing his healing ability. Or perhaps Ethan just didn't elaborate on how very dangerous Daniel was.

"Daniel." Danato placed a hand on his shoulder, but it didn't seem to do anything to ease his attack. Clark didn't struggle in the face of Daniel's threat. He seemed to sense the drastic change in the room.

Cori didn't wait for the threat to dissipate. She didn't care if Daniel killed Clark; part of her wanted that more than anything. She wasn't sure if it was her or Jill, but in the end it didn't matter, because Jill's vengeance belonged to her now. "I went upstairs to rescue Hirem. I wanted to talk some sense into Jill. I wanted to offer her hope, something she lost when Clark abducted Hirem six years ago."

"How the fuck do you know all that?" Clark sneered, barely taking his eyes off Daniel, who was still teetering on the brink of murder despite her interruption. That was fine by her.

Ethan turned his attention to her again. He was more than a little interested in the answer. She decided that was a conversation for another time. No sense adding possessed jewelry into a perfectly nice conversation about murder. "I stopped Jill before she could shoot Hirem. She was unarmed when Clark shot her."

"After she shot two of your guards, Danato." Clark turned to Danato, but he was still barely listening to anyone. His eyes were still on Daniel, the current locale of his directed anger. "I was within my right to defend my level."

"I had it under control!" Cori shouted, not able to forget the anger she'd felt at seeing a woman she now knew so well, being executed inches from her.

"You don't get to take control on my floor!" Clark overlapped her. "The only actions that need to be prosecuted here are hers. I am within my right to take her into custody. She breached the rules of our contract, and I expect you to allow me to question her, contain her, and sentence her for her crimes."

"I should have let you die like Garr wanted! He was right that you weren't worth saving!" Cori wrenched against the guards, despite the uselessness of the effort.

"I can remedy that," Daniel growled. The contrast between her screeching voice and his low drawl once again startled the room. Danato pulled on Daniel's shoulder a little harder, but he wouldn't let go.

Daniel didn't look at her, but she got the sense he was waiting for permission. She didn't understand him. His contradictions in personality thus far had perplexed her, but somehow she knew all she had to do was say the word, and Clark would be headless.

The temptation to sick her husband's weirdly heroic friend on Clark was nearly beyond her control. She even opened her mouth to say the words, *kill him*, but there was one thing that stopped her.

Heaton, Daniel's ever-present friend, babysitter, and designated leash-holder, was staring at him with pained eyes. He seemed to understand more than anyone what Daniel was, and he was the only one not trying to stop him. He was mortified by Daniel's potential homicide, but he wasn't about to get in the path of it. He was afraid; afraid of getting hurt, afraid of Daniel getting hurt, afraid of the consequences of what was about to happen. It didn't matter who the fear was for, but it reminded Cori that she was not a killer. No matter how much easier it would be that way.

"No, Daniel," she said calmly, and Daniel's intense gaze shifted as if he were uncocking his gun. "I respect Danato enough not to take the easy way out on this. Clark is the villain here, and as soon as Danato figures that out, he'll make this right." Danato looked at her, still baffled by so much of the night, and not quite able to direct his anger through the questions on his face. "But until then, I imagine Clark is right to detain me, because I did do it. I helped the elementals escape."

Danato's eyes fell slightly at that admission. His questions disappeared, but the anger that should have been revealed was hijacked by disappointment and perhaps a little embarrassment. He refocused his attention on Daniel, who still hadn't let go of Clark. He squeezed his shoulder tightly, making him wince, and pulled him away.

Heaton came to Daniel's side and tugged him away by his arm. Cori couldn't hear any exchange between them, but Heaton seemed to offer some advice that prompted him to look at the floor and breathe deeply. Clark stumbled away from Daniel and straightened his suit.

"All I ask for my cooperation is that we don't send the collectors until we can get this sorted out."

Danato looked at her over Ethan's shoulder. Now there were too many emotions to interpret. The mesh of all of them made him look vacant. His duty was telling him what to do right now, but his heart was saying otherwise. He didn't answer either way.

"You should have reported this to me," Danato said gruffly. At first she thought it was directed at her, but Danato shifted his attention to General Clark. "I have the right to investigate any mistreatment of your prisoners while in my facility. Including these most recent deaths, which, if I am not mistaken, you had no intention of reporting."

"Actually, Cori and I spoke at length about the meeting we would have with you tomorrow. She was present at the incident. I assumed that it wouldn't go unmentioned to you, so I told her we would discuss it with you together in the morning when our minds were clear. I had no idea she would plot a takeover rather than wait a few hours to discuss it civilly."

Cori felt the sting of that little jibe. Luckily, Danato ignored it. "I also have the right to review our contracts and revoke them if you have in any way lied about the circumstances bringing the prisoners into incarceration."

General Clark smiled, and Cori knew why. His documentation was just vague enough about the medical procedures causing their powers, and just honest enough about their crimes, that Danato would have difficulty revoking it based on that condition. She hoped his need to review them meant that he really didn't know or understand what he had read the first time. Perhaps there was hope that he hadn't knowingly housed innocent men.

"Be my guest." Clark displayed his palms like the end of a magic act.

Danato looked at her again, and she gave him the slightest nod before lowering her eyes. She knew this was coming, but it still felt like parental scolding. "Ethan, let them pass."

"What?" Ethan probably heard everything that was said, but he still looked baffled by the conclusion being reached. He looked back at Danato for confirmation.

Danato clenched his jaw, but Cori could tell it wasn't from anger. He was quite literally biting back his emotions. "Ethan, back away." Ethan's head whipped back and forth. She had once again put herself between Ethan and Danato. He was forced to choose between helping her or obeying Danato.

Cori wanted to apologize, but there was a laundry list of things to reveal before she could unveil her remorse. She didn't want a premature apology to signify her regret for her actions. The only thing she was truly sorry for was once again putting them both in this position.

"Ethan." There was almost a question in Danato's voice when he said his name. He was just as curious to see where Ethan's loyalties would land.

After a short, strongly deliberated pause, he made his choice. "Yes, sir." Ethan's cheeks tucked in as his mouth pursed his lips with resentment. He stepped back to let the men pass. The soldiers pushed her forward. She caught his eye on the way by seeing the pain he was hiding under his angry facade. She hated herself for putting it there.

As the men came upon Daniel and Heaton in their path, they paused, facing them down as well. Daniel and Heaton both crossed their arms simultaneously. There was a chain reaction of glances between the soldiers, the general, and Danato, which resulted in Danato shrugging. He wasn't going to exercise authority over them.

The soldiers bypassed Heaton and Daniel, letting them keep the stand they had made. She watched Danato as she passed. His cold stare did more to hurt her than Ethan's agony. She had wanted him to loosen his grip on her. Perhaps she should have specified not to drop her completely.

They didn't bother letting her grab her coat. Surrounded by three green berets was going to be warm enough, apparently. After several tries to open the door, Danato finally had to open it for them. The frame released the door with the squeaking crack of wood against wood.

As they hauled her through the door, she felt the fear of being separated from her home and her family. She dragged her feet at the last second and offered Danato one last look that hopefully conveyed her love. Since he pinched his eyes shut and turned away, it must have.

Without any hopes of redemption for her crimes, Cori let the soldiers drag her out to join the ranks of the prisoners.

FELICIA JEDLICKA

THE RING BEARER

Book 6

THE WARDEN

THE RING BEARER

Sneak Peek

DANATO LET THE DOOR to his office slam into the wall. The seemingly indestructible glass rattled loudly. Ethan unloaded his firearm into the bin beside the door, as he always did. The three men who accompanied General Clark to the late night—or rather early morning—meeting made no attempts to offer up their weapons.

"Put your guns in the bin," Danato instructed impatiently midway to his desk.

General Clark smirked innocently. "Really, Danato, I don't think all that is necessary. We are all gentlemen here. I think we can keep our tempers in check enough not to shoot each other."

Danato had never had much cause to associate with General Clark, but the little he knew of him, he didn't like. Clark was a typical high-ranking military officer who assumed that he owned every situation simply by wearing a uniform. Conversely, Clark knew little of Danato, and even less about the importance of his rules. "Given what I've heard this evening, I'm not so sure about that, but suit yourself." Danato gave Ethan a hard glance that would hopefully make him stand down without a verbal order. He didn't want to appear at odds with his successor in front of Clark. Ethan was no doubt struggling with his decision to let Cori be arrested and detained, but so far, he was still obeying him.

Danato headed to his chair, and Ethan took position against the wall like a stone statue. One of Clark's soldier drones entered the room with his gun still firmly holstered. He looked as smug as his commander—no doubt pleased that he could keep his weapon in hand. Men like that had the skill to use a firearm, but they lacked deference for its power. To them, it was just an extension of their cock. They didn't have any intimate understanding of its consequences.

Danato was certainly not anti-gun. Every guard in his prison was well armed. He just no longer saw any reason for a man of his stature and temperament to be holding a device that could kill with the flick of his finger. Most of his staff already quaked in their boots at his presence. He didn't want them pissing themselves as well.

Danato felt the air cool instantly in the room. He couldn't suppress a smile at the change in the soldier's demeanor. His prideful gleam melted into befuddled concern. He let out a solemn yelp before his body hurled backwards, disrupting his compatriots, who were entering behind him. His impromptu flight landed on the general, flattening him to the floor.

Ethan was doing his best to maintain his stern soldier-like exterior, especially with real soldiers present, but Danato knew he was shocked by the event. He had never explained to Ethan or Cori why they couldn't bring weapons into the office. He didn't believe in long-winded explanations regarding his orders—either you follow them or you don't. It doesn't matter if you understand them.

Clark offered Danato a glower as he got back to his feet, combing down his nonexistent hair before returning his beret. "You might have clarified the reasoning behind your request."

"I don't make requests. I give orders, and I *don't*... repeat... myself."

Thank you so much for reading. I hope you enjoyed the ride and if you aren't getting off here, I encourage you to sign up for my newsletter so I can return your generosity with new release updates and special offers.

Sign-Up

You can also find me on Facebook or visit my website. Keep reading!

Website

Facebook

AUTHOR

As a Nebraska native, and a small-town girl at that, I have very little to occupy my time beyond imagining a world outside of my own reality. By the grace of God and the seat of my pants, I have kept my waning attention span on the task of becoming an author.

So here I am, an indie author, peddling my words in cyberspace and enduring my comeuppances with an unwavering determination. I may not be a professional, and I certainly am not perfect, but if you've made it this far, you have to admit, this smartass yokel does spin quite a yarn.

From the self-inflicted sweatshop conditions of my unairconditioned childhood home, to the arthritis reaping positions of a sedentary lifestyle, I bring to you: my sarcasm, my oddity, and my heart. Take it with a grain of salt or a teaspoon of sugar, but take it for what it is: a story born of the mind, translated to paper, and gifted to you.

I thank you for your readership and even more for your support. Please recommend this book to your friends and family via any social media that you use. Word of mouth is still the best advertising and is greatly appreciated.

Most importantly, keep reading. I'll keep writing.